Theater District

By

Tim Wolter

Acknowledgements:

Jamie Wolter

Jan Child

Christy Connelly

Sue Moore

Paul Perret

Jennie Rosenblum

Connie Taylor

Coy West

Wes Wolter

Front cover art courtesy of Frankols

Dedicated to

Paul F. Cressy

Chapter 1

Monday November 25 1996

Another Monday drew to a close as anticipation of the holidays and season to come built in the minds of everyone. It was Thanksgiving week and the office was quiet all day, especially so by 5:30. Following the morning sales and management meeting, most of the principals with RPG Farnsworth Insco, or simply 'RPG' to most, had already escaped for the week. The rest of the staff took advantage and trickled out of the office one by one as the afternoon wound down. As it would be for any usual workday, the only folks still in the office at this time were Gabe Wagner, Kay Brightside and Nelson Bosch.

Gabe scarfed down one last handful of Funyuns as he shut down his computer and monitor, quickly calling out, "Goodnight!" to Kay over the grey cubicle wall and heading for the door – she responded with a quick, "Yeah." It was a cold, windy day so he wore rather than carried his suit jacket. Almost forgetting, he rushed back to his desk and grabbed his brass trimmed, dark green leather portfolio, mainly just to have something to hold. A yellow legal pad was tucked inside, while a small pocket contained a short stack of Gabe's business cards. Being a recent graduate and staff accountant rather than a producer, his opportunities to pass out business cards were very limited. But everyone in the firm had them and his brought cachet in the form of tangible evidence that he truly did have a real grown up job.

The Houston Club Building was built in 1954 and the elevators were always a crapshoot. Of the four elevators, only the middle two ever seemed to be functioning. RPG was on the twelfth and top floor, with floor eleven below being the only other true office space. Seven through ten housed The Houston Club itself with its multiple dining spaces, grand ballroom, barber shop and fitness center. Especially unique to this esteemed structure was the enclosed parking garage which consumed floors two through six, plus half of its first floor footprint. This mysterious lair was not accessible from the elevators or stairs, no buttons present to slow the descent. The potential for an express trip between twelve and the lobby was always there and today Gabe got lucky cruising nonstop down to 'L'.

He passed through the smallish lobby and out the front door onto Rusk Street, before hanging a right towards Louisiana Street, the main outbound Metro bus thoroughfare to Interstate 10 West. Passing the Houston Club Building garage opening, he watched for exiting drivers and gave a quick nod over to Cappy, his valet buddy.

Cappy was one of a dozen or so valets who orchestrated the daily movement of hundreds of vehicles. The garage was four lanes in and four lanes out funneling to and from a common steep narrow ramp which circled up to a mystery world of parking. Uniformed parking attendants rhythmically whisked an assortment of luxury cars through a maze of cross traffic flashing brights and snappy horn beeps. Most Houston Club guests, as well as some tenant visitors, pulled in to be parked by these strangers. Patrons usually felt the need to look away from the sight of their precious vehicles joining the controlled chaos, although no one ever recalled or spoke of any prior accidents.

Most of RPG's people had contracts with newer self park lots in the area, which were simply swifter and less stressful, plus cheaper for the company. As an alternative to a paid parking space, the company would reimburse the cost of mass transit. Gabe was one of only a few RPG employees to choose this relatively new option. He specifically purchased daily Park & Ride tickets so that he could drive in to the office occasionally sans the potential guilt associated with not getting full use of a pricey monthly pass. Thus every once in a while he had the pleasure of using the building garage - but not on this day, today he had a bus to catch.

A cold front had blown through and Gabe faced a biting north wind as he passed the Pennzoil Plaza en route to the full city block occupied by the Jesse J. Jones Hall for the Performing Arts. Jones Hall, home to the Houston Symphony, with its sixties modern lines juxtaposed against a classic white Italian marble veneer exemplified Houston's blend of the old and the new. In this section of Downtown, Jones Hall already was old, now surrounded by the sea of glass and steel skyscrapers that shot up during the most recent oil boom. Normally, its extensive overhang offered relief from the scorching late afternoon sun at the bus stops which dotted the four corners. Today it further tunneled the bone chilling air. These blustery gusts caught most off guard. Just about everyone was unprepared for the thirty degree temperature drop which had occurred during this particular workday.

Gabe was among the unprepared, though he did have a pair of thin brown leather gloves in his suit coat inner pocket. They definitely looked great while providing a tad bit of warmth. He could not stand cold weather; temps in the low forties certainly qualified and garnered some hate from him. Mumbling to himself, "I thought this was supposed to be the freakin' South..!" he quickly hustled towards the northwest corner of the block to catch the next 210 West Express.

Rounding one of Jones Hall's soft corners, Gabe noticed the silhouette of two individuals positioned near one of the massive columns outlining the building. One of medium height and slightly hunched over, the other very small and crouched down, these were the only bodies not in motion as a steady stream of souls marched by head down. With his eyes a little watery from the brisk headwind, Gabe's blurred view of these two came clearer as he quickly approached. Passing them, he noticed that it was a middle aged man, or at least one a few years older than Gabe, and a young boy. This child certainly stood out in this world of racing suits. The eyes of the two men met and Gabe slowed ever so slightly before hearing the stranger speak out, "Please help us." Gabe started to look back before noticing the red, white and blue busses lined up at the next corner, quickly scanning the destination signs for a warm '210 W Beltway 8' coach to climb up and into. None were in sight.

Everyone else around was scurrying towards and boarding the 221 and 228 Katy Line jumbo cruisers. Each and every trip out to far flung Katy, Texas, yet another sprawling suburb in full boom, was full. It was standing room only on all of those double length accordion style busses which had only recently been placed into service.

Gabe's commute was a short one and the relatively close-in 210 route was the least popular and, thus, least crowded of them all. This meant that the busses were also fewer and farther between, usually about twenty minutes apart. As he gazed back down Louisiana in search of his ride, Gabe caught another glimpse of the two shadowy figures and noticed another younger guy around Gabe's age sporting a ponytail and swiftly breezing by the pair. He watched the pedestrian's long hair whip across his neck as he shook his head 'No' once real quick, pointing at his wristwatch without breaking stride. He then heard another, "Please help." This time the higher pitched sound of the boy's voice echoed as the grown man's call faded.

Those words immediately resonated in Gabe's mind, he had conveniently dismissed the situation at first via his own haste to be home and get some food in his stomach. Now things were slowing down.

The homeless were a part of the Downtown Houston landscape and the various characters each seemed to have their own little territory carved out. Some pushed metal grocery baskets and mumbled incoherently, while others sat quietly in less traveled doorways with paper bagged beverages to keep them company. Still others had their chosen busy street corners from which to solicit donations from passersby. This city offered them a safe haven with its generous citizens, vast vacant after dark business district and allegedly mild winters. Most of these vagabonds became familiar faces over time and survived amazingly year to year without much noticeable physical decline, perhaps because they often appeared so rough from the start.

Gabe was single, but engaged, with no children. He had never really been comfortable around babies and toddlers, but having previously worked with school aged kids as a swim coach, he got kids around this boy's age. They were expressive and fun to be around, most at this age also had some semblance of self control. Gabe also realized that happenings at this age would be among this boy's first memories.

Hearing the voice of this young boy certainly got Gabe's wheels turning. Why were they here? What kind of help do they need: a handout, a ride..? Should he even look in their direction again? Money was surely what they wanted. But his wallet contained only cards, photos and bus tickets, no cash. What could he offer? Without cash, was there a low commitment and quasi-anonymous option? Besides, it would take more than a few dollars to help someone with a child on the streets.

After swallowing hard and taking a deep breath, Gabe pulled off his gloves, stuffed them in his coat pocket and casually made his way toward the guys in need. While making his approach he noticed their dusky golden complexions. Gabe cleared his throat as he soon observed that the man was clean shaven and neatly dressed in a white dress shirt and light grey pants, sporting black leather loafers with a dull finish. It took great effort to remain nonchalant and not stare. This man in need wore a casual dark grey jacket with the collar pulled up on his neck, his slight pooch belly poking out over his black belt.

Gabe's eyes focused mainly on the elder of the two as he asked, "What sort of help do you need?"

The man replied, "We're starving - I need to feed my son".

Gabe nodded slowly and bent over slightly at the waist to acknowledge the boy. He looked to be around five or six years old and wore a red and white rugby shirt with blue jeans and a pair of dirty white Reeboks. His next haircut was way past due. "I'm Garrett!" proudly stated the kid.

Gabe paused, then blinked long and hard before saying, "Well I'm Gabe, nice to meet you." Their potential rescuer took pause once again. "I don't have any cash and there aren't really any food stores around here," he calmly stated while rubbing his five o'clock shadow. Once again making eye contact with the father, Gabe asked, "Have you tried the Star of Hope?" The Star of Hope being the homeless family shelter on the southeast side of Downtown, it was about a fifteen block walk from where the trio stood.

The man sheepishly looked at Gabe saying, "They don't really help men there, plus it's not a safe place for Garrett."

Brushing his hair back, Gabe looked up to the now pitch black sky beyond the Jones Hall overhang and quickly considered just how involved he could stand to get.

Opening his portfolio, he pulled out the slightly tattered business card on top and gave it to the desperate man, "Contact me if you cannot find help, I will be in the office - my office, tomorrow."

The man looked at the card and said, "Thank you…Gabriel, I'm Jay. Thank you much."

Gabe nervously glanced at Jay's eyes and then at the ground and then at Garrett, carefully attempting to focus only on his youthful outline. Harkening for home, Gabe caught the familiar sound of bellowing air brakes, urgently looking up as the '210 W Beltway 8' luxury liner arrived. Cracking the slightest of half smiles, Gabe uttered, "Gotta go!" and jogged to the bus stop.

Behind him in the growing distance he heard the boy's voice once again, "Is that man going to help us, Daddy?"

Chapter 2

Through the open folding door and up a couple of steps Gabe sprung. He pulled a ticket from his wallet and handed it to the familiar driver, quickly stating "Here you go, sir." The driver's name tag read 'Alex Longoria' and he was one of the regulars for evening runs on this route. Gabe headed down the aisle and quickly found row two completely empty, settling into the right side window seat. Park & Ride Route 210's lower ridership, with fewer daily runs, allowed for tall Greyhound style coaches with plush, high back chairs and personal lighting. More importantly they were always nice and cool in the summer and warm in the winter, or in this case, the fall.

Settling into the warm cloth seat, Gabe stared at the back of the seat in front of him for a second and then looked out the window for Jay and Garrett. They were now walking away and Gabe wondered where they could be headed to spend this cold November evening.

His mind raced. Could he have done more? Do they not have family to help them? How to help? Did he go back to them only because a child appeared to be at risk? He knew that answer.

Considering this child seeking help on the city streets, Gabe concluded for now that someone more capable than him would get involved, if only for Garrett's sake.

As the bus pulled away from the stop, Gabe reclined his chair, located the footrest below and stared into the familiar evening lights. The white and amber hues of the buildings and streets respectively gave way to red brake lights as both remaining lanes of Louisiana Street veered left onto Interstate 10. Merging westbound, this coach had the right of way all the way. Tonight Gabe was not a bit reluctant to cede full control to the bus driver and move his thoughts to the rest of the evening as his commute's pace finally quickened. A cursory search found a lack of available reading material, which suited him fine.

A true accounting geek, his natural inclination was to observe objects in the world around him for their monetary value, often spiraling into an analysis of price, cost and profit. Anything was fair game, from buildings and vehicles to food and clothing. Even a random business along the way brought potential scrutiny. He would attempt to estimate revenue, expenses and profit, both gross and net, while calculating a value for the business and each of its assets, including the employees. But this road was all too familiar and already over-analyzed.

Gabe's thoughts turned to Laney Filas, his fiancé as of September. He would visit her at home this evening. Time with her, wherever, whenever, was what he treasured most of all. They were inseparable and saw each other every day with only a couple of exceptions in several years of dating.

Laney was now in her final year at the University of Houston, as an Education major this meant seven months of student teaching. Her assignment was first grade at an elementary school in the Alief area of town. Though classroom time consumed her weekdays, the lack of exams or papers to grade provided for free, and guilt free, evenings and weekends. Laney loved young children and had a part time afternoon position at South Hampton Montessori School, working with three and four year old preschoolers.

The holiday week allowed for plenty of wedding planning time, and Gabe was a more than willing helper.

Gabe comfortably relaxed as he intermittently closed his eyes. It took his full effort to stay awake. Now slowly moving along in the middle lane of I-10, or the Katy Freeway, as it is more commonly known, the driver eased off the gas and made a lane change to the left. They were approaching the High Occupancy Vehicle, or 'HOV', carpool lane entrance and a sea of brake lights appeared. Giving a stern nod to the Metro police screening the entrance, Alex the driver opened it up and gunned to seventy mph in no time.

Back to thinking about the wedding, Gabe was not the typical disinterested engaged guy. Of course he was most excited about having Laney as his wife, but the event itself would be so wonderful for them both. They were in the process of finalizing the guest list and excited at the thought of getting all of their Houston friends and family together with Gabe's from New Orleans and Laney's from mostly Texas and Ohio. Less fun was the process of paring down the list and weighting relationships to make the final adds to the list. They specifically did not want to cut anyone once they were added, so they each considered new friends they saw often versus old friends they saw rarely and exactly how far the extended family extended. Figuring on ninety percent 'Yes' replies, he had finalized his portion of the list in his mind.

As the bus was about to veer right and exit the HOV lane, Gabe noticed a Metro Traffic Police officer standing beside a patrol car as a just ticketed driver accelerated and pulled back into the flow of traffic. Most drivers felt as though they were immune from speeding tickets in this single, relatively narrow lane with full concrete barriers on either side. The road's shoulders widened at the exits, especially at this particular spot, where there was ample room for cops to radar and wave down those attempting to take advantage of the layout and lack of traffic. Surprisingly the heavily bundled officer aimed the radar gun at the bus, seemingly simply as a matter of normal procedure. Alex let out a big, 'Ha!' Gabe couldn't tell if it was a laugh type of 'Ha' or a busted type of 'Ha'. Though they were covering ground at a seriously high clip, surely a mass transit bus could not be stopped and ticketed, or so thought Gabe.

Sure enough, the patrol officer's right hand went up and began waving, while the left motioned the driver to pull over. Now hitting the brakes, Alex raised both hands as he exclaimed, "Really!" and brought the bus to a stop a hundred feet in front of the patrol car.

Gabe's wheels turned. First of all, the driver is getting the ticket, or maybe a warning. Gabe was completely innocent though he somehow felt guilty. Not a party or contributor to the deed, he was barely an associate, actually a mere observer. He liked Alex and hated the idea of him getting a ticket and, also, anyway, who pays this ticket..? Would it be Alex or Metro, his employer? It was somewhat comical with one civil servant sticking it to the other, funds moving from one government pocket to another. Gabe briefly appreciated the irony.

Alex exited the bus and began a discussion with the officer. Being the passenger closest to the front, Gabe had the best view and could hear, but not understand, the conversation. He also now realized that it was a female running this speed trap, she was attractive and fit. Random strands of long dark hair had escaped her official issue knit cap. As soon as Gabe began to wonder just how long the holdup would be, the officer pulled a small white card from inside of her 'Houston Metro Police' jacket, put it face down on the ticket pad and wrote something on the back. The military style name tag read 'Off. Kirby Chapman'. She handed the card to Alex and he put both hands in his front pockets as if to warm them, discreetly leaving the card behind as he pulled them out. This encounter slowly registered to Gabe as some weird, law enforcement mass transit pickup move. He liked Alex and was fine with it, especially since they were making good time this evening. Quickly back in their driver's seats, Alex and

Officer Chapman soon had the bus and the patrol car hastily on their respective ways.

The bus came to a gentle stop in the covered area at the Beltway 8 Park & Ride. Gabe popped up and gave Alex a quick, "Have a good one," as he bound down the stairs and out the door, behind him came a mumbled, "Sure, you too" reply. It was still windy and frigid.

Awaiting Gabe was his grey '92 Audi 100S, the tan leather seats were ice cold and he momentarily wished that they were cloth. Still wearing his thin driving gloves, he started it up and allowed some warm up time while quickly rubbing his palms and fingers together. After a couple of minutes, he pulled out of the parking lot and onto the West Beltway 8 feeder headed north; traffic here was also lighter than usual.

His breath still visible in the car, Gabe's thoughts turned back to the case of the odd traffic stop. Maybe they already knew each other and this was role playing, but she gave him what looked to be a phone number so probably not. She could have been giving Alex her supervisor's information, but that also seemed doubtful. Whatever it was, he could not wait to tell Laney about the strange incident.

Now turning right onto West Little York, he headed east and was only a few minutes from Laney's. *Better Man* by Pearl Jam came on the radio and he cranked it up.

More wedding thoughts came to mind, mostly honeymoon planning. This was the one area totally up to Gabe and to be kept secret from Laney. Acapulco was a strong candidate, since it offered 'exotic Mexico' and passports weren't required, but his parents' stories of gated security and rooftop guards armed with machine guns nixed that idea. He then considered New York, Niagara Falls was so cliché. Neither of them had ever been to New York City, but with so many sights to see, he decided that it would not be relaxing enough. So, now he had narrowed the choices down to either a Caribbean spot, Aruba sounded good, or California, exact area to be determined.

Turning the corner onto Brookstone, Laney's street, Gabe realized that his car had finally warmed up. Hot air began to flow from the vents as he pulled up on the curb and Pavlovian hunger set in.

Chapter 3

This was the place to be. Unpaid student teaching, plus a looming big wedding, found Laney living with her parents at this modest forever home. Approaching the screen door, Gabe could not wait to see her warm dark eyes and sweet smile, those full lips.

Laney greeted him at the door with a look of concern, not exactly the relaxed, holiday mode bride-to-be he was expecting. Gabe could tell that she'd been crying, but could also tell that he was not the reason. "Hi, Bunny," he said bracing himself for news as she replied with a simple, "Hey." They went to Laney's room, where an Adam Ant mix tape Gabe had dubbed from CDs played in the background.

Laney immediately opened up saying, "Regina Taupe left me a voicemail informing me that the Skyline Room was double booked for our date, even though it was supposedly available a couple of weeks ago when we were there. They have our deposit check, how is this possible?"

Regina was the Event Coordinator at the Warwick Hotel, Laney and Gabe's first choice of venue for their wedding reception. Now second in line, this meant of course that Gabe and Laney would have to choose either a different venue or a different date for the wedding. Just six months out and with so much already in place, changing the date was not an option.

Gabe was equally disappointed and replied. "She seemed so on the ball, how could this really happen?" he went on, "It will work out, let's call her back."

Laney replied, "It's too late, to call today I mean, it will have to be tomorrow, I'll do it. She did say that the Promenade Room, you know the big one on the ground floor, was available."

Sniffling a couple of times, Laney realized that they would likely just have to go with the Promenade Room. "That room's bigger and it's still the Warwick, maybe we can add more guests." They both had their hearts set on the Skyline Room, mainly because of the views offered by the surrounding walls of windows on three sides – envisioning a colorful sunset slowly giving way to the lights of the city as the reception began. Still, the Warwick was the right spot and they were quickly accepting that everything would work out fine. Besides her natural beauty and their chemistry, Gabe most appreciated this girl's inner strength and low drama tendencies.

She rubbed the back of her ring finger on Gabe's face along the jaw line and stated, "You really aren't shaving, huh". Smiling, he replied, "I just want to see how thick it gets, no one is around the office this week and, besides, maybe I can keep warmer with a little bit of fuzz."

Her mother, Shelly, or 'Mrs. Filas' to Gabe, poked her head into the room and said, "Hi Gabe, we have plenty of food leftover from dinner, some from yesterday too." Her distinctive West Texas drawl seemingly escalated with each subsequent word. Gabe replied "Hello, thank you!" and gave a quick smile, it was now 6:45. He loved the fact that there were always multi-course meals and leftovers at the Filas house. Multi-course in this case meant four or five course meals on weekdays and at least seven courses on Sunday. Mr. Filas loved to cook and Mrs. Filas loved to serve it up. Tonight Laney and Gabe warmed up some chicken, ribs, new potatoes and green beans. She nibbled while he ate a plate and a half. They then found some homemade confetti cake leftover from the weekend, just a regular old Sunday was occasion enough to bake in this house!

"Is Mr. Filas around?" Gabe asked. "He has graveyard tonight," replied Mrs. Filas. Laney's dad, Joker, worked at the Shell refinery in Deer Park and had the night shift this evening. Regardless of the shift Joker was working, Gabe often went long stretches of time without seeing him due to twelve hour shifts and occasional plant 'shut downs', which somehow meant that he actually worked more.

Now in the small dining area, Laney said to her mother "The Skyline Room is mysteriously not available for our date now, Regina, the lady from the Warwick, left a voicemail on my cell phone this afternoon."

Shelly replied, "You do mean the room we liked with the city views."

Laney sighed, "Yes, that's the Skyline Room, it will be alright. I will call her in the morning. That big room, the Promenade, on the first floor is available."

Shelly responded, "But we put a deposit down on the one you wanted weeks ago, let me call."

Laney preferred to handle this matter, "I'll call, this week I actually have time to do this stuff. We really want the Warwick either way - nothing else comes close."

Gabe chimed in, "Regina seemed to really have it together, hopefully she can handle this event, it can't be that hard…"

Shelly walked over and gently placed her hand on Laney's shoulder before kissing the back of her head.

Typical of Laney's inner strength, while others would have immediately gone crying to their mother or father, she had processed it internally, began the acceptance process and then calmly broke the news to Gabe and then Mrs. Filas, ready to handle it. He knew all along that this girl was a true keeper.

Along with Mrs. Filas, Laney and Gabe moved into the den and turned on the television. Monday Night Football was on and tonight it was Pittsburgh versus Miami, it sure looked nice and warm in Miami. Being an AFC game, Gabe would not normally be very interested, but it was football and he had Dan Marino in his fantasy league, needing twelve points to win his match up. Monday night offered the final NFL game of the weekend and his last chance to score any points.

They discussed the plans for Thanksgiving and were all very excited for the arrival of Laney's identical twin sister, Jane. She was coming in from Nashville, along with her boyfriend, Dion. Another engagement could be looming and they were flying in Wednesday morning.

With the game on in the background, the betrothed couple opened a Lotus spreadsheet on the Filas' Compaq desktop computer. A full blown discussion of the guest list ensued. It became a matter of predicting which of their newer friends would someday become old friends, trying to remember ever meeting distant family members and deciding which coworkers would be the best strategic choices.

For the most part this process was fun, the headcount was up to 230 and they figured to send a max of 240 invites in order to have around 200 guests in attendance. Again, they were careful not to officially add names that would have to be removed later. Shelly interjected "Don't forget my first cousins, Clint Jr., Eileen and Martha Swilling from Junction." Laney remembered them well "Oh, I remember them, I like them. Consider them added." With a few more spots left, they quit for now, knowing that other names would surely come up between now and Spring Break, when they would start the addressing and mailing.

Shelly retired to her room for the night, as a Special Ed teacher she was always early to bed and to rise. "Goodnight, it's already after nine," she yawned.

"Thanks for dinner," Gabe fully smiled.

Entering the hallway to her bedroom, she felt obliged to turn back and check for the return of joy in her daughter's eyes. All the while she remained the ever gracious hostess, "There's plenty more cake in there - be sure to get you some."

Laney looked at Gabe, raised her eyebrows slightly and shook her head side to side, "She's always trying to fatten us up, especially you."

Turning their attention to the next day, Laney and Gabe moved to the sofa and made plans for Party on the Plaza the next evening. It was a weekly concert series held at a Downtown park square near Gabe's office. This was the season finale and Adam Ant was performing and, best of all, it was free; they were going even if it was still bitterly cold out.

Both now sleepy, Gabe said, "So I know you know how to get there. Try to park in a free spot on the street in front of the main post office on Franklin - no need to feed the meters after six. Just leave here around 5:30 and your timing should be right."

She nodded, trying to recall that location.

He went on, "It would take me an hour and a half to come and pick you up and get back to Downtown at that time of day. I will follow you home after the show."

Laney said, "It's been a while since we've been to a concert. It will be awesome being so close and knowing the songs!"

Gabe replied, "Yes indeed, I will bring us something good to drink. Remember, exit Smith and take the first right onto Franklin, the Post Office is right there and you'll know where you are. I'll walk that way to meet you."

Laney thought out loud, "Won't it be super crowded for the last Party on the Plaza of the year, plus Adam Ant?"

Gabe thought out loud, "It will still be very cold then. You felt that wind, dress warm. Most people don't care much about Adam Ant, anymore…I think."

Gabe was so crazy about this girl and not really ready to leave, she could sleep late the next morning and he had a relatively light work week. Plus, he was dying to tell her about the 'bus driver meets traffic cop pickup incident', which he did in great detail.

"So they made everyone get home late for that?" said Laney.

"Traffic was actually light tonight, lots of people are off this week, we were really still pretty much on time," replied Gabe.

A little puzzled she rambled, "Did anyone else see it like you. It was probably totally innocent or, I know…could be some fantasy role playing deal. I've seen articles about this stuff in Jane's old Cosmo magazines."

Gabe teased, "Oh really? Tell me more about these articles…but I seriously don't think they knew each other. Remember, she gave him her card. Maybe they've just been waiting to meet - like we did."

They laughed and Gabe grabbed his jacket to leave as he took a last peak at the TV.

It was now halftime of the ballgame and Dan Marino had scored six fantasy points. Gabe had a very good chance to get another seven in the second half and win his fantasy game. They kissed goodnight and, after an extra long hug, he headed home.

Home for Gabe was a one bedroom apartment at the Princeton Club apartments, not far from his Park & Ride station. With no traffic it was a twenty minute trip, he switched the stereo over to AM so that he could listen to the game. It was smooth sailing tonight and the sign for Town & Country Mall loomed overhead as he approached. Through the access gate and pulling into his reserved spot, Gabe was ready to be home.

He quickly hustled up the stairs to his place, apartment number 214. There to eagerly greet him at the door was his springer spaniel, Brittany. It was a long day for her, but she was eight years old and very well trained, to the point that she would go out on her own to the grassy area, do her business and return with no problem. The temperature was now down near freezing and she would walk herself tonight. Gabe watched her all of the way out and back.

Upon her return he flipped on the game and checked his answering machine, just two messages - both from telemarketers. With teeth brushed and

18

alarm clock set, he watched the start of the fourth quarter of the game, eventually crashing on the couch.

Chapter 4

Tuesday November 26

A resonant buzz echoed throughout the apartment, the familiar daily rendition of Gabe's trusty Panasonic clock radio set to 'Max Buzzer'. It was 6:25 AM. The alarm sounded from the dresser in Gabe's bedroom, purposely placed so that he had to get up to turn it off whether he slept in the bed or on the couch. With blanket in tow he was up and the alarm was soon silenced, no snooze bar action here. He grabbed some fresh underclothes and hopped in the shower, this was a quick operation, especially with no shaving this week.

Business attire for Gabe meant selecting from one of the six suits that fit him well and matching a belt with shoes, usually both black but sometimes brown. Shirts were white button down collar oxfords, though the occasional blue was an option, but only on Fridays. The only things that slowed him down were buttoning his heavily starched shirt and selecting then tying a tie, any one which he had not worn in the past ten days would do.

By 6:45 he was ready and would feed and then walk Brittany, opting for a leash since other dogs would be out at this time. It was still dark and frost coated the thick St. Augustine grass. Back inside with SportsCenter on, he had a couple of bowls of Honeycombs with Brittany at his feet. Per the norm she had finished a heaping bowl of food in all of forty-five seconds. Realizing that Dan Marino hadn't scored more points, Gabe conceded that he had lost his fantasy game for the week, and to Kay Brightside of all people!

Normally he would grab and bring some workout clothes to run at lunchtime, but today would be his 'skip day' for the week due to the unusually cold weather. He turned off the TV and was out the door at 7:10, just as the dawning sun emerged.

With Party on the Plaza happening that evening, he would bypass the Park & Ride option and drive all of the way in to his office. Eastbound on I-10 he cruised, occasionally tapping the brakes along the way. Holiday week traffic was a breeze. Now flipping between sports talk and alternative, then classic rock, he thought about honeymoon and wedding band options – the two main items with which he was tasked and for which he was paying. He and Laney had agreed on a big band or jazz with vocals type of option, something in the realm of Sinatra and Harry Connick Jr., with some range and danceable.

Crossing Loop 610, the HOV lane emptied into the main lanes on the left as a bend in the road helped the sun find Gabe's eyes. He downshifted to match the tapping brakes around him while the Metro busses and carpoolers merged into the main flow, most were courteous. Up ahead he saw a '210' LED sign on the back of a bus and was reminded of the prior evening. He caught up to the bus as they exited at Smith Street Downtown and glanced over to see the driver, it was a familiar face but not Alex.

Stopped for the red light at Franklin Street, to his left Gabe saw homeless figures huddled below where the bottom of the concrete guard rail met the top of the embankment. He was able to make out a couple of faces and recognized the hats and eyes of two men, both were constants in this landscape and predated Gabe's tenure with RPG. He had seen these guys regularly, at least once a week, in this part of Downtown. The one with the black knitted hat was a tall, frail guy with extremely pale blue eyes. Gabe couldn't decide if his vapid look exhibited hardened inner strength or if it was simply that of a fearful lost soul. Wearing a dingy baseball cap was a shorter, healthier looking man with a strong stare that went right through him. His grey eyes met Gabe's before the slightly rattled commuter could turn his gaze back to straight ahead, in the background on 93.7 FM Led Zeppelin's *Heartbreaker* transitioned to *Living Loving Maid*. The two ragged strangers said something to each other and then pointed at Gabe in unison, peripheral yet clear to him. The target of their attention was ready to get moving and these synchronized traffic lights sure took forever to change!

Such a scene summoned thoughts of Jay and Garrett as the light finally turned green. Gabe wondered where they could be and what the cold night had meant for them. He accelerated and then kept his normal pace to keep up with the green lights as they rolled forward from intersection to intersection. All the while along the skyscraper canyons he scanned the sidewalks for any possible glimpse of the father and son. But this grid of one way streets was mostly barren, the exception being an occasional eight to fiver scurrying along.

Approaching the maroon Houston Club Building awning, Gabe took a left into the parking garage. It was obviously a slow morning and he was able to pull forward all the way to the valet stand. The half dozen or so attendants were all dressed warm enough, gloves even, and huddled in a nook with a newspaper and low volume soul tunes.

Gabe got out of the car and approached the group, "I need a ticket please".

Cappy grabbed one from the stack, tore it at the perforation, and gave the larger piece to Gabe, "Here you go, Cuz."

"Thanks, man, stay warm," Gabe replied with the coolest smile he could muster.

Passing through the lobby, Gabe nodded at the security desk to Marcus Dandridge, who was looking down at some sort of list. Without moving his head, Marcus peered over his reading glasses to note Gabe passing through. Marcus was generally a friendly old guy, but not so much early in the morning. The elevator cruised up to twelve, like an express, holiday weeks were great in this way.

Gabe was early. It was only 7:50 and so quiet at the offices of RPG Farnsworth, even the receptionist had not yet arrived. Upon reaching his cubicle, Gabe tossed down his portfolio and fired up his computer. It was a Compaq DeskPro 486 running with Windows 95 and a fourteen inch color monitor that had been passed down to him. His agenda for the day was very light, some journal entries, a bank deposit and some agent commission entry. Relatively few coworkers would be around to need anything and the phones would be refreshingly quiet.

He grabbed his plastic New Orleans Saints cup, went to the break room and rinsed it briefly before filling it at the water cooler. As the younger guys were always obliged, he replaced the nearly empty large water bottle with a full one, careful to be gentle with the thick glass containers.

In walked Lonnie Lesson, one of the firm's younger producers. Lonnie, or Lon, gave Gabe a friendly pat on the back and said, "Good morning, glad I'm not the only one here today."

Gabe responded, "Yes. Hey you gotta love holiday week traffic, pretty much nonstop the whole way in today…even after seven."

Lon was in the office everyday by seven o'clock, almost always first to arrive. He preferred to get ahead of the traffic in both directions, allowing him to return to his suburban Jersey Village home at a decent hour. Looking at Gabe he asked, "Any big Prudential checks come in?"

"None yesterday, maybe today…I'll let you know if any do come in today's mail," replied Gabe.

They returned to their respective offices.

Checking his email, the only new messages were a note about payroll and some office supplies to be ordered, this new email system was internal only. An inspirational quote from one of the firm's senior shareholders came through just as his final delete cleared the inbox: 'The only difference between ordinary and extraordinary is that little extra'. It was attributed to football coach Jimmy Johnson and evoked a slight smirk.

A single new voicemail, a sales call from a woman wanting to know the age of their copier, awaited and was promptly trashed. Gabe then realized just how quiet this day would be at the office. He updated and then saved an agent commissions spreadsheet before logging into the accounting software to print some vendor checks.

A few more coworkers had arrived and RPG was slowly coming to life this Tuesday before Thanksgiving. Gabe and the rest of the administrative staff officed in cubicles with extra high walls, allowing them to hear but not see each other. He was fortunate to have a corner unit with a window, affording him some degree of privacy.

Gabe heard his boss, Operations Manager Ivan Williams, unlock and enter his adjacent office. Ivan always took the Park & Ride from Katy in far west Houston and arrived at 8:30 sharp every day.

Ivan poked his head around the wall, "Good morning, Gabe J."

"Hey Ivan, good morning," Gabe replied.

Ivan asked, "Did Marino get you enough points? I only saw the beginning of the game."

"Of course not, Kay beat me. Why couldn't she be out of the office this week!" declared Gabe continuing, "Well, at least you got your 'W'; last night's game was just gravy points for you."

"Yep, my team should have overall high points for the week, I tell you it's feast or famine this season," sighed Ivan.

Gabe sat up in his chair, "I'll update and send out the league spreadsheet at lunch today, or maybe early tomorrow morning," he continued, "I'll get payables together for entry and check for possible accruals and, also, prep for month end payroll, it's really quiet around here."

Ivan replied, "Thanks for getting all of that together. Well it's tough to close on new business when everyone's either leaving town or has family visiting - I know the marketers won't be here much."

"Very true," answered Gabe.

Now flipping through the file marked 'Payables', Gabe pulled out a few invoices for entry. His phone rang and he barely recognized the number on the caller ID, it was Laney's new cell phone.

Picking up the receiver, he answered with a serious, "This is Gabe Wagner."

"Well, Hello Gabe Wagner," replied the soft voice on the other end, "This is your fiancé."

"Hey, Bunny, what are you doing up so early?" Gabe countered.

She responded, "I miss you, plus I don't want to create any late sleeping habits this week or else next week will be extra miserable."

Gabe replied, "Exactly, that's so you. How come you called me on your mobile phone, are you home?"

"Just because, I'm home and I just love my new flip phone that my future husband gave me," she answered.

"It sure sounds clear. I did the easy part, your parents are still paying the bill every month, for now…" said Gabe. He continued "I forgot to tell you about something last night."

Laney asked, "What's that? Any news, maybe honeymoon related..?"

"Oh, I can keep honeymoon secrets until the honeymoon, you know that. It's really nothing that exciting," Gabe affirmed. "Last night on my way to the bus stop, in the blustery cold, there was a man and his son asking for money, or help I guess, right there at Jones Hall. I am usually oblivious, well maybe indifferent. I couldn't help but notice the child…"

She immediately rattled off questions, "Were they homeless? Did you give them any money? How old was the son?"

"At first I passed them by, rushing to the corner. I was freezing but the bus wasn't in sight yet," he went on, "And I looked back and there was this little kid standing there and calling out for help. They weren't dressed too rough, you know they wore newer, nicer clothes than the usual homeless."

Laney wondered aloud, "So you watched…or you went back?"

Gabe's breathing quickened as he went on, "I went over and asked what they needed. The man said that the boy was hungry. I had no cash, anyway with no food stores, no above ground fast food anywhere around there…I gave the father my business card and they told me their names. The boy's is Garrett. I guess they could call."

"It sounds like they were presentable. Perhaps you could have charged something at a deli?" Laney countered.

"I guess I just really didn't want to get that involved" he concluded. "Anyway the delis around here close early. I have just never seen a kid out there like that though – you know, begging on the street downtown."

Laney paused and said, "Hey, you stopped, well went back to help. They know who you are now - maybe they'll come by your office. That'd surely liven up that place!"

"It sure is dead quiet around here this week. I'll have to turn on my radio," continuing he said, "They actually were clean and smell free enough to get through the lobby security. The dad had casual dress clothes; the boy was wearing Tommy Hilfiger."

Laney answered, "I really doubt you'll hear from them. Keep me updated."

Gabe paused then came back, "If they don't have money for food, they don't have money for a phone, or phone call. Maybe some family took them in. What are you doing today?"

"Helping my mom get the house, and food, ready for everything, Jane and Dion get here tomorrow!" she replied excitedly. "I also have to call Regina Taupe at the Warwick, not so fun".

"I know you can handle it, I will call you later on your new phone. I love you," were his last words for now.

"I love you too – bye," Laney returned softly back to him.

Gabe got back to the bills.

Chapter 5

"Top of the morning to Ya, Subs, or should I say 'Scrubs'!" came a loud voice over the cubicle wall. The Subs were Gabe's fantasy football team and the voice was that of Kay Brightside. She went on, "You are over there aren't you, Gabriel. Today would be a good day for you to be sick, or on vacation."

"I'm here, I can take it," Gabe mumbled sheepishly.

The other few folks around chuckled.

"You know I don't really care about this stuff, but it's fun to whip an alleged football guru," she proclaimed. "I'll just gloat a little, like the rest of the day, or perhaps until we match up again. Ha!"

Kay grew up locally and was the rare third generation Houstonian, the first Gabe had ever known in person. A math major, she had worked in an analyst position at the American General home office on the western fringe of downtown. There she came into regular contact with Mr. Ralph Farnsworth, a legend in the industry and American General's top independent producer. Mr. Farnsworth had recognized Kay's talent immediately and, after a few years of pestering, his irresistible charm eventually brought her to join his newly established agency. She was treasured as the firm's actuarial guru and could estimate premiums, both monthly and annual, in her head. Still, formal, computerized case illustrations which factored in the client's age, gender and health were required to quote policies for Houston's mostly rich and sometimes famous clients of RPG Farnsworth Insco. Nearly every single day she was the last to arrive and, also, the last to leave the office.

Gabe knew he had a little verbal abuse coming, but wow she was laying it on thick. He sat and wondered how bad it would be if Kay ever beat him by more than just a few points, or, God forbid, if she ever won the championship of the league which he had founded!

As he turned to look out the window, the phone rang. It was a direct call, no receptionist warning, the caller ID was his only screening aid. By the third ring he realized that the area code and exchange indicated a call being made from a phone nearby. At six rings it would go to voicemail. Only coworkers and Laney knew his direct number, oh, them and the few individuals fortunate enough to have one of his precious business cards.

"You there, Gabe?" announced someone over the wall.

"I am now," he answered and picked up as the fifth ring started. "This is Gabe Wagner".

"Hello Gabriel. This is Jay – you gave me your card last night…by Jones Hall," sheepishly replied the voice on the other end.

His heart now racing, Gabe slumped forward in chair and cupped his hand around his mouth as he spoke into the receiver, "I remember you, Jay. You were with your son."

"Yes, I am still with my son," said Jay in a now clearer voice.

"Where are you two?" was Gabe's quiet return.

Jay, relieved that the conversation was continuing, responded, "We are staying with a friend; he said we could crash here for a few days. It's nice and warm up in here."

Gabe realized that the office beyond his cubicle wall was extremely quiet. Everyone was either hard at work, in the break room or, quite possibly, eavesdropping on this phone call. Gabe said to Jay, "I am glad that you are warm, it's too cold out there."

There was a pause and Gabe moved his eyes side to side, scanning the row of wind whipped flags on the façade of the Texas Commerce Bank Building across the street. Gabe cleared his throat, "You still there, Jay?"

"Yes, I am still here," said Jay calmly, waiting for Gabe to offer more than chatter.

"So, were you able to get anything to eat?" asked Gabe.

Jay replied, "There was little bit of something here, my friend is generous."

Gabe was relieved that they had shelter and had eaten, but realized that there was some desperation or this call would not be happening. If Jay was calling to thank him for offering to help, then the call would already be over by now.

"So there is food for your son there?" Gabe went on, "I hope he's alright…I hope you're both OK."

Jay chose his words carefully, "I appreciate that but we need some help, while I continue to look for a job."

Gabe pondered this request, "What sort of help do you need? Isn't there a charity to help people with kids?"

Jay seemed to anticipate Gabe's questions, "I have tried the charities, they help women with kids – they don't want anything to do with men, even the United Way. I actually used to have money deducted from my paycheck for them, charitable contributions you know…but it's not like I get some kind of credit for that." He then went on, "We have a place to stay for now, my friend is not up to buying 'extra' food, even if I can repay him later. We need food."

Gabe took it all in and paused, once again debating his capacity to get involved, really involved. The silence soon became deafening and he realized that it was not as if any delay might be long enough for someone else to step in and rescue them. "Jay, I've been thinking about this. Are you still on the line?"

The response seemed so quick, "Oh, I am still here."

A sense of pride kicked in as Gabe looked inward; no child in this town could go hungry on his watch, certainly not a kid he now knew of anyway. He then felt compelled to offer, "OK, I can buy some food for you guys, but there's no grocery around here, do you have a ride? Can you get one?"

"I have a bus pass and the drivers will usually let Garrett ride for free, we could meet at the Randall's on Westheimer at Shepherd. We can meet anytime and it's not far," said Jay in full anticipation of Gabe's offer.

Again Gabe considered this predicament. He had offered help and his contact information and decided that he could do something small for them. "I can buy enough groceries for a couple of days. Can you be at that Randall's at noon?"

Jay remained fast to answer, "We will be there, at noon, out front."

"OK, Randall's – noon, I'll be there," were Gabe's last quiet words to him for now.

Jay got out a quick, "Got it, bye and thank you!" as Gabe hit the 'HOOK' button and ended the call.

Gabe noticed that he was actually getting warm and he felt his forehead, his skin was clammy and he realized that his right foot was tapping on the plastic chair mat below. He spun his chair a half turn and leaned back, staring at the ceiling tiles for more than a minute.

He wondered if others had heard this conversation and then figured it didn't really matter either way. Gabe was a young conservative and most of those in the surrounding cubicles were old liberals – Bill Clinton was the president and he had no reason to answer to any of them for wanting to help someone in need.

Concentrating on this day's light workload became nearly impossible as his mind continued to wander. First, he pondered safety; he was going to a safe place at a safe time. Then he considered the logistics of this meet up, he had driven in today so he had his car. Should he get cash or just bring a credit card? He decided that a credit card would be best. How much would he spend? His budget would be a basket nearly full, certainly not overflowing. But what he mostly determined was that it would be uncomfortable and that he would feel relieved when it was over…assuming it would really be over.

Gabe decided to that he needed to tell someone about this encounter and, perhaps, to seek approval to get involved. He went into his boss' office, the sign on the desk read 'Ivan R. Williams'.

"Ivan, I need to tell you about something," Gabe declared.

"What's up Gabe J., big news? Nothing bad I hope," replied Ivan.

"Well, on my way home last night I saw a man with a child begging by Jones Hall, I had never seen a kid out there like that." Gabe further explained, "It was freezing and the man was clean cut, so I went back and talked to them."

Ivan cynically squinted and said, "You do realize that the best con men sometimes use children, nice guys like you get suckered in. You didn't give them any money, did you?"

Gabe paused and then responded, "No, I did not give them money, but I would consider helping them. Seeing the kid definitely made me stop, whether it's a con or not, he probably needs help."

Ivan went on, "You're a churchgoer - you give at the office. Don't let your pity get you caught up in some situation."

Gabe ended the conversation, "You are probably right. I'll get the payroll data together today," before returning to his office.

He sat at his desk and considered just not going, but it was a short lived thought, and he knew that he had to follow through on this. Plus they had his address and knew his favorite bus stop. A little hungry himself, he practically inhaled a bag of Andy Capp's Hot Fries from his bottom drawer.

Chapter 6

It was time to go, Gabe grabbed his suit jacket. Originally planning to walk to an ATM at lunchtime, he still had no cash in his wallet. He stopped by Lon Lesson's office, "Can I borrow a dollar from you?"

Lon quipped "A whole dollar, are sure you're good for it? Take a five."

"Really just a dollar," a smiling Gabe replied.

"Sure!" was Lon's response as he reached into his top left drawer. "Here you go, you can pay me back after payday," with a wink.

Gabe said, "Thanks, you're saving me a bunch of time" as he took the single bill.

Next, he stopped by the front desk and reached over to get the 'RPG Farnsworth' stamp and stamp pad for official validation. He pulled out his parking ticket and, without adding ink, stamped it with full body weight before initialing the faint image.

Out the door and into the elevator, once again nonstop, he cruised down to the lobby.

Marcus Dandridge was still on post at the security desk, though now he was less serious and interacting with the folks waiting in the lobby for their cars.

Gabe breezed right on through the small crowd and went to find Cappy. He knew getting his ticket into Cappy's hand would ensure swift delivery of his vehicle. Cappy was nowhere in sight, so he handed it to the only guy available, another familiar face.

Now inside of the lobby waiting, Gabe made small talk with Marcus, "This cold came out of nowhere."

Marcus nodded, "It sure did. I like it."

Gabe countered, "I like it around Christmas; this is a little early. Isn't the building quiet today?"

Marcus, now more talkative, went on, "Very, we just have a few club members picking up turkey and fixins' - most will come tomorrow."

Somewhat puzzled, Gabe asked, "So they buy their Thanksgiving dinners? Here?"

"Oh yeah, the club's closed on Thanksgiving. But the chef prepares meals for those who don't want to cook themselves," he explained.

Gabe further considered this notion, "I thought that preparing the meal was part of the fun. Oh well, different strokes..." continuing, "You goin' anywhere for the holiday?"

"Yes, the lady and I are headed home to Texarkana, our kids will meet us there, with a new grandchild...a granddaughter!" Marcus went on, now boasting with a grin, "We leave at noon tomorrow."

Gabe began to get anxious, looked around for his car and glanced at the clock on the wall, replying to Marcus, "Have a great time...and, congrats on the new addition to the family."

Being considerate, Marcus asked Gabe, "Any big Thanksgiving plans?"

"Actually," Gabe spoke, "I am staying in town and spending it with my fiancé's family. I usually go back to New Orleans. This will actually be very relaxing."

"OK, I hope it's a good one," cordially replied Marcus.

"Thanks, here's my ride – see you later," said Gabe as he moved rapidly out the door and into his car, slipping the folded dollar tip to the valet.

Wanting to arrive at Randall's very much on time, preferably before his shopping guests. He cruised down Allen Parkway in record time. *High and Dry* by Radiohead came on the radio as he travelled along the edge of River Oaks, Houston's most exclusive neighborhood. Gabe thought of the comforts and excesses of the River Oaks crowd, many of whom were also Houston Club members and counted amongst the ranks of RPG's well-to-do client base. These privileged few indirectly paid Gabe's modest salary via executive benefit and other insurance products, million dollar life policies being entry level.

Naturally he contrasted their lives against those of Jay and Garrett. How did Jay come to lose his job, whatever it was? And, what about a wife...the mother of this boy?

Gabe reached and passed Westheimer, turning left into the bustling strip shopping center. He found a parking spot on the far edge and walked toward the main entrance. Although he was a good ten minutes early, Jay and Garrett were already there waiting.

They seemed to be wearing the same outfits as the night before, except that Garrett now had on a blue sweater with extra long sleeves.

Realizing that they saw him approaching, Gabe nodded as they turned towards him and smiled. Any possible opportunity to retreat now gone, he was all in, no turning back now.

He discretely cleared his throat and said, "Hello guys, it looks like we are all a little early," continuing as they nodded, "Good to see you again Garrett, and Jay."

Jay responded, "Thanks for doing this, I hated to ask anyone for help," his voice trailing off at the end.

Gabe also hated that he had to ask; especially now realizing that this man's pride was taking a big hit. It became particularly uncomfortable that his young son was witness to it all. Feigning enthusiasm, Gabe ended the moment, "Well let's get in there, it's a busy store".

Garrett seemed content as he drove the cart with occasional steering help from Gabe, the store was indeed packed. Jay selected the items as they stayed mostly in the middle aisles.

Attempting to find some common ground, Gabe inquired, "So Jay, who did you work for? Didn't you mention something about United Way deductions from your paycheck?"

Without hesitation, Jay sullenly shook his head side to side and said, "Compaq, Compaq Computer at the home office in North Houston."

"Oh, I know that campus, out 249, right?" Gabe affirmed.

Jay's eyes opened a little wider as the conversation developed, satiating a craving for some civil adult interaction. "Yes, towards Tomball, we lived out there." His more talkative nature began to emerge as he elaborated, "It was pretty good, I was with them for over seven years…first in manufacturing, as a supervisor, and then in 'corporate customer care', troubleshooting system problems on servers."

Gabe smiled and slightly raised his eyebrows, "That sounds pretty good."

Jay looked down "Yeah, pretty good until they reorganized me out the door…other good people too," continuing, "I got six weeks' severance and 'career counseling', our medical insurance was immediately cut off. It's been rough."

Jay continued to grab mainly junk food, Snackwells, Fruit Roll Ups, etc, each time looking to Gabe for approval, who repeatedly gave him the 'OK' nod or wave of approval. Except for a loaf of Wonder Bread, everything was non-perishable.

Gabe spoke up, "So, I guess the job market's not too good for you?"

Jay stopped in his tracks and looked Gabe straight in the eye, "The jobs that are out there are not any sort of professional or technology position like I've had, if I take a retail or manual labor position I'll never get back into the game. I have a degree."

Reluctant to press with further questioning, Gabe agreed, "That makes sense. Let's get some apples." He knew that apples were not too expensive and kept well.

"Sounds good," nodded Jay.

"What color apples do you like, Garrett?" asked Gabe.

Garrett pointed at the red, "These here, I like the red apples."

Gabe smiled, "Ah, McIntosh, let's get a bunch of these" knowing full well that these might never get eaten, but at least they were the cheapest. "Well, the basket's almost full," concluded Gabe.

Then Garrett whispered something in Jay's ear. "No, that's not a good idea," was his dad's quiet response, "We're good."

At first pretending not to notice their exchange, Gabe now saw that Garrett's eyes were welling up. "What else should we get?" asked Gabe.

"I think we're good to go," was Jay's quick response.

Gabe whispered to Jay, "Did he not want apples, or was there something else he wanted?"

Jay replied, "He'll be happy with what we got."

Pressing further Gabe asked Garrett directly, "Is there anything else we should get, but not something we put in the refrigerator..?"

"Apple Jacks!" exclaimed Garrett. Gabe was glad to see some excitement out of this kid.

Now sporting a genuine smile, Gabe's answer was, "That sounds very good, I love Apple Jacks too." He lifted his chin in a 'come this way' motion towards Jay and they headed towards the cereal aisle. Cereal was not cheap.

Jay found some extra large boxes on the lower, small box shelf where the price tag read '$2.19'. "Oh, they have to give it to us for that price!" he proudly claimed.

Gabe had no intention of making a fuss, "Let's get two; a customer probably put those there, in the wrong spot. They really don't have to give us that price, it's alright." He handed the large boxes to Garrett, who half hugged them before putting them in the basket.

They made their way to the front of the store, swinging through the dairy section for a quart of milk.

Once in the checkout line, Jay continued to go on about getting the lower price on the cereal. Gabe was just ready to pay and get this over with. He liked them both but was certainly way outside of his comfort zone.

"I'll watch the scanner," Jay repeated as they had now reached the cashier.

Gabe attempted to shush him, "No, it's fine," placing his index finger over his mouth.

Sure enough, the Apple Jacks rang up at "$4.79" and Jay was at the ready to speak up, "Hold on, wait a minute – the price said $2.19 for that cereal, can we get a manager here, now?"

Burying his face in his hands, Gabe could feel a major scene coming on as he softly spoke to the cashier, "It's fine, that is probably the right price."

"No it's not!" chimed in Jay. "They should be free, can we get a manager over here?"

The store was crowded and the checkout lines were long. People were on their lunch hours and Gabe was sure that someone he knew would see this go down.

The manager was there post haste. "Is there a problem here? May I help you?" she said to Gabe before looking Jay and Garrett up and down.

Just as Gabe began to reply, Jay jumped in, "The price said $2.19 for Apple Jacks, they rang up higher, much higher - that's a price error, they should be free."

His face now bright red, Gabe feebly tried to diffuse the situation, "It's no problem, someone probably just put them in the wrong place."

The manager, realizing how busy the store was, said, "Fine, just use the price he mentioned," to the cashier and then glanced back at Jay, before pulling out her special register key to do an override.

Relieved that this situation was settled, Gabe, too frazzled to get the manager's name, touched her elbow and said, "Thank you, Ma'am."

The manager yanked her arm away and said, "You're welcome. Now please get them out of here!"

The total came to $41.03, Gabe paid with his MasterCard and they walked out of the store.

Back outside and with Jay's hazel eyes focused square on him, Gabe flashed a nervous smile and said, "Hang in there and good luck with your job search." These guys were still strangers to him.

Jay replied, "Thank you for doing this - for answering the call and for showing up."

"You're a good guy, behave for your dad," Gabe said to Garrett as he crouched down and patted him on the back.

Jay went on, "We appreciate this."

Garrett said, "Thanks, Mr. Gabe."

As they parted ways, Jay with three bags and Garrett with one large but light one, Gabe's final words to them were 'Don't forget to say your prayers'.

Though he was curious to see which way they were going, Gabe was also ready for this most uncomfortable adventure to end. He got back to his car and noticed that it was only 12:30 – this shopping adventure hadn't lasting nearly as long as it seemed.

Now on Westheimer headed back towards downtown, Gabe hit the Wendy's drive thru for a quick value menu lunch. He couldn't help but think about where Jay and Garrett would end up. He felt good about helping them, but realized that his small contribution wouldn't hold them over for long.

Could Jay really find another job, a professional job with benefits? Without mention of a mother or wife, what were the circumstances?

Chapter 7

Gabe began to think in relative terms. Which of his friends, or family, would have done what he did? Shopping for food with a needy stranger, basket and all…never before in his life had he ever spent more than $40 on groceries…was he crazy?

His brother Les always empathized with the downtrodden and probably would have befriended them and his sister, Sissy, was always bringing home the neighborhood runaways. Surely they'd both be amused by Gabe's little charitable escapade.

He kept attempting to move his thoughts back to his little life. The sky was totally clear and Laney was meeting him this evening for Party on the Plaza, hopefully the afternoon wouldn't drag on.

Spotting a USA Today vending machine up ahead on the left, Gabe pulled over and hopped out to get a copy. This was where Chinatown met Midtown and gentrification was just beginning to sweep the area in full force - 'Finally' Gabe thought to himself. Pervasive new townhome and upscale apartment construction only made sense in this corridor so convenient to Houston's more meaningful areas.

As he got back into his car, he heard voices yelling, 'Get out of here, yuppie scum', 'Go back where you came from' and the like. He slowly pulled away and, without moving his head, peaked at his rear view mirror to see a couple of guys stumbling around on the sidewalk. They appeared to be local street people, outside of the usual downtown characters with whom he was familiar. These guys were younger and had colorful knit caps and dreadlocks, even their dark beards appeared tangled. Another guy with a partially grown out Mohawk emerged and gave Gabe the finger.

What were their stories? Were they just nonconformists without families? The one thing he did know was that the changing landscape would force them out of Midtown, though the new residents would have to tolerate them for a while as the neighborhood transitioned.

Gabe pulled into the Houston Club Building garage, right next to the valet stand. It was still not at all busy.

An unfamiliar guy quickly came to his car, opened the door and gave him a ticket. "Good afternoon, Sir," were his only words.

"Thank you, Sir," said Gabe to this stranger, who was all business.

Tucking the Sports section from the USA Today into his suit pocket, Gabe moved through the lobby quickly. He gave Marcus a quick salute gesture, scooting past the elevators to the stairwell. He was headed down, underground.

Below Downtown Houston was an extensive system of tunnels connecting all of the major buildings, including the Houston Club Building. This climate controlled oasis was constructed with one main purpose, protecting the workers from the brutal summer heat as they moved between the buildings and associated parking garages. Summer in Houston starts around late May and runs through late September, sometimes a little longer – a solid four months of ninety degree temperatures and relentless humidity. Fortunately, such as on this day, the tunnel system also acted as shelter from the cold and rain. Visitors often overestimated the effects of dips in the price of oil as full blown busts due to the lack of above ground pedestrian traffic on less than fair weather days.

Gabe needed money for the long holiday weekend and headed west to the Bank of America Center two blocks over. Along the way he passed a barber shop, the Wall Street Deli, General Joe's Chinese and a dry cleaner with a shoe shine stand. The tunnel below each building had its own unique style, varying from old school fifties to seventies carpeted walls and eighties modern to recently remodeled, a true hodge podge from one building to the next. Even the lighting varied from space to space and was not uniform in fixture style, intensity or hue.

Having withdrawn cash from the ATM and now heading back to his building, Gabe soon realized that even the tunnels were significantly less busy this week. Everyone still moved at a very brisk pace, staying to the far right except to pass, much more observant of the rules here than on the freeways. What he also realized, more than usual on this day, was that the ragged street people were nowhere to be seen. The lobby attendants basically acted as bouncers to screen those entering the tunnels. Those who desired to do so could park, work, eat, and even shop, without ever having to interact with the outside world.

Ascending the stairs and returning to the Houston Club Building lobby, Gabe quickly caught an empty elevator and entered his office through the back door. It was still not yet 1:00 and still very quiet at RPG.

A senior marketer and founder, Philip James, stopped by Gabe's office wanting to know if a monthly commission on a group policy had finally come in. Philip was the most serious and hard working person at RPG, and one of only three shareholders. He was extremely good hearted, but could be brash and intimidating to newer associates. Gabe was just now getting to be comfortable working with him. Gabe always remembered meeting with Philip his first day on the job. Their visit had concluded with Philip loudly proclaiming "I may be not always be the smartest guy in the room, but no one will ever outwork me - no one." Due mainly to Philip's diligence, he and Gabe had recently found together that a junior marketer had been stealing large commission checks, a case in which the carrier would only issue checks to individuals and not directly to the firm. They were in the process of finalizing a settlement and payment arrangement with the now former marketer.

Philip had suggested that Gabe consider going into policy sales, the firm's youngest producer was now in his late thirties. Philip repeatedly stated the he should 'consider the lifestyle' and all Gabe could think about were the lean months and extreme stress he saw the junior marketers endure. 'I'm considering it' would be Gabe's standard reply and Philip would always come back with 'You should, you'll be a married man soon'.

Though the established marketers at RPG all made high six figure incomes, the odds were solidly against someone in their twenties lasting more than two years in the field. Gabe was an accountant and not interested in playing those odds.

Clearly not as busy as usual, Philip was talkative and Gabe told him about Jay and Garrett and their visit to the grocery. For the first time ever, Philip actually took a seat in Gabe's office and considered the situation, before declaring, "I think that we all want to help those in need. It's human nature."

Gabe interjected, "Or at least it should be... I mean it should be to want to help."

Philip continued, "Yes, you do realize that most street people are there by choice, at least to some extent. Most are either addicts or mentally ill and some, probably few though, are just plain lazy."

"I would agree with that," conceded Gabe.

"You did the right thing not just giving him, or them, money – now you know what you gave will help the boy," Philip said with an affirmative nod.

Finally, the two of them exchanged details regarding their respective holiday plans. Philip was going home to Ruston, Louisiana on Wednesday morning. "Be thankful for what you have" were his parting words.

Getting back to work, Gabe went through his mail, sorting out the commission checks from the bills and junk. He also updated the Paradox database for agent license renewals.

His coworkers were returning from a long lunch and settling into their desks, mainly checking their few messages. It was eerily quiet for everyone. They then began chatting with each other and he heard one of them unzip a zipper. This meant only one thing: smoke break.

Typically smoke breaks were taken out in front of the building, under the canopy, according to the rules of the building and a recently enacted law. But it was cold today and they would just have their break in the nearest stairwell, which was always empty.

Gabe heard them gathering, two hardcore smokers and an occasional smoker, plus Kay, a non-smoker who was actually, for a change, not super busy. Gabe came around the corner, "May I join you all…for a second hand smoke break?"

"Sure, come on." one of them replied. "Let's go." They sat and stood on the stairs and discussed their lunch out together and holiday plans and the cold weather and light traffic.

Kay and Gabe had a running dialogue about fortune cookie lottery numbers from lunch the prior Friday. The numbers listed were nearly consecutive and any chance of winning with them had been laughed off by both of them as more unlikely than the usual impossible. As it turned out, Gabe would have matched at least five of six numbers if he'd used that fortune.

But he was mostly just trying to pass the time, as well as see if any of them had comments after eavesdropping on his earlier phone conversation with Jay. They were either being extra coy or just hadn't overheard him at all. He really had very little in common with any of them.

With the break over and now back at his computer, Gabe updated the payroll spreadsheet for changes and filed a few old forms.

Chapter 8

Laney was on his mind; Gabe needed to talk to her. He dialed the landline and there was no answer, so he tried her mobile number.

She answered immediately, "Hello, Gabriel." Gabe was especially glad to hear her voice again today.

"How's my best girl?" wittily replied Gabe.

Laney immediately quipped back, "Yeah, I'd better be your only girl…"

"Hey, your dad is the one who always says that. It's on Joker. Are you out somewhere?"

"I'm at the grocery with my mom," said Laney. "Not meeting up with my 'best boy' until later."

"Ha Ha, very good, hopefully that's me." Gabe went on "Were you able to call Regina Taupe?"

"Yes, she apologized and said that this had never happened to her before. They are giving us The Promenade Room top food and drink package at fifty a head."

"Fifty a head, really, fifty?" Gabe asked.

Laney quickly came back "Yes, you heard it right. That's for prime rib carving station, or sit down, and call liquor plus premium beer, imports included!"

Gabe sat back in his chair, "Nice, your parents will love that. OK, The Promenade Room sounds great after all, and, no elevator rides…"

"I'm good with that, I didn't want to sound too satisfied to Regina, though. I asked her to let me know immediately if the other room opens up," said Laney. "How's your day so far?"

"Way to play it cool, you always do. My day's been interesting, more interesting than I expected…" replied Gabe.

Laney asked, "Is something going on at the office - wasn't it supposed to be pretty quiet around there?"

"Yeah, nothing work related." He wanted to fill her in, "So you remember that guy and his son I was telling you about, the ones by the bus stop?"

"Sure, they didn't come by your office did they?" wondered Laney.

Gabe continued, "No, but the father called me, his name is Jay, and I offered to help them out."

"So they're coming over for Thanksgiving dinner?" she joked.

"I would have asked you first, but seriously, I bought them some food." Gabe replied.

"Where, how – like you bought them lunch?" asked Laney.

Gabe went on, "No, I have my car today so I actually met them at the grocery, Randall's. The son came along. They, well actually, we bought a basket full of groceries."

She became quite curious and quizzed him further, "Did you pick them up? Was that safe?"

He attempted to reassure her, "No, it was completely safe. They have a bus pass and I met them there."

"And then what?"

Gabe rambled, "I just paid, well after the father caused a mini scene over the price of cereal and we met the manager; but, really I just paid and they thanked me and I told them 'Good luck' and then watched them walk away."

"So that's it I guess? Is the dad able bodied, well spoken?" said Laney.

Gabe considered his answer "You know, I don't know. That should be it; surely he knows that I'm not any kind of millionaire. Yes, he's not handicapped and could do manual labor if need be, but he did mention that he has his degree. He is articulate and proud, but down – seriously needs to find work…"

Laney replied, "Yes, there are plenty of jobs out there. Afterschool care for his boy could be tricky though…definitely expensive, this I know."

"I know - I just wanted to help a little, mainly because of the kid," Gabe conceded.

"Ultimately it's up to him, the father, but I love that you have such a kind heart," she said sweetly.

Gabe paused then spoke, "Thanks. This may be a case where it is actually harder to be a man, I mean being homeless with a kid. I never got to ask about Garrett's, the boy's name is Garrett, I never got a chance to ask about his mom. Maybe I didn't want to know, or see their reaction to the question...Oh, well."

"Yes, surely there's some kind of story on the mom. Moms don't usually give up their kids easily...not at all, hardly ever. Oh, and, by the way, it's almost always easier to be a man, really come on..." was her retort.

"Yes, OK. Definitely, moms always care so much about their kids. We may never know that story, her story," Gabe continued "A story I kind of hope we never know anyway."

Laney agreed, "I hope not too, I hope they're fine and some family, their family, helps them and that he gets a job, a good one."

"Well, we have a concert tonight, you ready?" said Gabe.

"Definitely, even if it's old music," replied Laney.

Gabe countered, "Well, you know the songs, it'll be fun. Best of all it's free!"

"Oh, I know, free is great. It will be fun - poppy 80s new wave, soft punk songs."

"OK, six o'clock, right? You know the place, I'll walk over and find you...sometimes I could use a cell phone too..." said Gabe.

"Yes, I will be there. I know the spot," Laney replied.

Gabe sat back in his chair, "Great, can't wait. I love you."

"OK, gotta help my Mom finish up here. Love you," echoed her soft voice.

46

It was time to get back to work, so Gabe took a walk to check his mailbox. RPG was very quiet once again this afternoon and, sure enough, the mail had arrived. He brought his large stack back to his office and sorted out the commission checks, preparing a bank deposit.

His boss, Ivan, stopped by to check on the deposit, "Any big checks come in today?"

Gabe replied, "About 35K total, mostly group plan commissions and a couple of life renewals, Prudential and Pacific Mutual."

"OK, thanks, I am heading out, do you need me to drop it off?" he offered.

"No thanks, I still need to make copies - plus I want to get out, it's dead around here," answered Gabe.

"Alright, take off a little early," offered Will.

"Sure, I will, though I do need to get the fantasy football stuff done."

"That's right; there are Thursday games this week. See you tomorrow, I'll probably just be here in the morning," said Will.

"OK, see you in the morning."

After making copies, Gabe grabbed his suit jacket and headed out of the office and down to the ground floor. Once again it was a quick descent, he could get used to this.

Texas Commerce Bank was located in the former Gulf Oil building, which was the tallest building in town until 1963. Completed in 1929, it was also off the tunnel grid, which meant that this would be an outdoor trip. The venerable landmark was right across Travis Street to the east and Gabe casually jaywalked as the massive flags above whipped in the wind.

Once inside the grand lobby, Gabe was surrounded by hundreds of school aged carolers. This was a dress rehearsal and workers were installing the last of the massive Christmas decorations, specifically, extra large wreaths and a life sized angel above the Nativity Scene.

Gabe was greeted at the teller window by 'Vernon Norwood', as his name tag read. Mr. Norwood was one of a dozen familiar faces here. Though he and Gabe knew each other by name, they seldom addressed each other as such.

"What may I assist you with today, Sir?" was Vernon's greeting.

"Just a deposit today, thank you Sir," countered Gabe.

Vernon continued, "Great, I'll take care of that. It still freezing out there?"

Gabe replied, "Thanks, it is too cold too early this year. At least we work indoors, right man?"

Vernon concurred, "Absolutely, you got that right guy," as he sorted and examined the checks for endorsements.

Suddenly the teller's eyebrows raised and his jaw dropped as he now addressed Gabe more seriously, "Mr. Wagner, watch your back, get down!"

Gabe whirled around quickly as a haggard older man wielding a shiny, and apparently sharp, object made his way through the crowd of singing children.

The kids were oblivious to the situation as the man swung his weapon of choice high above their heads. Teachers and parents now realized the danger and began to herd the youngsters away; it was like a parting brown sea of pipe cleaner reindeer antlers.

From the opposite side of the lobby, a bulky security guard made a beeline to the scene. But the scene was moving towards Gabe, actually the man seemed to be targeting Vernon and Gabe was in his path.

Vernon yelled, "Oh, I know who that is, stop that hobo!"

Gabe's instincts kicked in and he charged the assailant low at the waist, easily toppling him and sending the weapon flying straight up in the air. The man's head hit the hard marble floor and the weapon, which turned out to be a box cutter, landed blade first on Gabe's back. It pierced his suit jacket, oxford shirt and undershirt before ever so slightly breaking the skin between his shoulder blades. Lightly trickling blood was immediately soaked up by the layers of fabric.

Everything in the lobby settled down quickly as the bank security team promptly arrived on the scene. They then debated whether to shut down the bank under standard robbery protocol or to classify the event as a simple assault and return to business as usual. Neither party was seriously injured and they were both hustled into a secure area just outside the walk-in vault.

The carolers resumed their singing and the groggy attacker soon joined in, "Deck the Halls with rah rah rah rah, blah blah blah blah blah blah blah blah blah…"

Ted Bowers, the bank facilities manager, and an arriving Houston Police detective escorted Vernon the teller into the area as the caroling stranger was being handcuffed. Gabe answered a few informal questions and then listened as Vernon did the same. For some reason the attacker was spitting at them.

Vernon said that the man was a 'familiar bum' in the area and often harassed people on the street. He went on to say that the man had been in the bank lobby the prior afternoon trying to stay warm and was hurling insults at customers. In response to Vernon's request that he leave immediately, the man said, "I'll get you one day, Vernon Norwood!" and stuffed his pockets with handfuls of free lollipops and mints before bolting out the door.

The police were struggling to settle the suspect down and get his identity. At first Gabe thought he was the guy who was always selling newspapers on the corner of a main intersection near his apartment. But then he recognized him as a homeless man he often saw roaming the area near Jones Hall, the exact area where he had first encountered Jay and Garrett.

Ted Bowers informed Gabe that the bank would reimburse him for the cost of his damaged clothing and any medical bills, should he choose to go and get checked out, which the bank 'strongly recommended'. It would be a single stitch wound at most, he was fine.

While the police wrapped up and made photocopies of Gabe and Vernon's drivers licenses, the two men briefly chatted.

Vernon thanked him, "He was coming my way - great form tackle!"

"I just knew to go low, thankfully he's pretty frail. That old guy was about to go postal on you, with a box cutter," Gabe chuckled.

"Yeah he almost went Waco on me, but really with a razor and across a tall counter? The odds were against him big time. I don't know what's wrong with some of these people…" replied Vernon, shaking his head.

Gabe agreed, "I'm glad nothing serious happened, but some people are just out of it…you know, just not operating like the rest of us are."

Vernon went on, "Yeah, here we are working for a living and they are wanting to live off of us and endanger our lives. I have little sympathy at this moment, very little."

The lead investigator gave each of them their drivers license back and stated, "You are free to go, sorry about this ordeal. You will possibly be contacted if there is a trial, which is highly unlikely - so probably not."

Gabe wondered aloud, "So what happens to him now?"

The officer responded, "We will bring him in for further questioning and fingerprinting, booking etc, mainly trying to get an ID on him at this point."

"What kind of time will he do?" continued Gabe.

"It's likely a Class A misdemeanor, assault with a semi-deadly weapon," he winked. "Probably a couple of years in the county pen and then we'll have to deal with him again. These guys tend to go back to what's familiar. They are rarely salvageable and surely don't save themselves."

Gabe expressed his appreciation, "Thanks for everything, you take care," and the police left.

"See you Vernon, have a great Thanksgiving. And watch your back," a winking Gabe said as he headed back to his office.

Vernon replied, "Thanks again, Gabe, see you next week."

While on the way back to his office, he replayed the day's events and considered the plight of the nameless prisoner to be. He was a little proud that he had reacted instinctively and seemed to have done the right thing. The takedown was impressive despite the soft target. As he exited the building, a spirited rendition of Silent Night faded leaving the repetitive melody in his head.

He then thought about the fact that the old guy was now off the streets and would be fed and have a warm place to sleep. Gabe also realized that he'd now be indirectly providing for this man, there's always a cost.

As the elevator ascended towards floor twelve, he anxiously anticipated telling the story of his afternoon adventure. Making his way through the office, he soon realized that it truly had emptied out.

The only one still around was Kay Brightside and, though they rarely visited socially, he figured that she'd want to hear this. As he revisited the details, a true sense of compassion came across her face and she simply stated, "It sounds like he's probably an addict. You know it can happen in any family?"

"Oh, I can definitely see how," Gabe iterated and then continued, "It's extra sad around the holidays."

Kay smiled and said, "OK, well don't go getting yourself into trouble and have a Happy Thanksgiving – I'll be out tomorrow."

Gabe replied, "You too, thanks," before heading to his cubicle.

Chapter 9

It was now almost 5:00 and Gabe checked a couple of voicemails, both were from telemarketers. He then did a little reading and tossed out some junk mail.

Next he retrieved the USA Today Sports section to complete the week's scorekeeping for the Prime Time Players League. He opened his '1996PTPL' spreadsheet file, scanning the box score from the Steelers vs. Dolphins Monday Night game and entering the player points. Though he, and Kay, already knew the result, now it was official. He printed the week's results to be passed out to his coworkers and faxed to friends in the league. The league had ten members, six RPG employees and four friends of Gabe. Since he had some time to burn, he would get the faxes going and then pass out the coworker copies in the morning.

The first three faxes went through on the first dial. However, as usual, Trent Hovercraft's line was busy. He worked at Compaq Works, where they sold closeout PCs in a plush warehouse setting. Connecting to their fax machine was always a crapshoot. After a couple of failed redials, Gabe decided that he'd just have to retry later.

Gabe returned to his office and left the fantasy result copies on his keyboard to remind him to get them distributed the next morning. After shutting down his computer, he grabbed his portfolio and suit jacket and then headed for the door, nearly forgetting to stamp and initial his parking stub.

Down the elevator and back into the tunnels, he headed to the south and then east through a seventies era section which terminated at Woolworths. Once inside the store, he went up a flight of stairs to the street level and straight to the beverage cooler. Checking prices, he determined that the Bud Ice twelve pack was the best deal and grabbed one and a mini pack of red Solo cups. At the cash register he noticed that even this normally very busy store was quiet, only a meter maid buying cigarettes was ahead of him at the checkout counter.

Now quickly on his way with his goods and some cash back, he remained on the street level and ventured out onto Travis Street. He was in the holiday spirit and thought to himself, "I'll give a beer to the first homeless person I see, whether they ask for anything or not." Of course he was back at the Houston Club Building in no time and failed to run across a single one.

Gabe quickly got his validated parking ticket to Cappy and slipped into the warm lobby, where *Forever In Blue Jeans* by Neil Diamond was the current background tune. He considered the irony of his failed offer to make some street person's day and smiled to himself. His stepfather, Pops, was from Iowa had often told him that the homeless up North disappeared after Halloween due to the cold – they were apparently hunkered down in a similar manner here this late November evening.

He soon heard the familiar double eurobeep of his horn and scurried out to his car, the normal hustle and bustle of the garage was absent. Cappy left the door open and strolled over to Gabe who slipped him a five for his effort. "Well thank you, Sir!" exclaimed Cappy, noting the extra generous tip.

"You're welcome, thanks for being so quick," was Gabe's response.

"Hey, it looks like you're set for a good time tonight," said Cappy noticing Gabe's libations in the clear plastic Woolworth bag.

"Oh yeah, want one?" offered Gabe.

"Sure, but I can't - not on the job and…and certainly not from the job, if you know what I mean," reluctantly responded Cappy "Thanks though dude."

"You're welcome, and, in case I don't see you tomorrow, have a Happy Thanksgiving," said Gabe with a smile.

"Will do, you too," replied Cappy and Gabe was off on his way.

It was only a few blocks to Jones Plaza, which he could have walked, but Gabe wanted to be around where and when Laney parked, since the sun was quickly setting.

He turned onto Franklin Street and, sure enough, there was Laney parking her maroon Mazda in front of the massive main post office. Just as she got out of the car, Gabe slipped into the spot right behind her and shouted, "Hey hotness, hop in."

"Sounds like a great offer," she replied as she got in on the passenger side and kissed him.

Gabe pulled out a couple of beers and put in a cassette titled *Antmusic: The Very Best of Adam Ant*. As it played, he asked her about her afternoon and the feast they were preparing for Thanksgiving.

He then gave her the full detailed story of his adventure at the bank. She felt the punctured clothes on his back and said, "Oh Gabe, does that hurt? I am so glad that you are OK, I wish you would have called me."

"I didn't want you to worry about something that was really nothing, plus I wanted to tell you in person – it's a pretty exciting story, right?"

"Yeah, well, I want to know if something happens to you - right away, understand?" now somewhat jokingly.

He smiled and hugged her, "I am glad that you want to know 'right away', I understand. Tonight will be fun, you remember these songs?"

She nodded and furrowed her brow, "Of course I do, D. John had them."

"Wow, your brother was into Adam Ant. It doesn't seem edgy enough for him," said Gabe.

Laney continued, "He had a little of everything and this is cool, or at least fun, music. So Jane and I would take his tapes. We played these songs all the time."

Gabe reminisced, "Paul Cressy brought the *Friend or Foe* tape one night when we all went out; his older brother always had lots of non-mainstream stuff. It was the first Adam Ant I'd heard. We literally wore that tape out - I miss my New Orleans buds. Our eighties drinking songs always bring me back…"

Laney grabbed his hand, "Well, guess what, all of those guys will be at our awesome wedding."

"Yes!" replied Gabe. "It will be great, and kind of strange, to have them all here. You know, those guys together with all of our Houston friends."

"Yeah, it will be a blast. Remember, some of them sort of already know each other or they'll connect during the extensive pre-wedding festivities." Laney reassured him and then went on, "Guess what? I have great news!"

Gabe sat up a little, "Great, what's it about? Maybe the holidays..?"

"Well, it's about our big event of course," replied Laney.

With a big smile Gabe responded, "Of course I figured that. Wait, what event? What is it? Something big?"

Laney nodded and gave him a loving smack on the shoulder, "Yeah, you'd better know it's about the wedding and it is pretty big news!"

"I can tell. So, what is it?"

Laney half closed her eyes and shook her head side to side with a huge grin, "On the way back from the grocery, my new phone rang and I didn't recognize the number, but answered anyway and it was Regina with the Warwick and…"

Gabe interjected, "And..?"

Laney continued, "And, we got the Skyline Room for our date, and time, and we are still getting the same cheaper rate 'for our troubles' as she put it."

"OK, that is awesome. I mean, the other room would have been just fine, but now it will be perfect, or at least the room will be," said Gabe before continuing, "Did the other party cancel, cold feet perhaps?"

"She was just looking at the calendar wrong, the room was never double booked," said a smiling Laney. "She checked it again after I called back and apologized for freaking us out and thanked me for being understanding about it all."

Gabe sat back and said, "Oh, I bet your mom's happy, actually your dad will really be. I know that your mom doesn't really care too much about which room and all, but now they are getting an awesome deal."

Laney raised her beer, "Everyone's happy, cheers!"

"Cheers, everyone's happy!" exclaimed Gabe. He then leaned in to kiss her when something caught his eye.

Two shadowy figures were approaching his vehicle, one tall and lean, the other short and stocky.

"Look out!" Gabe warned Laney as they approached the passenger side and cupped their hands around their faces, peeking in the window.

Laney turned and responded as her eyes met theirs, "Whoa! How creepy!"

Gabe quickly confirmed that the doors were locked and started the car, then glanced over at the peeping faces. He immediately recognized both of them. They were the familiar homeless guys that he had seen that morning, the ones with the spooky eyes and juxtaposed statures.

It was still very cold out and they immediately fogged up the glass. One banged his fist on the roof, before backing off. Gabe floored it and got them out of there, "I recognize them; they hang around this area and ask for money. I saw both of them this morning, and they saw me; I was stopped at a red light and they actually pointed at me."

Laney wondered, "So are they after you or something?"

"Not really, how could they be?" Gabe pondered, "They don't know me. It's a big city."

"They seem to think they know you, or at least your car," countered Laney.

Gabe paused and then said, "No, they saw a cute girl get in and wanted a closer look. They are too out of their minds to keep track of random people, or random cars…"

Laney replied, "Out of their minds, maybe, but they still can remember things, people, you!" now giggling a little and popping the top on another Bud Ice.

"Hey, well let's just find another parking spot," said Gabe "Look here we go right here, half a block from the show."

He grabbed the pack of Solo cups from the rear seat and both of them filled a cup to the brim for the walk to Jones Plaza. It was now nearly 7:00.

Chapter 10

It was a relatively sparse turnout and Gabe and Laney could hear the opening band playing as they approached. The two of them made their way towards the front where the crowd was only about three deep. "We are Banana Blender Surprise, thank you for coming!" shouted the lead singer as they wrapped up. "Adam Ant is next!"

Snuggled up close, they did some people watching as the stage was set up for the lead act. Yuppie suits and city workers mixed along with aging punks, scattered goths and street people to create quite the eclectic scene. The time passed quickly as they finished their drinks and listened to funky jazz and techno filler music. As the lights began to dim for the headliner, Gabe spotted the two homeless guys from earlier across the crowd "Laney, over there – but don't look, it's those creepy guys, the two of them." Gabe was unsure if they had seen him, or even knew who he was away from his car. The crowd crushed forward in anticipation of the start of the show, insulating them from the lurking degenerates.

Taking the stage was Adam Ant, or possibly Adam and the Ants, there was no introduction – only those who cared more than Gabe knew the answer and those who cared less than Gabe didn't know there was a difference. He looked the same as they remembered from his music videos and album covers. The show was good and the music was great. They kept commenting to each other about how close they were to the stage and the songs, 'I remember this one' or 'another good one'. They had mild buzzes and the show was quickly over after a single encore of *Goody Two Shoes*, which remained in their heads as the overhead lighting returned to full brightness.

Gabe and Laney made a point to move with the thickest portion of the crowd down the street to the car, all the while looking back over their shoulders for the apparent nemeses. They were nowhere in sight.

Now safely back in the vehicle, focus turned to clean restrooms downtown, after regular business hours no less. Short of buying a meal or theater tickets there were two options known to Gabe, the Hyatt and the Houston Club. They chose the latter.

He pulled into the parking entrance, which was down to a single lane this time of day. Cappy was comfily nestled in a lobby chair, drinking from a metal thermos and watching a rerun of *The Jeffersons*. "Back so soon?" he coolly chimed at Gabe, "Bringing me a beer?"

"Actually, we have plenty of beer left," Gabe offered. "This is Laney, Cappy. Laney meet Cappy, the slyest of the sly around here."

"Yep, nice to meet you," said Cappy politely.

"Good to meet you as well," responded Laney.

Now hurrying, Gabe said, "Back in a few," and then, "Hi Marcus," as they passed the front desk on the way to the lobby restrooms.

Finishing his restroom business before his intended, Gabe visited with Cappy and Marcus, "Seriously, I have plenty of beer if you guys would like one." *Atomic Dog* was playing on a jam box in the garage and could be heard in the background.

"We just can't," chimed in Cappy, "Would love to though. Thanks man."

"OK, one of these days," said Gabe, turning to address Marcus, "Now please tell me again when you are heading out of town, Texarkana, right – Texas or Arkansas?"

"Noon tomorrow, I have half a morning shift and then we will be on our way." Marcus reminded him. "There will be a sub from another building coming in. Oh, and it's the Texas side of Texarkana - Texarkana, Texas."

"Oh okay, that's what I thought," said Gabe now looking Cappy's way, "How about you, heading anywhere for Thanksgiving?"

"My family's all here, so I'll work until the garage closes and then just hang tight," Cappy replied.

"Hang tight?" questioned Gabe, "So your family's all in town, near here, downtown?"

Cappy proudly stated, "Oh yeah, we all stay in Freedman's Town, off Dallas Street."

Gabe responded, "That's definitely close by, so you really will hang around."

"I usually walk to and from home and I work as many hours as they'll give me here - keeps me out of trouble," said Cappy.

"So you are like on call?" Gabe quipped then questioned, "And you said the garage closes tomorrow?"

"Yes, the club's closed for Thanksgiving. So only the building is open; but no parking here after eight tomorrow night," he answered.

Gabe nodded, "That makes sense, glad you all get time off to be home. Now stay out of trouble."

Laney now returned and gestured towards the door, "Let's roll."

"The keys are still in there man," said Cappy. "You two have a good one."

"Great, thanks," expressed Gabe before he and Laney scampered out to the car. He grabbed a couple of beers and ran them back into the lobby, where he gently slid them onto the desk in front of Marcus exclaiming, "Happy Thanksgiving" and taking off before a reply could be offered.

Now back cruising the deserted streets of downtown, Gabe and Laney talked about how much fun the concert was and then revisited the 'vagrant attack', as Laney called it.

"They were probably harmless, just curious," Gabe tried to reassure her.

Laney was only somewhat comforted, "They are obviously whacked out of their minds. Let's quickly get my car and get out of here."

"Definitely!" agreed Gabe, "I'll drive your car home, let's switch places here."

He pulled the car over and they kissed and swapped seats and then kissed again, before exchanging 'I love you's.

Back on their way with Laney now driving, they headed back towards her car. "I'll follow you home." He then quickly jumped into her car, started it up and got moving in short order.

Now moving and feeling safer, Gabe scanned the area. No one was in sight.

***

But, his departure had not gone unnoticed. Tucked comfortably below the berm at the bank across the street were Ace 'Preston' LeGrande and Reginald 'Walker' Townshend. Preston, the tall and thin one, was finishing up assorted drinks leftover and scavenged from the concert. Though warmly nestled against a grassy embankment, they both heard the cars and felt the need to get up and peek. They recognized Gabe, and his car, and shook their heads at each other.

Walker, clearly the alpha dog, sounded off, "That bastard has got something coming. Besides, I don't like the way he looks at me, at us."

Preston chimed in, "Really, what's the deal with him?"

"Oh, he thinks he's a hotshot and stares at us from a distance, but then ignores us while he struts on by," continued Walker, "This morning he gave me a serious 'go to hell' look from his car."

"Wow, you really do remember this guy out of all these random people...lots of randoms," replied Preston now sipping the remains of a Bartles and James wine cooler. "Then we'll have to catch up with him - get together with him, you and me."

Walker proclaimed, "Oh most definitely, he's a Violator." The two of them soon drifted off to sleep.

***

Gabe cruised along in Laney's car as an *Alanis Morissette* cassette played in the background. He kept a close eye on his car up ahead, as the outline of the top half of Laney's head shadowed above the headrest; her sharp driving would have her home safely in no time. He did his best to evoke inner confidence that he could always be there to protect her. The concert was well worth it and that music brought him back to cruising Uptown New Orleans in high school. Waxing nostalgic about those old friends and times, he pondered his and Laney's future kids and their future exploits, strategizing all possible means to keep them in the neighborhoods and off the freeways. His mind moved back to Laney. He simply could not get enough of this girl and had no doubt that she was the one for him. With zero traffic, they were quickly at her house and he pulled into the driveway.

He walked her to the front door and they kissed.

Laney spoke up, "OK, I love you and you're a great kisser but please shave soon, like before you come over tomorrow."

"I know, it's time – pretty impressive though, right?" he wondered aloud.

"Sure, impressive, but it's time," she responded. Gabe truly had no business attempting to grow facial hair. It was scraggly, like a case of mange.

Now smiling he said, "Are you patronizing me? Because you should be and I'll shave it in the morning. Did you have fun tonight?"

"Of course, it was great."

"Great, and worth the drive?" he asked.

She responded lovingly, "Always worth the drive, just to see you alone is worth the drive."

"OK, thanks for coming my way. I will see you tomorrow, clean shaven. Call me at the office in the morning," said Gabe before another quick kiss goodbye and genuine, "I love you."

Laney nodded and said, "I love you, too!" as she went in the screen door and turned to watch him drive away.

Back in the comfort of his car, *Buddy Holly* by Weezer came on the radio as thoughts of the days' events raced through his head and questions arose.

Who are those creepy homeless guys, the ogre and his sidekick? And, why had these Mutt and Jeff characters seemingly invaded his world, at least for this day?

What about the bank lobby attacker? Was he feeling the effects of the form tackle Gabe had laid on him?

Finally, what about Jay and Garrett? Their hunger had to have been relieved by now, but for how long?

How many beers were left in the back seat?

With his mind racing all the way, Gabe found himself at his apartment access gate sooner than expected. He had always gotten a kick out of how the apartment management labeled it an 'access gate' rather than a 'security gate' to absolve themselves of liability.

It was still very cold out, but much more bearable since the wind had died down. Gabe grabbed the now warm Bud Ice bottles and headed up to his apartment. Brittany was ready to be out and they went for an off leash walk. It had been a long day and she needed to be able to run. He felt bad that, except for when Laney came over, Brittany had become somewhat of a weekend pet; thankfully she was getting older and had lost some of her hyper puppy energy.

He gave her a treat and swapped out the warm bottles for a single ice cold Bass Pale Ale. Next he laid out running gear for the next day and loaded it into his brown leather briefcase, which he leaned against the front door. He carefully laid his keys on top, in the handle nook, so as not to forget the two items as a package deal. Next he set his alarm for 7:00 AM and got ready for bed, finishing his beer while falling asleep to SportsCenter.

Chapter 11

The sun peeked through the gap between the undersized mini blinds and the window frame, reflecting off of a coaster and onto Gabe's face. One eye opened to notice repeating bursts of red light on the wall in the bedroom. The led on the clock radio flashed *12:00*, it seemed brighter than usual and what day was it anyway? It was Wednesday and what time was it? He hopped up and scrambled to grab his watch, which read 7:24. Relief set in, he could deal with this start - late but doable.

Immediately, he opened the front door to let Brittany walk herself, playing the odds that other dogs, leashed ones with owners attached, would not be out. She was eager to do her business. He then wet and combed his hair, brushed his teeth and dressed quickly, saving tie tying for the bus. Brittany had returned without incident and pushed her way back through the cracked door opening. Gabe gave her a big scoop of food, before grabbing his briefcase and keys together while rushing out the door.

Now in his car, the clock read '7:36'. If everything went well he could catch the 7:45 bus and be in the office no later than 8:15, no big deal on this quiet eve of Thanksgiving. He caught a single red light and checked the stubble on his face in the rear view mirror, it wasn't pretty. He would just have to shave after work before heading over to Laney's.

The light changed and up ahead in the lot he spotted the on schedule and patiently waiting '210' bus, which he quickly eased by before turning in and finding a primo parking spot. He briskly walked up to the bus and saw a familiar face in the driver's seat, before realizing that he did not have his wallet.

"Hold on please, Mr. Longoria. I'll be right back," he said.

"No problem, we still have a couple of minutes," replied Alex.

On the walk back he came to conclude that his wallet was at home, but he did have a bus ticket booklet in his glove compartment. Eight hours without cash or credit seemed doable. He tore out a pair of tickets for the round trip and was back on the bus in no time greeting the driver with a quick, "Thanks for waiting, Sir." The only fully open seat was right behind the driver and he gladly took it.

Feeling a mini crisis averted, he eased back into the seat and said his usual morning prayers. The bus pulled out of the station right on time at 7:45 sharp.

Traffic was extremely light and seemed more like the flow of a weekend morning. Gabe relaxed and looked forward to the fun, extra long weekend ahead as they cruised nonstop into downtown. He had nothing to read or listen to and did not mind at all.

Considering his unusual interactions of the previous days, Gabe felt like sharing with Alex. "Mr. Longoria, you spend lots of time downtown – I know, you have to."

The driver turned his head slightly and said, "Uh huh, sure I do."

Glad to receive some sort of response, Gabe began to quiz him, "Do you ever interact with the homeless?"

Alex wondered if he should further engage, but felt as if he knew Gabe and found himself saying, "Not particularly. I pretty much just give a wave to some regulars, you know, the ones you always see in the same spots…ones who might be up to responding."

"Oh yeah, I know them. Us bus riders are forced to walk the streets and know those familiar faces," concluded Gabe before pressing on, "I decided to help one of them the other day and now I view them a little differently. It seems like they're everywhere now and know me, watch me. I know that must sound strange to you, Mr. Longoria."

The bus was emptier than usual and its driver grew more comfortable in openly conversing. "You can call me 'Alex', I work for you. Nothing surprises me anymore, but you are probably just extra aware now that you helped one of them."

"Yeah, you're right," said Gabe. "It's probably like when you buy something new and then notice everyone else who has the same something, which was clearly there all along."

Alex nodded, "Exactly".

Now more curious about his new buddy, Gabe asked Alex, "So did you really get a ticket from that Metro cop the other day?"

Alex paused and then replied, "I got a warning; she's a nice lady and totally concerned about safety."

"OK, glad to hear that - I'd hate to see you get into trouble," responded Gabe.

"Oh, I might still get into trouble. She's that type," Alex stated with a grin.

Gabe read further between the lines and quit prying, "All right, you know what you're doing."

"Definitely," became Alex's final word on the subject and Gabe would not pry further.

It was 8:02 as they exited I-10 onto Smith Street and stopped at Franklin by the main post office. Gabe was on the left side of the bus and just had to take a look around for his vagrant acquaintances from the prior day and night, moving his eyes much more than his head. He scanned the area they had occupied the morning before and spotted no one. To his right the door opened for some departing passengers and he gained a partial view of nothing of interest.

However up ahead in the bank parking lot something caught his eye. As the bank employees were arriving for the day, the hostile strangers were vacating their comfy spot. Gabe was disappointed to see that they were still around, but didn't really expect that they would just go away. He also realized that the two of them had probably watched him rescue Laney's car the night before.

Soon enough the bus reached Gabe's stop and he told Alex, "Have a Happy Thanksgiving," as he exited the bus. "You do the same, make it a good one," was Alex's reply.

Chapter 12

Down the street, through the lobby and up the elevator, Gabe was at his desk by 8:13. As far as he could tell, only the receptionist had made it in before him as others immediately began to trickle in. He was relieved but starving. Fortunately an email came through stating 'Donuts in the Kitchen'. After waiting a couple of minutes to be somewhat polite, he hit the kitchen and found a couple of dozen glazed from Shipley. Being still warm and the best of the best, Gabe discreetly snagged a few and practically inhaled them within seconds of returning to his office.

Besides keeping up with email, mail and phone calls, Gabe had two must do items for the day. First, he had to run the payroll, which he completed immediately. The second was somewhat beyond his control. Vendor invoice payments were due and he was waiting upon the return of a signed check file.

He rotated the privilege of check signing between the two managing principals: Philip James and Nelson Bosch. This week was Nelson's turn and the file had been in his office since Monday.

Of all of the eight or so principals at RPG Farnsworth, Nelson was definitely the most free spirited. He drove a Porsche, was the only Democrat in the bunch and occasionally even wore non-button down collars. A graduate of Rice, he was intellectually gifted and one of the few who could hold their own with Kay Brightside on math and financial matters.

Gabe stopped by Nelson's office to see about the status of the checks, but he was not in yet. Nelson was the only principal with a cubicle rather than an enclosed office; though it was an extra large corner cubicle, it demonstrated his egalitarian mentality. Gabe was fond of Nelson and always enjoyed visiting with him.

He swung by the kitchen for one more donut and some water. As he rounded the corner back towards his office, Gabe heard his phone ringing and hurried back to check the caller ID, which read 'Hyatt–Hou'. It could be anyone and possibly important so he answered, "This is Gabe Wagner." There was no immediate reply but he heard shallow breaths on the other end. Gabe persisted, "Hello, this is Gabe. May I help you?"

A voice on the other end quietly spoke up, "Hi Gabe, it's Jay."

Gabe covered the receiver and sighed to himself before replying, "Hi Jay, how are you?"

Jay replied, "Not so good, we need more help." His words echoed and Gabe could tell that he was in a lobby or some other large empty space.

Gabe paused before answering, "What kind of help do you need? There should be enough food for a few days."

Jay, now sounding more forlorn than ever, responded, "My friend kicked us out. We were able to take some of the food but need some cash."

Gabe quickly responded, "I am sorry to hear that. What do you need cash for?"

"We obviously will need some money in this material world," Jay defensively countered.

Gabe next said, "I know that, but do you have a plan?" before covering the receiver and whispering, "A way off the streets?"

Jay hurriedly answered, "I have a plan to fix this situation, but need help from a good guy like you."

"OK, so how much cash do you want, do you need?"

Jay was slower to respond now, "Twenty or thirty dollars would go a long way. Of course more would go further."

Gabe responded, "When do you need it?"

Jay quickly replied, "ASAP, as soon as possible, before the holidays start - for my plan."

Not having his wallet or cash, Gabe pondered a proper response. Was this just a deepening scam? "Well, I actually do not have my wallet with me today, but I can work out a way to meet you with a twenty."

"That would be great, we really appreciate it. When can we meet?" Jay graciously asked.

Gabe stated very clearly, "All right, I will meet you at noon at Sam Houston Park by Allen Parkway and I-45. There's a grey house with columns and a porch, I will meet you there."

"I know the spot and will be there."

"Great, see you there and then."

"OK, I've got to get out of here. See you," were Jay's final words for now.

So now Gabe was in a bit of a bind with a promise to deliver cash not in hand, but he really knew that it would be no problem rounding up a twenty. He would start with the neighboring offices and work his way towards the front if necessary. And, if all else failed, he could get an advance from petty cash.

The light was on, so he knew that Lonnie Lesson was in. Knowing him fairly well, he headed there first. Lon was wearing a striped shirt, a sure sign that this was the eve of a holiday.

"Good morning, Lon," said Gabe as he entered Lon's office.

"What's up Gabe?" replied Lon.

"Nothing much, I just need to borrow a twenty from you," Gabe answered. "Please don't ask why, I will pay you back on Monday."

"No problem, I know where to find you," responded Lon with a wink before pulling a thick money clip from his front pocket. "You have a Happy Thanksgiving, I am heading out early today."

"I really appreciate it, this. You have a Happy Thanksgiving too."

Gabe had figured that it would be fairly easy, but was still relieved that he was able to get the money right away.

Upon returning to his office, Gabe called Laney, but had to leave a voicemail on her cell phone. He assumed that she didn't hear it ring; perhaps she was sleeping late or taking a shower.

He then returned to Nelson's office and found him there. Gabe addressed him politely, "Good morning, Nelson. How are you?"

Nelson responded, "Pretty good, got in a good long run this morning – nine miles."

"Very good. I am running at lunch today. Have you had a chance to sign the payables?"

"No, not yet - I know that you need to get those out before the holidays. I will get them to you this afternoon."

"That'll be great, thank you."

Only a couple of the payments truly needed to be mailed before the · weekend, but they were important ones: rent and medical insurance. He was relieved that Nelson was in the office and that the checks would get signed.

Gabe then checked in with Ivan and informed him that the payroll was complete and that the invoice payments would be made on time. Ivan let Gabe know that he would be leaving early and that he should do the same. With both Ivan and Gabe being Park & Ride commuters, the earliest either would get away was 3:30 due to the bus schedule. Nevertheless Gabe would try to get an early jump on the weekend, but also knew that he may be waiting on Nelson.

Next, Gabe grabbed the stack of fantasy football score sheets he'd prepared the night before and passed them out around the office, using inboxes for those not present. He placed a copy on his chair in order to remind him to fax a copy to Trent Hovercraft before leaving for the day. Thanksgiving Day games were being played the next day and everyone, especially Trent and his hardcore buddies in the league, needed the lineups and matchups before the games kicked off.

Chapter 13

It was 11:20 and Gabe grabbed a Barq's Root Beer and the last of the now stale donuts for a quick power lunch before getting his running gear from the overhead bin in his cubicle. The stiff north wind of the prior day and a half had waned and it was now sunny and warmer out, '59°' according to the clock on the First Interstate Bank Building on the corner. He would wear an off-white long sleeved t-shirt with barely baggy cotton shorts.

He took the stairs down to the eighth floor where he dropped off all of his dress clothes less the jacket and tie. The firm had eight memberships for the various marketers. Gabe always made a point of hand delivering the monthly dues payments in order to become a familiar face and create a hint of presumption that he was a member. A cluster of empty lockers stood at the far end of the galley style men's shower area. He claimed one for the moment. His old Master combination lock from high school conveniently matched the club issued locks, with their red dials and white numbering and dashes.

The elevator actually had some traffic for a change. A middle aged woman, likely a club member, and a staff porter with a cart were bringing down a fully prepared Thanksgiving meal to be served as homemade. Gabe took in the savory aroma of the turkey and fixings, but was able to divert his attention quickly by clutching the twenty in his pocket and focusing on the impending meeting. Mild nerves overrode strong hunger.

Gabe had fifteen minutes to make his way over to the park and carefully considered what he might say to Jay, as well as what would be appropriate in front of Garrett. He would get details on Jay's plan and options and more about possible family and friends to also help them. But his main point to convey would be the fact that his willingness and ability to offer help had reached their respective ends.

This was the route Gabe took two or three days a week, since it acted as the gateway to the winding and slightly hilly jogging path along Buffalo Bayou. He was going this way anyway today, but was starting to regret choosing a meeting spot that he would frequently have to pass, potentially ruining a happy escape place should the meeting have an unpleasant outcome.

It was a very pleasant day and lots of people had chosen to forego the tunnels for the fresh air to be found above ground. Familiar joggers passed him as they approached the main trail on the western edge of downtown, where the far edge of true skyscrapers gave way to parkland and wider roads. Gabe scanned the landscape for signs of the cretin duo seemingly stalking him. In the distance he could see some of the many restored historical homes in Sam Houston Park.

***

Meanwhile, a mile or so to the northeast at the Harris County Corrections intake center, Ricardo 'Clay' Hidalgo was being bailed out and released back onto the streets of Houston. His bond was posted by none other than Reginald Townshend.

Reginald, who was now known only as 'Walker', was born the only son of Charles Townshend and Tomeka Collins-Townshend of Montgomery, Alabama. Charles was an attorney and had come to Alabama from Rochester, New York in the late sixties as a civil rights activist. His mother Tomeka was a school teacher turned librarian. Walker's parents were happily married and still lived in Montgomery.

Unlike his kind and gentle parents, Walker had a mean streak from a very young age, which he had eventually learned to channel and control, somewhat. He also bore the brunt of mixed race teasing and taunts throughout grade school. Walker grew into a handsome and athletic teen and was a high ranking member of the junior ROTC at Jefferson Davis High School. Though a great student and high school baseball star with preferred walk-on offers to play college ball, Walker decided to enlist in the US Army right out of high school. Somehow he had now found himself a hustler on the streets of downtown Houston.

Walker came to the realization that he had overestimated Clay's physical ability to take out Gabe, or perhaps they needed to step up their choice of weapons. But with Ace 'Preston' LeGrande passed out drunk half the time and other unreliables within his ranks, Walker needed Clay on the streets to act as a scout or decoy at the very least. Also, Walker was not comfortable with Clay in police custody, potentially spilling his guts.

***

Back at the park, Gabe and Jay simultaneously arrived in front of the grey Greek Revival home they had agreed upon, the sign read '1870 Jack Yates House'. Jack Yates was a former slave and minister, who founded the first predominantly black church in Houston following the Civil War. The home had been relocated from Freedman's Town to the park and was set for a post renovation grand opening within the next couple of weeks. The fresh paint smelled and sparkled in the high noon sun.

Jay's look was approaching ragged as was Gabe's, unshaven amplified by scruffy workout clothes. With no sign of Garrett, Gabe immediately expressed his concern, "Hi Jay, is Garrett not with you?"

Immediately Jay's eyes expressed nothing but total sadness, "His aunt on his mother's side has him," he continued, "I had no choice to call her once I knew that we were out of my friend's house." In full sunlight, Jay's slight wrinkles and salt and pepper stubble were fully visible; his white shirt was yellowing in some spots.

Gabe asked more, "So where is he?"

"Well, he's safe, much safer than he'd be around here," Jay replied "Right now he is in a car headed for Lake Charles, probably more than halfway now."

"OK, I am glad that he's safe and I know that you miss him. He seems like a great kid – from what I could tell."

Jay nodded and thought for a second before conceding, "He will probably be best off there, and back in school. My wife's kin are good people."

Though curious to know more upon the first mention of a wife, Gabe kept it moving, "That's good to know. So let's talk about your plan."

"I will really miss my little man. Garrett keeps me going. My plan is all about getting my son taken care of, him and his mother too."

Gabe paused and, though he was now becoming emotionally and financially involved, he again chose not to pry into the issue of Jay's wife. "So what is your plan to take care of them?"

Jay took a deep breath and went on, "This big city has gotten the best of me and it's time for me to move on and settle."

Gabe wondered what this meant. It was getting warm and glary so Gabe motioned for Jay to move into the shade with him. Gabe spoke again, "Jay, what do you mean by settle?"

Without hesitation Jay responded, "When I came here it was for college and a career and to be a success. None of that matters now, I want to go home and be able to take care of my family."

"Where is home?" said Gabe.

Jay replied, "Home is Beaumont, really Port Arthur. Greyhound will get me there for $25."

Gabe nodded in approval, "Not a bad trip at all, just over an hour."

Jay went on, "I have brothers there and can get some work plus find a very cheap place to stay."

Now with a slight smile Gabe said, "Well I am so glad to hear that you have some family not too far away. I am sure that they miss you."

"Yeah, I hate to come crawling home with my hat in my hand, but they're good down home folks, my people."

Gabe attempted to console him, "You might catch a little grief, but I bet they'll just be happy to have you around. Besides, you're not obnoxious or anything."

Jay looked all around and then right into Gabe's eyes, "You're a good man, a fine man, Gabe Wagner. Thanks for meeting up with me."

"Honestly, Jay, I mean thank you, but I really hated to see your boy out in the cold and wanted to help. Please do know that I am not super charitable, or well off, but felt the need to see what was up with you guys the other night..." rambled Gabe.

Jay wondered out loud, "Do you regret doing that?"

"Not at all - I do not regret it at all. As I told you on the phone, I left my wallet at home today, idiot move, but was able to get you a twenty." He pulled the folded bill from his pocket and handed it to Jay.

An appreciative Jay responded, "Thank you, man. This is just about enough to get me there. I will remember this and pay you back someday. I still have your card."

"No problem, wish I'd brought enough to get you home. You pay me back when you are able. I can tell that it will bother you a little until you do."

"I still have a little pride," was Jay's sanguine response.

"At this point in our lives you just happen to be less fortunate than I, that's all," stated Gabe, who then asked, "So how will you get the rest of the cash for the bus ticket?"

"Oh, well I'll ask around here and over at the library by city hall," responded Jay before going on, "You know it will be tougher to get any sympathy not having Garrett with me. If I strike out today, well, then I can surely find some generosity at the charity feast at the convention center in the morning."

Gabe now inquired, "So where would you sleep?"

Jay shook his head, "I doubt it will come to that, but maybe I'll sleep in this here house," nodding his head towards the grey Jack Yates house currently providing them shade. He went on, "You know for people without homes, this park is kind of like a little neighborhood, even though the fixed up houses are double locked with alarms and extra thick plexiglass windows."

"OK, I know that you can take care of yourself, I guess your friend's place is not an option?"

"Being that he kicked us out because he had folks coming in for Thanksgiving, it's really not. His place is tiny and we were really invading his space."

Continuing with the intention of wrapping up Gabe asked, "How often do the buses leave for Port Arthur?"

"Four or five times a day, my friend," was Jay's response, "The schedule is no issue at all; departure and travel times are really non factors."

"OK, I will let you get on your way," Gabe said as he shook Jay's hand and touched his shoulder.

Jay was happy to be having an extended adult conversation and was fond of Gabe beyond his ability to give him some food or cash, but was also ready to get moving. "You cannot know how much I appreciate your help."

Gabe quickly popped back, "You would do exactly the same for me and you know it. Tell Garrett 'Hello' from me when you see him again and I hope that's soon."

"Will do, soon, very soon," answered Jay as he started towards the main library.

Chapter 14

The crisp fall day was perfect for a long run. In his haste to get out the door, Gabe had neglected to wear his Ironman training watch, but he knew all too well how long the various courses took. The conversation with Jay seemed to last forever. But in actuality it had lasted all of five minutes, just long enough for Walker and Clay to walk up on the scene and view the tail end of the meeting.

With the Tenneco Marathon less than two months away, Gabe needed to get in all the miles he could. Not knowing the exact time, he chose to do the five mile Allen Parkway Shepherd Drive loop. Plenty of runners were out, enjoying the weather and getting in a last run before the long holiday weekend of feasting and sedentary visiting with company.

The first mile was always his toughest, and slowest. Jay and Garrett's plight consumed all thoughts. His mind raced between images of their faces and the bus station and the road to and between Port Arthur and Lake Charles, which was very familiar to Gabe. He felt good about getting involved and offering genuine help. He was pleased that they seemed on their way to a better place and relieved that he was once again removed from their struggles, however minor his involvement had been. Realizing that he may never know their ultimate fate, he also realized that he wanted to know how things turned out only if they were for the best.

***

Walker flanked by Clay trekked around the perimeter of the park and then methodically approached before reintroducing himself to Jay. "Aha, my sharp dressed friend, welcome back to the neighborhood."

Jay had encountered Walker once before. Monday night in the cold, after he first met Gabe by Jones Hall, Walker and Preston LeGrande had appeared out of nowhere. Walker rarely worked alone. He had seen Gabe hand Jay his business card and mistook it for money. They emptied Jay's pockets and found only the card, which was promptly crumpled up and tossed in the wind. The marauders also made a point to threaten Garrett's well being. Jay had been wise enough to leave his wallet at his friend's house that day and also wise enough to scoop up Gabe's card as they left the scene.

Jay attempted to step up his pace towards the bus station before quickly remembering that he needed another five dollars and that the bus station was full of takers, not givers. He slowed just enough to allow Walker and Clay to slip in front of him and stop him in his tracks. Not about to go without an answer Jay responded, "I already told you that you're not the boss of me and I am not your friend."

Walker did the speaking and Clay did the nodding, "This is my neighborhood and you are in it," he went on, "I get a cut of everything that happens in or near The District." Jay was familiar with the Theater District, the northwest area of downtown containing several theaters home to the performing arts.

Though definitely intimidated by Walker's scowl and thick build, Jay was not backing down. "This is a public right of way, it's ours, not just yours. Move along."

The truth was that Walker ostensibly ruled this area for those living on the edge; Jay was precariously close to being a part of this world. As vulnerable as he felt at the moment, he was filled with inner comfort knowing that Garrett was safe somewhere else now.

Walker came closer and spoke again, "I will show what's mine. Normally I just take a piece, a 'guardinar' as we call it, a fee to keep you safe. But to show how things can be, this time I'll take 100%." Jay attempted to head butt Walker, who stepped back and grabbed Jay's shoulders, turning him around and lifting his chin in a cocky nod to Clay, "It's in his front pocket," referencing the bill he'd seen Jay receive from Gabe.

Clay pulled out the twenty, along with the now wrinkled business card and then commented, "Ooh, this will go far." This was a huge sum in this world of ones and an occasional five or ten.

Grabbing both the cash and the card, Walker in the most ominous voice said "This may go even farther?" as he read the card, "This 'Gabriel J. Wagner' has chosen to go messin' up in my world, in our District. We deal harshly with Violators, such as him, and you."

A large group of office workers scurried along the sidewalk and a couple yelled for the thugs to let Jay go. Walker and Clay had little to lose and just ignored them, fully aware that these lunch breakers weren't interested in getting mixed up with street people matters.

As the two prepared to check Jay's back pockets, a mounted patrol officer rounded the corner and they immediately released him, before smiling like middle school bullies around a hall monitor. Jay was safe for now, but broke and starting over in his quest to raise the bus ticket cash.

***

Though not sure of his exact pace, Gabe was running well, surprisingly well, especially considering the fact that he was being fueled by donuts and soft drinks.

Going into the second mile, the tempo picked up and his runner's high kicked in. As always, he reminded himself that this feeling was the main reason he ran. All of the slight aches and pains subsided and the rhythmic ticking of his shoestrings moved from being an utter nuisance to being the perfect metronome tuning his cadence.

His thoughts turned to Laney, not only how beautiful she was, but how beautiful their life together would be. He marveled at the incredible weather, so clear and not windy or humid or cold, just ideal for running. The effects of the season's first freeze were not yet showing, so the grass was still green and the crepe myrtles still bore leaves and fading flowers. Buffalo Bayou was blue with the reflection of the sky above.

Turning back towards downtown, he'd reached the halfway point. Gabe loved working downtown. A strong push was on to bring more residential and night life there, and tangible signs of changes to come were popping up all over. The modern skyline shimmered in the sun, with towering skyscrapers perfectly varied and spaced. He considered his path in life, how he'd always wanted to wear a suit and work in a tall building, one with a shoe shine stand. As a huge sports fan, he also cherished the evening and weekends off a professional position afforded.

This extra long holiday weekend would be just perfect. A tremendous, delicious meal with leftovers and football, pro and then college and then pro again, shared with his family to be. He especially loved it when Jane and Dion visited, partly because he genuinely liked them, but even more so because Laney's happiness elevated. Elevated until the last day, when everyone realized that the visit was wrapping up with an airport run to remind everyone that work and school and the real world loomed. His reality was that he was glad to have Laney to himself again and that her sadness diminished ever so slightly with each of Jane's subsequent departures.

Gabe jogged back into downtown and wrapped up mile five passing through Sam Houston Park. He realized that he'd probably think of Jay every time he came through or by the park, particularly when seeing the grey Yates House. His little extra favor to Jay would be their little secret, no pats on the back for offering charity or chastising for brushes with 'danger' were necessary. Their two worlds were once again safely separate.

Coming around the corner at One Shell Plaza and about to slow his pace, Gabe noticed a pair of familiar characters seated on the steps. It was Walker and Clay. His mind raced, his runner's high instantly waned. He maintained his pace and casually veered from the usual course, attempting to discreetly keep his distance.

Walker, with his wits always about him, saw Gabe right away and nudged Clay, "Hey look, there's our friend Gabriel."

Clay perked up and then called out, "Let's get him." Gabe now knew that they'd spotted him.

Walker rocked back and said, "Oh, let him go for now - now that we know where to find him."

Being the lackey he was, Clay chimed in with instant affirmation, "Yeah, man – exactly where to find him."

Out of pure instinct, Gabe ran up the parking garage ramp at the Houston Club Building. He wasn't quite sure why but felt that it'd be his safest route. He was sure that they had lost visual on him but did not want them to see him enter through the main lobby.

His avoidance route had entered a maze of columns defining extremely tight parking spots fit only for trained valets. Headlights and constant honking were their lifelines in this world; Gabe was amazed at how fast they drove other people's vehicles in this surreal world surrounded by fake, louvered windows offering little ventilation.

"C. Ellis" read Cappy's name tag as he stepped off the conveyor during his descent from an upper floor and approached Gabe, "Mr. Wagner, is that you?"

Gabe was tired and, perhaps, feeling the effects of serious exhaust fumes. He responded, "Hey Cappy. It is me, Gabe"

Cappy was puzzled, "Are you trying to check on your car, is it in the garage today?"

"No, it's nothing to do with my car," Gabe replied and then went on, "You probably won't believe this, but I am positive that there are street people, homeless guys, after me."

Knowing that Gabe was a customer, both a tenant and a member, Cappy attempted to take him serious. "I guess that's possible. So how did they come to know you, to choose you?"

"I don't know how or why, but they are almost stalking me," said Gabe before continuing. "At first I thought it was a coincidence that I kept running across them, then they called me out today, just now."

Cappy sat on a nearby stool and said, "Stalking you? Are they threatening you? What started this?"

Gabe, now sensing some patronizing on Cappy's part, replied, "I know that it sounds crazy - but it started this week. I will just have to be more selective about what bus stops I use, or just drive in more for a little while."

Now needing to get back to work, Cappy offered some help. "I'll let you in the building through the staff door here," pointing and then opening a red, windowless door to the stairway.

"Thanks, and again, you have a great Thanksgiving," said Gabe before entering the stairway.

Cappy patted him on the back and gave a farewell, "You take care, Mr. Gabe," before hopping back on the conveyor and heading down.

Chapter 15

Jay wandered around a while before finding a safe alcove in a vacant store front on Market Square. Moving toward the bus station would be futile without the necessary fare. It was time to have a seat and regroup.

First, he removed his current drivers license from his wallet and put it under the insole of his left shoe. The wayfarer didn't want it to be lifted from his person if and when he endured another shakedown. He actually had an expired license too, which he put in the other shoe just in case. The lifeline to Gabe was now severed and he started to weigh his options.

Going back to the Hyatt to make a call was somewhat of an option, but the folks who could rescue him would be a long distance call away, not doable from a courtesy phone. Besides he'd sort of already been run off from the Hyatt.

After a hearty breakfast this morning, Jay had not eaten a thing and was getting hungry. He got a strong whiff of the Cajun lunch offerings at Treebeard's across the square. The aroma of crawfish etouffee, as well as oyster and shrimp poboys on buttered bread filled the air and reminded him of home. With the clock on the square reading '1:10', his plan was to grab a bite from some leftovers on a sidewalk table. As he nonchalantly drifted closer, Jay realized that he could time his arrival with the departure of a table of five and was able to discreetly snag some bread and butter. A couple of other diners noticed, but didn't really care.

Jay located another shaded spot in front of the Majestic Metro, finding a ledge against which to rest and comfortably enjoy the bread. It was very filling.

***

Safely inside the worn stairwell, up went Gabe as a hint of stale cigarette smoke further motivated his ascent to the eighth floor locker room. Upon gathering his business attire, he caught a glimpse of the clock which read '1:17'. He hurriedly washed up and dressed, leaving his tie around his neck completely untied, then jumped into the elevator for the short ride up to the twelfth floor. Time for a proper shower would come after work before heading over to Laney's.

No one was around the office, even at the front desk. Gabe returned to his office and checked email where the header to his only new message read 'Happy Thanksgiving – Office Closing at 1:00'. It had been sent at 11:45, right after Gabe had left for his lunch break. This pleasant semi-surprise prompted a chair spin, complete with a contemplative look out the window. Clouds were beginning to fill the bits of sky visible above the surrounding buildings.

Tucking his loose tie into his suit pocket and undoing the top button on his shirt, Gabe was comfortable but realized that he was hungry. The best option was to rescue a leftover half sandwich from the refrigerator, which would surely spoil by the time everyone returned on Monday. As a compensatory good deed, he moved some room temperature soft drinks from a storage cabinet into the refrigerator, being sure to remove the plastic rings and pop the loops so as not to trap scavenging landfill birds as per company policy.

Now back in his office and kicked back with his feet up on the desk. Gabe remembered that he had some payables to get out and checked his box for a delivery from Nelson. It was bare.

The only choice now was to go over to Nelson's office and check on them. After a brief internal debate, Gabe decided to forego bringing the tie back out since it was now technically after hours and Nelson was least likely of all to care.

Nelson was in and seemed to be in a great mood. Noticing Gabe he said, "Hey Gabe, the checks are ready. I signed them and they are over there," motioning towards the folder at the other end of his long formica desk.

"Great, thank you. Have a Happy Thanksgiving," replied Gabe as he went over to get the file.

"Do you have big plans for the Thanksgiving?" asked Nelson.

"No super big plans, just staying in town and relaxing. How about you all?"

"We are staying in town, too. Hey, would you want to grab a drink and some oysters in a little while?"

Gabe thought for a second and then replied, "Sure, I'd love to. When?"

"How about 4:00 in the 1894 Room?"

"That sounds great, see you then," answered Gabe. It was plenty early enough for him to still catch one of the first busses out.

Nelson concluded "OK, very good – catch you then."

Gabe returned to his office and pulled out the payments that had to be sent immediately. There were just a few and Gabe stuffed and stamped some envelopes before heading downstairs to the lobby mailbox.

Once again there was a club member's Thanksgiving dinner heading down in the elevator with Gabe. This time it appeared to be hired house help doing the pickup. They exchanged greetings and both commented on how great the food smelled.

After completing the mail drop, Gabe stopped by the garage area. It was dead quiet and the older valets were playing dominoes. Cappy was seated near the radio and appeared to be half asleep; Gabe tapped his shoulder and said, "Hey, man. Thanks again for helping me out earlier, I really appreciate that."

Cappy pointed at him with his pinky and responded, "No problem – any time."

Gabe gave him a quick, "Later," and headed back into the lobby.

An unfamiliar fellow sat at the security desk and Gabe said, "Hello there," as he breezed by.

Entering the elevator lobby he heard the stranger call out behind him, "Hold on, sir. Sir, may I ask – which tenant are you visiting?"

After confirming that he was the target of the question, Gabe replied, "I am actually on staff with RPG Farnsworth on the twelfth floor." He glanced at the stranger's name badge. It read 'Norman Cline'.

The overzealous Mr. Cline responded, "OK, let me check my records," he then continued, "It shows here that RPG Farnsworth closed their offices at 1:00 today and won't reopen until 8:00 on Monday."

"Yes, well I am still working. I just mailed some checks, didn't you see me come out of the elevator a minute ago?" countered Gabe.

"No Sir. I am focused on those entering the building," was the doorman's snarky response.

Gabe now started to become indignant, "Really, shouldn't you also care what's coming out of here. What about all of these carts of food – or is it really food rolling out of here?"

"May I please see your ID? So that we may both return to our business," demanded Mr. Cline.

Really, of all days to not have his wallet, Gabe was more than perturbed when Cappy appeared behind him and said, "I will vouch for this man. He is Mr. Gabe Wagner and works here just like you and me and the rest of us."

Mr. Cline continued with his strict protocol routine, "Mr. Ellis, I appreciate your concern, but this is a security matter and I just need to see your friend's ID to clear him for entry into the building."

"Really, just let the guy in and quit being such a prick," replied Cappy.

"Name-calling will not be productive in this situation," responded Mr. Cline. "He is requesting to visit an office that is closed for the day. I simply need some identification to allow him entry."

Cappy looked at Gabe and conceded, "Alright, this guy 'Mr. Cline' is insisting on harassing a tenant and, therefore, needs to see your ID."

Gabe realized Cappy had no reason to think or know that he didn't have his wallet ergo ID. This would go nowhere and so he said, "Out of principle, I will head directly to PM Realty Group's main office and file a complaint right now with Mr. Ellis as my witness, specifically citing that Mr. Cline is indeed a prick." As the primary payer of RPG's bills, Gabe was able to recall the name 'PM Realty', the property manager and Mr. Cline's employer, which also happened to be a client of RPG. He then put his arm around Cappy's shoulder and walked him out to the parking garage.

Once outside, Gabe informed Cappy that he didn't have his wallet and got the OK from him to ride the conveyor up to the employee entrance to the stairway. The rest of the valets were still engrossed in their game of dominoes.

Cappy's response was, "I told you 'anytime' and I meant it. That clown will be out of here at eight tonight and you probably won't see him again until next Thanksgiving, if ever."

"I owe you one, at least one," said Gabe with a smile.

"You're OK, Mr. Gabe," said Cappy, once again pointing at Gabe as he trotted up the ramp.

The door was still unlocked and Gabe was back in. He took the stairs up to the eighth floor once again since it was a proven route.

Once in the elevator, Gabe caught a glimpse of his own reflection in the shiny door and realized how bad he looked - absolutely ragged and unshaven. Upon further review, he might not have let himself into the building either.

A quick grazing pass through the kitchen yielded some crackers and another root beer, which would hold him over until he met up with Nelson.

Chapter 16

Steady rain began to fall at the Majestic Metro and Jay further settled in to the cover it afforded. Foot traffic came to a halt, the employed stayed in their tunnels, while the disenfranchised sheltered in place for the time being. Vehicular traffic kept moving and the road noise was amplified by the water, echoing off of the surrounding buildings. For the first time ever, Jay noticed that tire noise trumped engine noise. His mind was clear and ready to formulate his next plan. The goal remained the same: return home to Port Arthur.

Raising enough money for a bus ride would be almost impossible at this point. Walker and his cronies seemed to be lurking around every corner and would surely keep ripping off each bit of cash he could possibly garner from strangers. His prospects for collecting donations were further diminished by the fact that he no longer had Garrett to set him apart from the common panhandlers. Furthermore, the workers were rapidly clearing out of downtown, most for the duration of the weekend, and the ones that were left certainly wouldn't be stopping and passing out money in the rain.

Still, Jay's resolve remained strong. With or without money, he would get to Port Arthur and save his family.

Actually, he had chosen this locale for a reason. The north side of downtown Houston was bordered by Interstate 10, which ran east-west less than a quarter mile from this very spot, Jay would take it west to east. No longer willing to be fully at the mercy of others, his decision was to go full pioneer style. He would walk his way home, a full hundred miles.

Along the way hitchhiking would be an option, indeed not turning away any help that may come his way. Surely some Thanksgiving travelers would let him hop in the bed of their pickup.

Gabe had told him to remember to pray and so he did, the light steady rain soon became a torrential downpour. He would leave in the morning and be home no later than Sunday.

***

A few blocks to the south, Gabe was snacking on crackers and catching up on his Far Side daily calendar, tearing the sheets away one day at a time. He even went a few days ahead since he'd be out until Monday. He noticed the very heavy rain outside his window and phoned in the 401K contribution for the month end payroll.

He called Laney again, starting with the home phone first to preserve her mobile airtime. She answered on the third ring, "Hello."

Gabe paused for a second and then went on, "Hello, is that you Laney?" When her twin sister Jane was in town, Gabe always double checked to see who it was before continuing - they and their voices were identical.

Laney responded, "Yes, it's me – of course. Jane doesn't really answer this phone anymore."

"OK, just being sure."

Laney continued, "So what have you been up to all day, I thought you might call me this morning."

Gabe replied, "I did call, but there was no answer and I figured that you were either sleeping or in the shower or, maybe headed to the airport" he continued "I left a voicemail on your new cell phone. Did you get it?"

"Oh, I saw that cute little envelope picture, but don't know how to retrieve voicemails on this phone yet," answered Laney.

"Jane will show you, she works for Sprint after all," Gabe said before continuing, "So what are you up to?"

Her voice lit up now, "They have arrived and we are ready for you to arrive. How has your day been?"

"Excellent, I can't wait to see them, everyone, and just chill. This has been a hectic day, mainly because my alarm did not go off and I left my wallet at home," responded an exasperated Gabe.

"Are you OK?" replied a concerned Laney, "Oh, and did you bring a lunch, or are you starving?"

Gabe elaborated, "The power went out last night - it's just been a hassle. I did not have time to grab a lunch, so I've just been eating scraps around here. It started with Shipley donuts, soft warm glazed, and has pretty much gone downhill from there."

"Oh, I won't ask what junk you've consumed. There's plenty of food here…and junk too," Laney quipped.

"Hey, well I did get my run in and one of the Principals is taking me to the club, the main bar that is, for drinks and oysters."

"Very cool, who is it?"

"Nelson Bosch - you've met him. He's the Rice guy who lives right by the campus. Remember we went over there for Bloody Marys before the UH-Rice game last year?"

"Oh yeah, I remember his wife. I like her. She's very nice, and actually down to earth. So why did he invite you to the club?" she wondered out loud.

"Probably because I was his only option - I pretty much had to say 'yes'," explained Gabe, before going on, "I like him though! He's fun and always has interesting stories. Plus I'm getting hungry for some real food, protein, like oysters."

Laney understood and said, "OK, as long as you show up here hungry, and not too late."

"Absolutely, traffic should be a breeze. So I will see you soon, 'My Bride'," he kidded. "I do need to stop by the apartment and get my wallet." He also really needed to shave and shower, which he chose not to mention.

"'My Bride, huh, I sort of like it, the way it sounds. But it's sort of too 1950ish if you know what I mean…" she teased and then countered, "OK 'My Groom', I will see you later."

"Well that's fine, I like that, I have no problem being yours," stated Gabe, "I love you."

She giggled and answered, "I love you too." The call ended.

With almost an hour to burn until it was time to meet Nelson, Gabe had completed everything due and considered possible alternatives to playing solitaire or watching the rain.

It was time for a little Mavis Beacon.

Gabe had entered the workforce, the professional workforce that is, right about the time that everyone started having a computer on or at their desk.

He shared an office with plenty of folks like him, mostly men, who never bothered to learn to type. In high school, only the remedial students took typing, usually as a blow off course like shop for an easy 'A'. In Gabe's mind, when he entered the real working world, a secretary would do all of his typing, perhaps even take dictation and use shorthand.

At RPG only very few executive types were still using transcribers with dictation and secretaries. Personal assistants were becoming shared assistants and just about everyone was migrating to email, composing their own messages.

It was laborious and painful, and especially so to watch, as the well educated and highly successful struggled along, hunting and pecking their way through this new world.

Knowing how competitive this group was, Ivan had come up with a great idea.

RPG Farnsworth would conduct the First and Only Novice Typing Skirmish, or *FONTS,* at some point in the future to determine a champion, but really to speed everyone up. Frankly, none of these Type A guys were comfortable with appearing so feeble; it was a win-win proposition.

Ivan floated the idea and the principals bought in. Only two conditions were added.

To start with, a significant cash prize with money from the competitors, and matched equally by the firm, was a must.

Secondly, the contest had to be renamed with the word 'Typing' being replaced by the word 'Keyboarding', despite the fact that the name of the program being used was 'Mavis Beacon Teaches Typing 2.0'. It was simply impossible to underestimate the value of collective pride within this crew.

The contest was scheduled for February 15th and Gabe was one of the favorites. He would practice on this day to keep it that way. The one-hundred dollar entry fee meant a lot more to him than any of the others and the prize would cover two months worth of rent.

Chapter 17

With the decision to leave the next morning made, Jay knew that he needed to find a safe place to spend the night. And, it would be great if he also happened to score some food along the way.

With a fresh new plan and his bearings now straight, Jay realized that the Harris County Criminal Justice Complex was just across Main Street from his current location. After serving as a juror on more than a couple of occasions, he knew that there were about five court houses and a county prison not too far away. He also knew that there was a steady stream of released suspects and convicts heading in all directions at all times.

His options were limited.

Staying put or heading east as daylight began to fade would expose him to the criminal element he'd just recollected.

Going south would only bring him farther from I-10 and make his upcoming trek to Port Arthur that much longer.

Due west was 'The District', Walker's territory, and he wanted no piece of that.

His only option was to head northwest, to the area around the main post office where Buffalo Bayou and multiple bridges converged. He wanted the most secluded, dark spot possible – invisible and warm suited him best to rest up for the journey ahead.

The rain had subsided and was down to a drizzle with intermittent sun. Jay decided that it was time to move and made his way past Treebeard's, which was now closed for the day. But next door was Warren's Inn, it was open and he was daring enough to open the door and venture into this mysterious place he'd always wondered about. As expected, it was extremely dark inside, especially for his weary eyes transitioning from the now bright and glary outdoors.

His presence only managed to turn the heads of a couple of regulars. Amongst the dim, Jay pretty much looked like any guy who had just gotten off work and removed his tie before getting caught in the rain. The wet weather acted as an equalizer for him. He was less than a day removed from his last shower and, thus, not yet odiferous. Warren's was the consummate dive bar and he felt as though he had entered a different era. Everything was vintage, mostly in a good way, and certainly good enough to take care of his business. On the way out he discreetly grabbed a paper bowl full of shelled peanuts; only the barflies noticed and not a word was said.

He crossed the street where he leaned against a concrete wall and ate the peanuts.

His next task was to make a sign for his hitchhiking adventure. Cardboard was scattered about, but everything he saw was either rain soaked or too small.

Across the square, he spotted lights on at La Carafe, reputed to be the oldest bar in Houston, or at least the one with the oldest liquor license. As he approached, he realized that he had passed this place many, many times before but never noticed it. The large wooden door was propped half open in order to take advantage of the mild day and fresh air and Jay stepped inside. A single patron was seated at the bar near the front door and visiting with the bartender. They both smiled at Jay when he walked in, before returning to their conversation, apparently a deep one.

Jay remained standing and scoped the place out for the supplies he needed. He marveled at the charm of the old place with its exposed brick walls and soaring ceilings, massive beams and old ceiling fans. Admiring the charming ambiance, he struck up a conversation with the two present, "What a great place, I've always wanted to come in here"

The bartender replied, "We hear that all of the time; people have heard of us but don't always find us. Can I get you a drink?" *Rikki Don't Lose That Number* by Steely Dan was playing on the jukebox.

"Maybe just a water for now," answered Jay, "I am supposed to be meeting someone here, well actually on the square, but the storm may have held them up." He noticed a wooden staircase at the back of the room; it appeared to be open to customers, as there was a sign with an arrow pointing up.

"OK, Sir. Just let me know if you need anything," said the bartender, while the other patron comfortable rocked slightly on his barstool.

Jay took the glass of water and responded, "Thank you, I will," while conspicuously looking all around the space. He then stated and asked, "I can just feel all of the history in here. Is the upstairs open?"

The bartender replied, "You are welcome to go and look around, but there is no service up there now."

Jay quickly scanned the whiskey offerings available at the bar and said, "I think I'll go and take a look."

The bartender paused and then asked, "So what about the friend you might be meeting?"

Slightly taken aback, Jay took a second and formulated a response, "Oh yeah, my friend. He's a yuppie guy in his twenties, with a scraggly beard if you want to call it that, a 'beard' I mean…name's 'Gabe'. Please let him know that I'll be right back." He then strolled toward the back.

The staircase was steep and squeaky. At the top Jay observed that the upstairs was not quite as grand and also noticed how narrow the building was. He snagged a pen from the bar and looked around for anything he could use to make a sign. There was a small cardboard menu, which was a possibility, so he folded it up and stuffed it in his back pocket.

Next, Jay noted the whiskey selection at the upper bar, he noticed lots of dust. Then he went to the front and looked out the windows overlooking the square. It was raining again and time to move on.

Jay walked over to the stairs at the back of the room, once again carefully checking stocked whiskey options once again as he passed the bar. He took a deep breath before descending.

Back in the main bar, Jay wondered out loud, "So, no one came in looking for me, did they?"

The bartender responded, "Nope," and then asked, "Would you like a drink now?"

Jay answered, "It looks like it's raining hard again. You know, I'll have a Maker's Mark, a double straight up on the rocks."

"Maker's Mark, huh? Definitely not our most popular," said the bartender, "We don't have any down here; I'll have to check upstairs. There may be some there."

"I think I saw a bottle up there, it'd probably be out of line for me to go back and grab it for you," quipped Jay.

"Yeah," responded the bartender, "The TABC would be all over that, you're not the TABC are you?" Smiling big, he looked over at his obviously tipsy buddy and pointed at the door saying, "Keep an eye on the front for me, will you? I'll be right back"

Right inside of the front door was an easel with a small dry erase board and a couple of markers, one black, one blue.

Jay could clearly hear the bartender's footsteps echo on the wooden stairs and once he was clearly about halfway up. It was time to make a move.

He hustled over to the dry erase board and scooped up the two markers, which he shoved in his pocket. Next he tucked the dry erase board under his shoulder and slipped out the half open door before lifting the board above his head to block the rain. An eraser went flying into a gutter puddle and old multi colored ink seeped into the flowing water. His next destination was the main post office and Subjects were watching.

Chapter 18

Nelson called out, "Hey, Gabe, are you still over there?"

From his cubicle, Gabe shouted back, "Yes, and I am done and ready to shut it down."

"Great, I'll see you down there in a few, 1894 Room alright?" said Nelson.

Gabe replied, "OK, sounds great", before going to check the transmittal report for the fax he was attempting to send to Trent Hovercraft. The report read 'Line Busy – Auto redial pending'. It would be a huge hassle for everyone if the report didn't eventually go through, especially with the first game kicking off before noon the next day. Either way it was out of his hands and he was ready for a drink.

While his computer shut down, Gabe debated and then decided not to bring his coat and tie, especially since it was no longer cold out. He had already planned to come in over the weekend to swap out his running gear and could get them then.

Just like the city after which it was named, The Houston Club was genuinely Southern with some Western influences. The 1894 Room was a fine case in point, its massive mahogany bar elegantly adorned with carved magnolias and scrollwork. An enormous mirror with columns and lone stars above provided a great backdrop along with ubiquitous model oil derricks to remind everyone what had built the club and the city.

Nelson was saddled up at the far end of the bar and chatting up Buster, the server. An open bottle of Pinot Grigio chilled in front of Nelson as he told Buster tales of his most recent visit to Italy. He was learning to speak Italian and becoming an expert on the culture, especially the food and wine. Gabe had already heard most of these stories, but humored Nelson and listened to their retelling.

"Here, have a glass," said Nelson, nudging an oversized Bordeaux glass Gabe's way before looking back at Buster and stating, "Fill him up".

Buster did so and said, "I won't ask for an ID," insinuating that Gabe looked too young, but that it didn't matter since he was with Nelson.

"Thanks, very good," said Gabe with a smile.

Nelson turned slowly and addressed Gabe, "So, I've got to ask, what's with the new look? I mean, are you trying to grow a beard, perhaps full Grizzly Adams?"

Gabe responded, "Not really, I was really trying to grow sideburns but there is just nothing there, so I am going to shave it all off tonight."

Tilting his head to the side Nelson said, "You look alright, just don't let your hair get too long," before looking over to Buster and saying, "Right? Oh to be young again…"

Buster walked over to close out another customer's tab and Gabe and Nelson exchanged the details of their respective Thanksgiving plans.

Nelson was volunteering at the 'Thanksgiving Big Feast' with his family and said to Gabe, "Hey, you should come down, bring Laney. They need something like 2000 volunteers."

"Wow, that's a lot. Maybe we'll be there, what time?"

Nelson answered, "I'm thinking it's for 7:00, or 8:00, there's the Turkey Trot beforehand; but we're not running this year."

"We might be there, Laney's sister is in town so we might be out late," was Gabe's non-committal response, "It's great of you, and so many, to help the homeless."

"Yeah, it's homeless and, really, any of the poor, lots of families," replied Nelson as he finished off the first bottle of wine.

Gabe agreed, "Yes, it's especially hard to see kids go hungry, though I guess it shouldn't matter how old someone is if they're starving."

"It's nice to see the food going directly to them, like at this event," said Nelson before continuing, "I mean you see these people begging on the corner, and know that they probably just want money to feed an addiction, probably…"

With some fine wine in him, Gabe freely spoke about his interactions with the homeless during the course of the week. He finished with the story of the bank attack and the possible connection to the 'steely eyed' guy.

Nelson, considering the business angle of the events, particularly at the bank, said, "OK, well it seems like you're fine," before joking, "As long as you're not filing a workman's comp claim, that is."

Gabe shook his head and conceded, "It's been the longest three day work week ever, totally weird stuff."

"Hey Buster, we'd like to order some drinks and, also, may I see a grill menu?"

Nelson ordered a Jameson neat, plus a dozen and a half oysters on the half shell for them to share, while Gabe ordered a Wild Turkey on the rocks.

Then Nelson dug deep, "So did you choose to help your new friend, Jay… right? Because you felt sorry for him, and his son, or was it mostly about guilt over being better off than them – you know, living comfortably?"

"Oh, there's definitely some guilt sprinkled into the equation. I am fortunate, we are so fortunate," replied Gabe, but then concluded, "I really just hated the thought of him and his son being on the streets and hungry."

Nelson summed it up, "So basic human decency, compassion for your fellow human beings prevailed."

"Pretty much, simple compassion, plus my faith definitely played a part too," replied Gabe, "But you know, I really just hated seeing this man appear to be so defeated. I can't imagine feeling like I can't take care of someone I love, someone I helped create."

"So, some empathy too," added Nelson.

"What's your primary motivation for volunteering tomorrow, getting up early and all?" quizzed Gabe.

"Definitely have the same compassion and empathy angles that you do," responded Nelson before going on, "But really we as parents feel the need to set the example for our girls and expose them some, safely. They are growing up sheltered, well actually I guess 'pampered' would be more the word to describe their world."

96

Gabe agreed, "Oh, I know what you mean, most people are fairly insulated."

Nelson then said, "I see them, street people, more from the car, like beggars on the corner at a stop lights and will give them a buck or two if they seem to be disabled or something."

"Yeah, us bus riders get to interact with them close up - it can definitely be more threatening, and personal."

Nelson then paused and said, "Sure, using my parking garage and the tunnels definitely keeps them at a distance, by design I guess. Wow, these oysters are perfect, fresh and good sized." Gabe agreed.

At this very moment, Walker and Clay were in the lobby of the building attempting to get past Mr. Cline. In their efforts to get at Gabe, they first begged to use the restrooms and then to access the tunnels. They then offered him cash and even special privileges and protections in The District, all to no avail. Mr. Cline held firm and they were forced to wait out Gabe on the street.

***

The journey from Market Square to the main post office was only a few blocks. Once Jay felt that he was clear of any possible pursuers from La Carafe, he slowed his pace and was extremely careful not to step in deep puddles. Wet socks and shoes would make for a miserable night's sleep, or any attempt to get rest anyway. More importantly, he had a hundred miles to travel in the next day, or days, and needed to be able to travel as comfortably as possible.

Reaching Franklin Street, Jay spotted another open bar up ahead. The signage was tough to read in the dark, but the right front door was propped open. He stashed his dry erase board behind a planter and stepped into the entryway, before picking up a Greensheet and a Houston Press, actually two of each. He stood there and looked into the main bar area, realizing that this was The Brewery Tap. A few bikers sat at a long table as a waitress took their order. Behind them he noticed a very large cluster of beer taps; he would love to go for a sample but thought better of it. Then he decided to grab a few peppermints from a tray right inside the front door and move on. He took a few steps toward the post office, before thinking to turn back and retrieve his dry erase board.

Unbeknownst to Jay, Preston LeGrande was lurking in the shadows. Preston was working through a hangover after gorging himself on the spoils of the prior evening's concert leftovers. Those wine coolers had gotten the best of him. He was somewhat out of it, but the stranger with the large whiteboard caught his attention – Jay's slightly bowlegged gait jogged his memory. Preston soon recalled that this was the man with the well dressed little boy from Monday Night. He immediately sent another of Walker's lackeys, or 'Subjects' as they were known to spread the word and ultimately notify Walker that Jay was in the area.

***

Back at The Houston Club, Gabe and Nelson had moved on to lighter topics like college football matchups and finer drink options from premium ale to single malt Scotch and Vintage Port. Feeling a comfortable buzz, Gabe chose only to sample a few of Nelson's selections while appreciating the free education. His measured sips were still too many.

"OK, Gabe, I know that you are taking the bus home, right..?" said Nelson. "Please tell me that's correct."

Gabe replied, "That is correct, I will have a large iced tea to go and be fine to drive in an hour when I get to my car."

Nelson agreed, "Yeah, you seem fine. You're just not always easy to read."

A smiling Gabe shook his hand and replied, "Thanks for the invite, and the visit. I am glad that we met up to kick off the holiday."

"It was my pleasure," responded Nelson, taking a final sip of port. "Glad you could make it - have a great one, and be careful out there." He then signed the check and headed for the exit.

Gabe decided that he was comfortable at the bar. NBA highlights were on and he enjoyed an iced tea and some crackers with Tabasco and horseradish.

Buster checked on him, "You doing alright there young man?"

"Definitely, thanks though," replied Gabe. "I let him do the real drinking, his tolerance on the heavy stuff beats my game big time."

Buster agreed, "Mr. Bosch holds his liquor extremely well. You know Mr. Wagner, I'll call you a taxi if need be - it's not like you can just hail one around here…"

"That won't be necessary," was Gabe's slurred response. "So what time do you get to shut down?"

Buster answered, "8:00 tonight. The club shuts down for Thanksgiving; it's actually the best holiday for us, the staff." He then slid a glass of ice water to Gabe, "Drink this before you go."

Gabe took the cue and prepared to leave, finishing the water and then woozily standing for a visit to the restroom. The drink variety and empty stomach had gotten the best of him. Somehow it was already 6:59 and the last bus on his 210 Park & Ride route hit his stop at 7:10. He stopped by the bar on his way out and said, "Thanks, Buster, and you have a Happy Thanksgiving!"

"You do the same sir," called out Buster as Gabe's departure now became more hurried.

Chapter 19

Jay had reached his destination, the main post office. It was a massive facility swarming with activity, even on the eve of a major holiday. The mail drops were open around the clock, so customer traffic was nonstop. In addition, a gigantic bank of PO boxes were accessible just inside the lobby so there was a constant flow of folks parking, coming and going. A very non-imposing security guard was posted to keep out vagrants. Jay figured he was still presentable enough to go in and use the restroom. The guard looked him up and down, checking out his dry erase board and folded newspapers, but did not stop him.

Back outside, he realized that the immediate area was too busy to hunker down for the night. So he lumbered along to the opposite side of the building. Now on the western end of the property, Jay observed another twenty-four hour customer mailbox with slightly less steady traffic. However, he found an even greater nuisance in the form of truck traffic. Eighteen wheelers steadily streamed in and out of a large double gate. He felt that he could slip past the gate and actually find a safe spot to bed down, but the noise and bright lights were overwhelming.

Behind the post office was a raised section of I-10, but the barbed wire fences were much too tall for him to risk taking on. To the southwest he could see massive Fire Station #1, but it was also loud and well lit, plus it would take him farther away from his ultimate destination. In the distance, he saw other wanderers trickling into Sesquicentennial Park. Behind the Wortham Center on the north end of the Theater District and being extra careful not to venture that way, Jay soon came to notice that everyone he spotted there seemed to have spotted him first.

The prudent move was to turn around and start over.

***

Gabe decided that he still had time to go and grab a drink from the RPG fridge before leaving for the bus stop. He took the stairs and went in the back doors. Thankfully, his fax to Trent had finally gone through.

As he rounded the corner to head out the front door, Gabe noticed masked strangers all over the place and his heart began to race. He then turned and quietly jogged to and out the back door, noticing caution tape across the front door. Approaching for closer inspection, a makeshift sign read 'Warning: Do Not Cross Due To Possible Asbestos Exposure (All workers must wear protective gear at all times)'. New ethernet cable was being run for the computer network; he now recalled seeing some sort of notice of such work in the old building. Sighing, he approached the elevator bank and pushed the 'Down' button before deciding that he should toss his asbestos contaminated Coke.

The vintage elevators had been a breeze all week and Gabe was comfortably set to catch the last bus home. He'd probably visit with Cappy for a couple of minutes on his way out in order to reduce the time spent waiting at the bus stop like a sitting duck.

The workers suddenly turned out the lights and locked up, just in time to hop in the arriving elevator with Gabe. They removed their masks and one greeted Gabe, "Hey man, what's up? We didn't scare you, did we?" in a tone that indicated hope that they had.

Gabe smiled and replied, "You startled me - you definitely startled me."

"We checked the space before we started. Were you in a locked office?" asked the worker.

"Oh, I just came up the stairs, from the club, and used the back door. I forgot that you all were coming this evening," said Gabe.

The worker responded, "Yeah, well so did the building management. They want us out of here early; so that they can close up the building. But we really don't mind and will come back on Saturday."

Gabe's buzz was hardly waning and he was ready for a break from his work and the downtown scene. Over the long weekend, Gabe would certainly not miss his new acquaintances, some destitute or addicts, others just plain old bums. He figured that Jay was surely halfway to Port Arthur by now.

Gabe was so ready to be home and to shower and to shave. And it seemed like he hadn't seen Laney in forever. It had been an exceptionally long day, despite the late start.

They stopped at the eighth floor, and a crowd was waiting with their prepared and packaged Thanksgiving meals. Gabe took a long deep breath and then blinked a long hard blink as everyone tried to pack into the elevator.

Meanwhile, Walker and Clay had grown tired of waiting for Gabe to emerge from the building and began to walk back to The District. Walker grumpily said to Clay, "He must've taken the tunnels out."

Clay agreed, "Yep, definitely the tunnels. Next time we'll surround him better, with more Subjects."

"He can't hide forever - we'll get him," grumbled Walker. "I just can't wait."

Gabe's heart began to race as the full elevator descended; he knew that it was now after seven and that the bus would be reaching his stop at any minute. With lighter than usual traffic, it would surely be right on time, unless somehow the rainy weather had slowed up the route.

They reached the lobby and Gabe attempted to remain polite and calm as the people slowly filed out. He mumbled to himself over and over, "Let's roll, let's roll..." and finally there was an opening. Bolting out past the militant substitute security guard and through the garage, he called out, "Later, Cappy," as he emerged onto the sidewalk. A bus that could be his was stopped at his usual favorite intersection and he went into a full sprint. From half a block away, he could make out Alex's profile in the dim light and knew it was the 210.

The light turned green and the coach pulled away, away in a hurry. Gabe wasn't the only one ready to start the weekend - Alex was blazing a trail to the next and final pickup stop. The synchronized lights were now Gabe's enemy. Only another braking bus or a wayward pedestrian would impede the determined driver's charge towards the Texas Street stop.

In his desperation, Gabe failed to notice the now familiar figures shadowing him to his right. Walker and Clay had just rounded Jones Hall and were reenergized by the good fortune with which they'd just been struck.

Nary a single passenger was waiting at Texas Street. Alex tapped the brakes and kept rolling, easily outpacing Gabe's valiant pursuit. "Woah, Alex!" shouted Gabe, but the driver was completely oblivious to his call and entered I-10, disappearing from sight.

Walker turned to Clay and murmured, "Let's go!"

Another bus pulled up to the stop where Gabe was now waiting and puddle soaked him from the waist down.

Gabe boarded the bus and spoke with the driver, "Does this route stop at the West Belt Park and Ride?" He already knew that answer but felt the need to ask.

The driver replied, "This is Kingsland, 228 to Katy, my next and final stop of the day. Do you have a ticket?"

"Yes, I have a ticket, for the 210. But I think I just missed the last run," said Gabe, as he reached into his pockets with both hands, one felt his keys the other felt the ticket.

The driver replied, "Yes, that was the last 210 for the day. Your ticket isn't really good for this bus, but I'll let you ride."

"Can I get a transfer to get back to the 210 Park & Ride station?" wondered Gabe.

"Not really," answered the driver before clarifying, "I mean I can print you a transfer, but there won't be any busses coming through the station to pick you up...to get you there."

Gabe's best bet now was to call Laney from his office, so he said, "Thanks, I'll have to pass. You have a great evening."

The door of the bus slammed shut behind him just as he stepped back down onto the curb. The mammoth bus pulled away and Gabe was promptly greeted by the now familiar rag tag miscreants, "Welcome to The District, Gabriel."

Chapter 20

At about this same time Jay was skirting The District as he redirected back to the east. He considered options that would be relatively deserted, yet safe.

The Spaghetti Warehouse quickly came to mind. It was mainly a lunch destination with a smaller dinner crowd, which would surely be particularly light this night before Thanksgiving. He was well aware of the boundary between Walker's territory and his path. Eyes following him from the park and bayou below faded as he moved down Franklin Street.

He could now see, and smell, his destination. Desperately seeking shelter, his intention was to find a dark, dry place behind the building, preferably some sort of corner blocking the wind. Rest, maybe even sleep, and some leftover pizza or pasta would be great added bonuses.

Jay was extremely alert and constantly scanning the landscape for threats, particularly just released criminals. The county jail was now just a couple of blocks away.

Inside of the restaurant he could see a group of wait and bus staff standing in a circle, they wore matching white oxford shirts with colorful ties and black pants. The servers appeared to be sharing a bottle of red wine, random puffs of cigarette smoke wafted into the air and Sinatra's rendition of *Stardust* played in the background.

Around the back corner of the building, Jay passed some employee cars and a dumpster before coming up on a chained link fence. He found a gate with an opened padlock hanging on the latch and began to open it up. Just then a large dark body lunged toward him out of nowhere; he saw only sharp white teeth. It was a dog, a hundred pound plus Rottweiler tasked with protecting the area. Its head came in contact with Jay's hand on the gate latch and he quickly pulled back, dropping his whiteboard. Thankfully he had no cuts or bite marks and the gate had not opened.

Someone from the restaurant opened a screen door and said, "Who's out here? Make yourself known," before calling out to the dog, "Hey Knuckles, everything OK back here?" and tossing the canine a cannoli. Jay gathered himself and decided to move on.

***

Gabe was now surrounded. In addition to Walker and Clay, at least two other Subjects had appeared on the scene.

Walker spoke up, "Are you familiar with The District?" and then restated "Of course you are familiar with The District. It's here and you are here. I therefore shall ask, 'Why you are challenging The District?'"

Gabe attempted to brush him off, "Pardon me, but I need to get by."

"You are not pardoned and you are not getting by and you did not answer my question," responded Walker as the Subjects came closer.

Looking around at this odd menagerie of characters, Gabe answered, "So what is this about?"

Walker calmly replied, "Since you are challenging The District and think you can ask your own questions, I'll tell you how it is."

Gabe looked straight into Walker's eyes and further challenged him, "I have no business with you and we all need to move along." As Gabe tried to brush them off and push through, Walker nodded to Clay and another of the simpletons who'd shown up. They grabbed each of Gabe's arms from either side.

"Actually, we do have business to handle," said Walker before motioning and continuing, "Walk with us."

The group trudged along together past the Alley Theater and Wortham Center to a stairway leading down to Sesquicentennial Park on Buffalo Bayou. Up above Gabe noticed stainless steel towers of artwork forming a mini skyline and Walker instructed them to stop directly below the middle tower. More of Walker's followers suddenly appeared, many of them familiar to Gabe from the daily street scene above.

Walker once again stood directly in front of Gabe and called out, "Check his pockets!" All four of his pockets were promptly pulled inside out. His keys, the single bus ticket and an old tissue were found and handed to Walker. He promptly pocketed the bus ticket and threw the keys and tissue in the bayou.

Walker then spoke to Gabe, "Now that you understand who's in charge of The District, let's take care of our business." Walker looked him up and down and then went on, "Where are you hiding your money, your wallet?"

Gabe refused to answer and Walker became more forceful. Walker brandished a box cutter and held it to Gabe's throat stating, "Where are you hiding your wallet? Do I need to start slicing?"

"I don't have my wallet today," Gabe finally uttered.

Walker cut the sleeves of Gabe's shirt and said, "We'll see about that," before frisking him head to toe.

Gabe still wondered what this was all about and how he could get away. From what he could see, Walker was the only one who was actually fit and physically imposing. He felt that he could outrun them all if given an opening.

Walker continued to address him sternly, "This is The District and we all are its Subjects. I am in charge and you are a Violator."

Gabe realized he was serious and, despite his racing heart, gave a dismissive look.

Walker was relentless, "Why so quiet, Gabriel. Do you have anything to say in your defense?"

Gabe responded nonchalantly, "Why are you calling me a 'Violator'?"

Immediately Walker responded, "By virtue of aiding Pops, a Violator, you became a Violator. Your minor violation would normally be overlooked, but you are a repeat offender and just kept getting in our way."

Pausing to process what he had just heard, Gabe looked up and noticed the contrast of the glimmering artwork against the dark night sky. He tried to figure out who 'Pops' was and remained quiet so as not to further dignify the charges or the situation.

Walker raised up the box cutter and said, "Besides, you are extremely disrespectful. You attempt to ignore us on the streets, but watch us out of the corner of your eyes and then decline to donate when asked."

Gabe remained quiet and hoped for a break, perhaps more rain or some other sort of distraction.

Unrelenting, Walker pressed on, "Respond now or be dealt with harshly."

Gabe finally spoke, "Who is Pops and how did I aid him?"

Walker fired back, "So you want to play dumb…you don't give a dime around here for years, and a dressed up guy with a kid shows up and suddenly you're passing out bills."

Now nodding Gabe questioned, "OK, you've been watching me, and I wanted to help out a man in a bad place and now you're coming after me?"

Walker immediately quipped, "We were watching a Violator and you came into the picture. You were immediately recognizable to most of us as a regular Snubber, actually an arrogant Snubber." The brazen enforcer smirked as he realized that he'd just made up a new label.

Gabe understood now, but feigned puzzlement, "So what's a 'Violator' and, what's that other one you said…'Snubber'?"

"Finally you ask a meaningful question," replied Walker. He then explained with an evil grin, "Everyone is defined once they enter The District. We here just happen to be the most aware."

Gabe nodded slowly, fully processing the situation.

Walker went on, "If you live in The District you are a Subject by default and must pay a daily 'guardinar', a sort of tariff if you will, on your collections within The District. It is paid to ensure the overall well being of the Subjects as well as The District itself. Subjects are not permitted to collect outside of The District and we pay the guardinar on the honor system. Most are extremely trustworthy. Any questions so far?"

His predicament was so surreal and bizarre, but Gabe was slowly realizing that his nemesis was real, and that he was totally serious. Still flanked by the mildly capable goons in Walker's ranks, Gabe felt Clay and another both still holding his arms tightly. He gave a negatory head shake, methodically back and forth.

"Great, no questions so far – we might get along well," said Walker. He then continued, "Subjects who choose not to pay the guardinar are not welcome and, as Violators, are asked to leave The District. To our knowledge, which is extensive, a Violator has never spent a night in The District. Makes sense, right?"

Gabe spoke up, "So how does one know when they've entered 'The District'," envisioning air quotes in his mind.

Walker sensed the sarcasm but remained serious, "There are signs all around, but anywhere there's a big, but not necessarily super tall, building or hall that patrons pay big money to attend shows is considered The District, plus everything in between those places of course." He looked at Gabe and nodded, "I think you know the area well."

Taking a deep breath, Gabe replied, "So basically The Theater District," before dropping his head down.

Walker responded, "We don't phrase it that way," raising his voice and then emphatically stating, "Do you understand!?!" He chose not to await a reply from Gabe and finished his explanation, "Which brings me to the topic of outsiders, people who live elsewhere but enter The District, people such as yourself."

Remaining indignant Gabe wondered openly, "So what are we?"

"All persons who choose to visit The District are Patrons," answered Walker. "You, however, Mr. Gabriel are also a Snubber, one who sloughs us off and doesn't even have the decency to look us in the eyes. But you really crossed the line when you enabled a Violator, repeatedly, and please don't act like you don't know who Pops is by now."

Gabe nodded his head as stark quiet and full darkness set in. The last remaining bit of bustle up above seemed to quickly wane, with any remnants of such out of reach. Imprisoned underground, the air soon chilled as his breathing slowed, though the rapid pulse remained. Modern office towers loomed in the above distance. Their floors illuminated a couple at a time, forming fluorescent rings of alabaster as cleaning crews worked their way up from the ground, patterns dictated by executives on the upper floors. Those barons of industry, mostly oil, some banking or legal, tended to work longer, or at least later, hours. The captive's current predicament summarily suppressed any thoughts or ambitions of reaching such esteemed heights.

Challenges of the past instantly lost all significance. Never before had he truly been struck to the deepest core of his very being. What was this ultra surreal tribulation really all about..? Had the simple gesture of providing bread to his fellow human in need swiftly followed, passed and brought him to this place? The sliver of light he'd sought for others had majorly dimmed his world, and he found himself living by the light of a vanishing moon.

Chapter 21

Jay departed the Spaghetti Warehouse and started to notice small groups of shadowy figures to the east. He wasn't quite sure if his imagination was taking over, but they sure seemed to be moving in his direction now faster and faster. The post office was just too bright and busy. He needed to avoid Market Square, especially since he had absconded with the dry erase board from La Carafe. Out of options and not wanting to go too far south, away from I-10, he decided that he'd go back to Sam Houston Park and perhaps find a safe haven around the Yates House.

This meant he'd once again have to skirt The District, a fact not at all lost on him. Glancing back over his shoulder again, his eyes had not fooled him and three big and bulky guys were rapidly gaining ground. Jay picked up the pace and went into a jog. Though he was a Violator, passing through The District might actually provide for some good interference since a bunch of hobos on his tail might distract or redirect these big jailbreak guys.

Once again Preston LeGrande spotted Jay as he neared the area, this time from the top of the Alley Theater Garage. He immediately sent a page to Clay which read 'pops at alley'.

Clay immediately showed the message to Walker who instructed him to take two men with him saying, "I want Pops to join us here. I'd love to successfully reunite our new associates."

Walker pulled out a chunky choke chain and formed a slip knot over Gabe's wrists before hooking the end to a fence with a carabiner. This life was now subject to the terms of others and bound like a junkyard dog, with no hope for outside help. A cleaner cut character with an eye mask suddenly emerged from a secret opening behind a brick wall and whispered something into Walker's ear. Gabe noticed a worn bank bag in the new stranger's hand, which he discreetly handed over to Walker.

Walker then went over to another ragged underling, a much older looking man, and said, "Keep an eye on him," motioning towards Gabe. Walker and the masked stranger then disappeared into the secret opening.

The elderly man said loudly to Gabe, "Don't get any smart ideas, just stay calm". Gabe couldn't help but notice this man's deep wrinkles and sunken eyes as he passed and then took up his guard post.

Well aware that any sort of tugging would only tighten the hold, he needed to catch a break, one that would have to come from the inside. Was there a single ounce of grace to be found amongst the horde of hoodlum captors? This life still felt so young and new, with much to come and to lose. The confinement of his wrists naturally kept his tired hands pressed together at the palms and the cold soon prompted interlaced fingers.

Desperately in need of some inside help, this gentleman seemed neither willing nor able. Quiet set in as the rest of the ruffians scurried away in pursuit of another prized prisoner. Time stood still while Gabe surveyed the grim scene. His heart raced furiously, his body shaking enough to noticeably move his head and distort his eyes' view of the skyline up above. Seconds felt like minutes as his folded hands remained together and he called upon his spirituality. An instinct to pray trumped all others, perhaps his call would be answered.

Nerves did not prevent him from recalling scripted prayers he'd recited his entire life, but he just kept racing through them without meaning. In the moment his prayer soon took on a less formal tone. Gabe reached out to God directly, augmenting his pleas with specific calls to all familiar holy ones, repeatedly attempting to summon the aid of his patron saint.

With the coast all clear an eerily quiet movement finally came. The feeble watchman slowly approached and stuffed a note in Gabe's back pocket, while whispering, "Back into the fence and the knot will loosen when you raise up your hands as high as you can. Bend over and jump if you need to. But don't you dare go running while I am right here."

As it turned out, the old man was a former stock broker and now a street veteran by the name of Crawford. Crawford was comfortable living as a vagabond but he wanted Walker, and hence, The District, eradicated. He had worked these streets and theaters since the mid eighties and despised the structure Walker had created through intimidation and coercion. Crawford wanted independence and saw Gabe as an avenue by which it could be gained.

***

Preston quickly raced down the stairway to the ground level of the Alley Theater. Though he lost track of Jay as he moved through Jones Plaza, Jay's other pursuers moved into view, revealing his course as reinforcements from The District arrived. Preston and a younger subject were the quickest of the bunch and they took off after Jay. Clay and the rest, which numbered at least five, ran interference and eventually spooked the three roving criminals into vacating The District.

Finally ditching the whiteboard as he approached Sam Houston Park, Jay ran full speed ahead until he spotted the grey Yates House. He slowed up and attempted to look like he belonged, well aware that curious eyes were watching.

Though the restoration of the old home was nearly complete, the legacy burglar bars remained for now and Jay was relegated to the back porch. There was a half dry piece of drop cloth acting as a back door rug, which he augmented with the remaining pages of the newspapers he'd stuffed in his front pockets earlier. Though he was exhausted, his heart raced as he went to his knees and leaned against the door where it met the frame. He listened for any sounds not identifiable as road noise from the Pierce Elevated section of Interstate 45 which bounded the park to the west.

Jay thought back to his rendezvous with Gabe in this very spot earlier in the day and wondered where the kind stranger might be now. He then marveled at the fact that it was still Wednesday - his longest day ever. How had he lost so much? The bit of relative peace and kindness Gabe had brought was quickly becoming an ancient memory. He also knew that Garrett was in Lake Charles by now, comfortably getting ready to climb into a warm bed or sofa after reuniting with relatives and, probably, hopefully, thinking about his father. Jay said a quiet informal prayer to himself, his intentions focused on the destination. Any graces received along the journey would be lagniappe.

***

At the Filas house, Laney was becoming concerned. Gabe was known for being a little late for holidays and special occasions, but it was usually due to last minute gift shopping and this was Thanksgiving, not Christmas Eve.

Jane and Dion were there waiting with her and joked that perhaps a big family gathering and all of the wedding planning was giving Gabe a case of cold feet. Laney was not remotely amused.

Once again she checked the home phone to make sure that no one had dialed up AOL and tied up the line.

They had talked about all going out together tonight, before the marathon of feasting and football began. Those plans were off.

Laney knew that Gabe would be stopping by his apartment to get his wallet, plus it was raining. Maybe the bus was delayed. Maybe the driver stopped for another civil servant hook up. She pulled out the owner's manual for her new phone and attempted to decipher the instructions on checking voicemail. She had a single message. It was from Houston Cellular welcoming her to their service plan.

The dinner leftovers were still warm, and it was not yet time to openly worry.

***

Still chained, but subtly testing the looseness of the chain's slip knot, Gabe carefully considered his path up and out of these bowels of The District.

Walker reemerged from behind the brick wall, while his masked associate remained in the shadows. Even with his eyes now fully adjusted to the darkness, Gabe could not get a better look at this mysterious character.

After motioning to Crawford and relieving him of his guard duties for now, Walker addressed Gabe, "Glad to see that you didn't attempt to depart our locale while I was away." He then spoke further, "I have been considering your fate and we could use a guy like you up in the glass, those buildings, steering our endeavors at the corporate level. You know, someone on the inside, with full tunnel access, etcetera, etcetera."

Gabe calmly listened, while considering his wish to honor Crawford's request that he await his departure from the scene before making his breakaway. His potential accomplice was now out of site.

Walker noticed that Gabe was distracted and tugged on the chain before saying, "You're quiet again, Gabriel. Do you have anything to say about this?"

Following a long pause, Gabe attempted to placate him and replied, "I'm interested in hearing more, what specifically would we do? You know, with me operating at the corporate level…"

Considering that his initial intention was to simply ruin Gabe's long weekend, The District's leadership had now determined that their prisoner knew far too much and would expose them if he were to ever escape. He would have to be killed and dumped in the bayou downstream, as close to the ship channel as possible. The plan was to string Gabe along until after midnight, when the bulk of the chemically dependent Subjects were bedded down for the night.

With a wide grin Walker excitedly bluffed, "Well of course we'll make lots of cash, money to sustain The District. Many of the subjects must be rewarded for their loyalty with basic care and we have certain relationships to maintain. Not a cop in the area misses a chance to supplement their paltry base salary. Of course there is always a cost."

Gabe had no idea how he would ever help them, but wanted to buy time and perhaps gain trust. "I think I can make things happen and would like to hear more of your ideas," said Gabe before pleading, "Also, I am so hungry, I don't guess there's any extra food around. Maybe some water?"

Walker looked down at the bayou, "There's the water. We'll get you some shortly though it may take your system a while to get used to it." He then stated, "We will get you more details on our business plans. First though, you will have to prove your loyalty to The District, though we are not really concerned about loyalty on your part. First of all, you'll come to find that we are noble and, dare I say, likeable - our mission is worthwhile. But, also, we know that there's a sweet young thing near and dear to your heart. If you are loyal you're safe, and if you're safe, she's safe."

The tug at his heartstrings only heightened Gabe's resolve to make an escape and he knew that his best chance was from this location. He'd have to make it happen soon, while he was still held by this vulnerable chain and before Clay and the other strong arms returned.

Chapter 22

The air was dry and still, Jay was settling in well. Seemingly safe outside The District, he cherished the rest afforded him now and hoped for some light sleep.

He would soon come to know that neutral territory was scarce in Downtown Houston. The daytime resources dictated the evening landscape.

His scamper to the Yates House had not gone unnoticed, nor had his meeting with Gabe earlier in the day.

Sam Houston Park was full of restored homes from different eras and areas of Houston, each with historical significance. The Heritage Society maintained the properties and had limited resources, particularly to provide for security. So an informal arrangement was made with certain needy individuals who were allowed to stay in the park during the day as long as there was no vandalism at night. This select group was called 'The Caretakers' and they were known and respected throughout the homeless community. The Caretakers were also fed a square meal every morning for their services, following an inspection of the structures of course. Additionally, they had access to a guard stand with a phone via combination lock. Local calls were free and the police department was on speed dial.

Each of the park's buildings housed a single Caretaker and guests were not welcome or allowed. No less than six of them had seen Jay reenter the park. They had also seen Clay, Preston and their cronies following behind and searching.

After conferring, the lead Caretakers determined this unanticipated onslaught of visitors to be an in house matter and chose not to contact The Heritage Society, or the police. One representative from The District, Clay in this case, was allowed to accompany them as they approached and surrounded the Yates House. The Caretakers carried only mace and handcuffs, though billy clubs were stashed in each of the houses. Clay carried a switchblade.

Before Jay could react and attempt to elude apprehension, the hands of multiple Caretakers were lifting him by the shoulders. One of them spoke up, "Sir, we are going to have to escort you out of the park."

"OK OK, I will move on," responded Jay, "I don't see how I was causing anyone harm."

The lead Caretaker spoke up, "The park closes at nine on weeknights. We are required to keep it clear of all visitors."

As they moved into the light Jay noticed Clay in the group and reacted, "Hey, what is he doing here?" and then continued sarcastically, "This isn't 'The District'."

"As a condition of our alliance with our neighbors to the north, they maintain extraterritorial jurisdiction," replied the very serious Caretaker.

Shaking his head, Jay countered, "What is that about, you people act like you have your own little governments." He attempted to wrestle away, but there was no chance with multiple Caretakers holding on tight.

The Caretaker was very matter of fact, "We all choose to do what we can to maintain order throughout the area."

Jay then realized that they were bringing him in the direction of The District and saw more Subjects waiting in the shadows to take him into custody.

A smooth handoff was made and Jay's new captors were less polite. The waiting subjects had picked up the dry erase board and Preston searched Jay, pulling the markers from his pocket. Clay wrote 'Pops – Violator' on the board and ordered Jay, who was shocked that he actually spelled it correctly, to carry it. Preston proudly sent a page to Walker which read 'pops secured'.

***

As Walker gave a fist pump and let out a 'Bam! Got him'. Gabe seized the opportunity caused by the momentary distraction, backing and lifting on his tip toes. The pressure on the slipknot was relieved; his left hand squeezed out and his right quickly followed. He was able to quietly unhook the carabiner.

A sole subject, Bagby, was on watch guarding Gabe with Walker close by. This Bagby guy also looked feeble and could be easily outrun.

With Walker now turning his back to him, Gabe realized it was time to tackle his tormentor. His adrenaline kicked in as he rushed the stout, barrel chested villain, pulling the chain over his head and around his neck. He knew of Walker's strength and just wanted to buy some time and get a good head start.

116

Walker's neck was very thick and there wasn't as much slack in the chain as Gabe had expected, but catching him off guard did the trick. Walker attempted to wrangle him off but Gabe held on tight as they spun.

Slow to react, Bagby called out, "Smith!" as he approached and jumped into the fray, attempting to pry Gabe's hands off of the chain. But the action was simply too furious for him and Gabe was able to head butt and then kick the gimp out of the picture. Walker went down to his knees and Gabe pushed him down the embankment to the edge of the bayou. Walker hit his head and was disoriented, though not fully incapacitated. Still Gabe's surprise attack had left him unable to immediately call out for help or give chase.

In accordance with the plan in his head, Gabe headed back out the way he was brought in, passing a single, somewhat oblivious, Subject along the way. The masked man emerged from behind the brick wall, pulled a pager from Bagby's pocket and sent a group page 'violator loose'.

Now back up on the ground level in front of the Wortham Theater, Gabe looked ahead at his two best potential avenues of escape.

Straight ahead was Jones Plaza, a wide open space surely full of Subjects. So he chose to take Prairie Street to the left, behind the Alley Theater. Normally, Preston would be perched atop the Alley Garage watching the area, assuming he hadn't excessively imbibed Olde English. But tonight Preston was out on a mission, off amongst a pack moving slowly towards the dungeon Gabe had just escaped. Gabe noticed the mob as he rounded a corner and recognized Jay as the figure in the middle. He also noticed little lights being pulled from at least a few of their pockets. The group page had alerted them of Gabe's escape and most of them peeled off and started running in his general direction.

Gabe felt that his best option was to get to the Houston Club Building and call Laney from there. He would keep running and zig zag with the green lights. Gabe's gait varied as he considered his odds of encountering a good cop and the consequences of not. The streets were deserted and he reached his destination in no time.

The garage doors were down, all of them, something Gabe had never before witnessed. He immediately went over to the revolving front door, it wouldn't budge; neither would the locked doors on either side. Looking through the window, he saw a single light above the security desk, where a familiar acquaintance sat. Mr. Cline was still on guard duty and attempting to ignore Gabe's presence.

After some banging, the stubborn substitute stood and walked over to Gabe. He pulled out his wallet and pointed to his driver's license, signaling and yelling to Gabe that he'd like to see some sort of identification. Gabe knew that he'd get nowhere with this fellow and that his pursuers would be nearing.

Walker's brief tutelage brought him to distrust the local police. Stealing an idea from Jay, his next option was to make a phone call from the Hyatt Regency Hotel.

***

Laney had enough of the waiting and was now fully worried. She called his apartment and the phone just kept on ringing and ringing. There was no answer and no answering machine greeting or chance to leave a message.

After calling and leaving a message at his office, it became more difficult to remain calm. But Laney was her usual strong self. Next she decided that it would be best to go over to his apartment. She would bring her key just in case. Jane and Dion joined her. Laney drove, with Jane in the front passenger seat and Dion scrunched into the back.

They travelled her usual route. *The Macarena* was playing on the radio; it was overplayed but still catchy. Changing the station was not a priority.

Approaching on the right was the 210 Park & Ride station and they turned in. Gabe's car was still there and he was not in it. Laney had mixed feelings about this discovery. He was certainly in trouble now, either with her or with the world.

Gabe's apartment was just a few blocks away and they were quickly at the gate, waiting to follow in someone with an access card. Laney's best hope at this point was that Gabe was drunk and had been given a ride home by Nelson, or maybe a taxi, or even a concerned Metro bus driver.

After some awkward silence, Jane attempted to console Laney, "He's probably fine and couldn't get to a phone."

"Jane, OK so he missed the bus, probably drank too much or whatever, but he could call. He was supposed to be going for drinks in his building, that's it," Laney replied, still worried but also perturbed.

Jane nodded her head and said, "Gabe's so level headed - surely he's stuck somewhere or something and will call soon."

They were finally able to follow a car in. Greeted at the door by Brittany, Laney quickly checked the apartment. He was not there and his answering machine had not been reset after the power outage; it showed only a flashing red dash. They called the Filas home to see if Gabe had called there. Shelly had gone to bed for the night and Joker was logged on to America Online. The call would not go through. Laney did not want to dial '911' and was more comfortable just going to a police station. Dion walked Brittany while they decided what to do.

Chapter 23

Back in The District, Jay was secured with oversized zip ties as soon as he arrived at the underground section of the park along the bayou. He was searched and only a couple of Slim Jims leftover from the grocery outing with Gabe were pulled from his back pocket. How had his starving self overlooked them?

Though they were certainly thrilled to have Jay, the repeat Violator, captured, Gabe's escape sent ripples throughout The District. He certainly wouldn't just go home and forget about all of this. After all, his gainful employment brought him to traverse The District twice daily. Plus, he likely knew that Jay was being held captive in this same place.

Walker was injured and angry, and in the eyes of the leadership, not fit to interrogate Jay. After being held outside for a few minutes, it was determined that Jay would be brought inside. With all that Jay knew, there would be no harm in his seeing the inner workings of The District since he'd now either be indoctrinated or terminated.

Crawford appeared and said, "This way, follow me Sir". Jay was shocked to hear a kind voice and wondered who this old guy was. A plywood wall covered by frost burned ivy was pulled back, revealing a dark tunnel of more plywood supported by 2 x 4 framing. This section of the park was still under construction. Crawford led him through the tunnel with a six volt flashlight, Jay kept expecting to descend or drop in a hole, but it was level and smooth. After a slight turn, a faint light appeared ahead.

Finally, they entered a concrete room that was tremendously wide and deep, but with low ceilings. Large sheets of insulation foam acted as partition walls, creating a few smaller rooms.

A handsome and fit older man appeared; he was clean shaven and his skin was barely weathered. He immediately smiled at Jay and said, "Welcome to The District!" before turning to Crawford and politely demanding, "Please remove the restraints from his wrists." This man was clearly in charge, and, to Jay's surprise, quite well spoken. Crawford pulled out a box cutter and sliced the zip ties, freeing Jay's hands.

The leader then spoke again, "I am Smith and we are truly glad to have you here. You may not appreciate our means and, technically, you are a Violator, a repeat offender, but we are here to serve each other."

Jay was utterly confused, "Why am I here and where are we?"

"I knew that you'd have plenty of questions," the man said as he now looked around the space proudly. "In due time you will find out what this is all about."

"This is a criminal operation and you have kidnapped me," stated Jay contentiously. "That is what seems to be going on."

Smith smiled again and responded, "We need to visit, please follow me," before turning and walking towards the rear center of the room. Now seeing Smith from the rear, Jay noticed a thin ponytail tucked into his collar. Crawford walked beside Jay. They passed a thin old mattress on the floor where Walker had been ordered to rest, though he appeared to be fine. Jay was sure not to make eye contact with him.

They entered an area where the ceiling was slightly higher and he noticed that all floors, ceiling and wall surfaces were extremely rough, as if they'd been chiseled. This area was full of seventies era vinyl chairs, in orange and brown.

"Have a seat," said Smith extending his hand to allow Jay to choose from any of the dozen or so options.

Jay sat and said, "Thanks, I appreciate it - but I'd prefer to go now."

Smith responded, "We have some things to cover, important things. Would you like a cup of tap water?"

Jay was indignant and answered with a simple 'No'.

He then went on, "First, have you officially been introduced to Crawford?"

"No, no I haven't," answered Jay.

"Well OK then, please meet and know Crawford," said Smith as he nodded towards Crawford, "Crawford is a senior Subject of the District and most valued, as are all Subjects."

Crawford humbly replied, "Thank you Sir" before turning to Jay and saying "Good to know you."

Jay grudgingly nodded back, shrugging his shoulders.

After an awkward pause, Smith pulled a note from his pocket and spoke more sternly, "Let's continue and discuss your status. You have been frequenting The District and collecting donations without paying a guardinar, on at least two separate occasions. Particularly troubling was the fact that you brought a juvenile into the situation. After fair warnings from a Subject, Walker in this case, you returned to The District and its territories earlier this evening as a Squatter and now we find ourselves here."

"Is this some sort of trial?" asked Jay.

Smith continued, still stern and still polite, "This is not a trial - this is a Statement of Determination. By nature of your actions, we have determined that you desire to inhabit The District. Thus, we are offering you the opportunity to become a named Subject."

Jay protested passionately, "You have no right to be deciding what I want and making decisions for me."

"Our rights extend to those who choose to solicit and indwell within The District. We control and protect these streets for the good of all who enter," professed Smith, coming off as a polished professional. He then went on to proclaim Jay's fate, "You are now a provisional Subject and shall be called 'McKinney'. As a Subject you will be fully protected. And as a Subject with family ties you will be placed in quarantine indefinitely."

Now completely morose, Jay realized that his situation was profound beyond anything he could have ever imagined.

***

Gabe knew that there were eyes everywhere on these downtown streets and that every move had to be calculated but quick.

The Hyatt was about eight blocks to the southwest. Once again he would run the whole way and once again he would zig or zag based upon the traffic light patterns and any unsavory characters he may notice ahead in his path.

He started south on Milam Street, completely unaware that he was entering The Neutral Zone. Short of being at the police station, this was the safest he could be downtown without actually being inside of a building. Subjects of The District were free to come through The Neutral Zone, but would have to deal with Independents, unaffiliated vagrants generally tougher than anyone in The District except for Walker.

But what made The Neutral Zone even more safe was the police presence. This was the main business district, full of modern, tall and shiny office buildings with top notch tenants. Every building had a full security staff, with cameras and monitors and well lit gated garages. Additionally, The Zone was well patrolled by the Houston Police Department and Harris County Constables, as well private security patrols. Could he trust any of them? At this hour, the tenants were long gone, at home in their tony, mostly mid suburban, homes. There was no business or begging to be done now and law enforcement was freed up to be vigilant about checking out suspicious characters and keeping vagrants from camping in doorways and sleeping on stairways.

Running along at a brisk, but comfortable, pace, the safer feel of these streets and thoughts of speaking with Laney comforted him. Gabe was ready to be rescued; her sweet voice and face would make it all the better. He caught his second wind and was quickly through the covered entrance to the hotel on Polk Street, where the building covered the road. A valet and a doorman each caught a glimpse of the speedy guest out of the corners of their respective eyes. They would keep a close watch on him.

The Hyatt was the main major hotel in Downtown Houston and very familiar to Gabe. He had been there on many occasions and quickly recalled dances, business conferences and lunches with his visiting grandfather. He slowed to a jog and was quickly up the elevators and into a partially walled section with private courtesy phones.

Instinctively, he first dialed the Filas' home phone. The line was busy, since they had call waiting he instantly knew that Joker was probably on AOL, likely checking prices on the stocks and funds in his retirement plan.

Gabe didn't panic, he could call Laney on her new mobile phone, or could he? He had the number written down somewhere in his wallet. Though he instantly remembered that it was a Motorola StarTac flip phone and how much it cost, he had not learned the number in the few days she'd had it. His clever idea to immediately program the number into speed dial at home and at the office had backfired on him.

The new '281' area code had just been added and so he knew those first three digits. He also knew the exchange '855' those were the next three numbers, that part was easy too. But his fogged out brain just could not recall those last four new digits. When she first powered up the phone, they had tried to make a word with the number - but the last four numbers had a '1' and a '0', ruining their little game. The other numbers and the order simply escaped him. Realizing very quickly that his efforts to remember those digits were futile, he once again dialed the home phone number to no avail. The long day he'd endured was now transitioning into a long night. Exasperated, he buried his head in his hands.

Gabe decided that he would stay there as long as possible. It was warm, safe and semi-private. He'd sit in this spot all night redialing if that's what it took. Who knows maybe they'd eventually 'star sixty-nine' him, if such was possible with a busy signal. The still hastened his fade.

Suddenly the courtesy phone at the next desk over rang loudly and Gabe rushed over to answer, as if it could somehow be Laney calling him back. Unfortunately it was coming from a guest room, and the caller was looking to order room service. Delirium had clearly set in.

As he leaned back in the chair, Gabe caught a glimpse of himself in an oversized mirror. He sure was looking awfully ragged with hair flowing in all directions, a dirty shirt with ripped sleeves and dark circles around his eyes, plus he hadn't shaved in days. He could smell himself too; mainly sweat from running, and stress. He dialed the Filas home once more to no avail before dozing off.

Chapter 24

Light tapping on Gabe's left shoulder became harder poking, ultimately giving way to full shaking, eventually waking him. Startled, "Sir, Sir – please wake up" were the words he heard from a black vested hotel manager 'Englebert Breaux', as his Hyatt name tag read.

Now only slightly awake, Gabe's head tilted as he blurted out, "Englebert?"

Flanked by a security guard, the manager quietly spoke, "Please call me 'Mr. Breaux', I apologize for disturbing you, but do you have a room in the hotel to which you could retire? We'd prefer that guests not sleep in the lobby"

Gabe rubbed his eyes and shook his head, "No, I don't have a room. Been here many times, but not booked for tonight. Seriously though, I love The Spindletop," attempting to make small talk by referencing the rotating restaurant atop the hotel.

Mr. Breaux remained polite, "I am sorry sir, but this area is exclusively for hotel guests and event visitors. Unless I am mistaken, no events are scheduled for this evening."

"OK, no problem. I'll go," replied Gabe, who then made a request, "Sir, Mr. Breaux, my fiancé may be calling back to the hotel later and asking of my whereabouts." He thought logistics for a second with a faint hope that caller ID could save him, while also realizing that Breaux definitely wouldn't go for them meeting up at the Hyatt. Gabe then took a pen and a sheet from the notepad and quickly wrote 'Laney calling for Gabe Wagner – meet at Power Tools'. Gabe placed the paper on the desk in front of him and pointed, "If she, Laney, calls looking for me, please let her know that I am fine and she can pick me up at Power Tools", before folding the note and handing it to him.

Mr. Breaux looked back at the security guard, expressing serious doubt with a quick raise of the eyebrows, but stuck the note in his pocket anyway. "OK, sir, I will do that," was his response, though less than sincere, since he really just wanted to get their unsightly guest to the exit.

As they cruised down the escalator, Gabe once again communicated his message for Laney, "If she calls, please remember 'Power Tools' and to stay there if I don't come out right away…Oh, and not to come alone."

"It's the least I can do Mr. Wagner; I have no reason not to help you," said Mr. Breaux, relieved that Gabe was leaving without incident. The security guard rode along a few steps back.

Gabe began to map out a route to Power Tools in his head, considering the layout of The District and the horror it offered before recalling the slip of paper Crawford had slipped in his pocket. He needed to check it immediately, in the light. What could it possibly reveal?

He reached into his back pocket and pulled out the note. They were now at the bottom of the escalator. Gabe walked slowly toward the same door through which he'd entered and turned to Mr. Breaux with one last reminder, "Thanks, I know the way out from here. Remember Laney calling for Gabe – pick up at Power Tools."

Mr. Breaux nodded in agreement and watched him deliberately saunter towards the exit.

The note was written in jagged script and simply read 'find defector lamar at north foley'.

    ***

By now, Laney and Jane, with Dion in tow, had decided that they would go to the police station. The closest one that came to mind was Northwest Station off Gessner Road in the Carverdale neighborhood. Dotted with serene urban cowboy ranchettes, Carverdale was a suburban area with some rough pockets. Though somewhat wary, most typically avoided entering this area at night, they were mission driven. Laney showed little regard for the speed limit, almost daring to be pulled over. They arrived at the station problem-free in no time.

Officer Cassius Allen greeted and offered to assist them. But upon hearing Laney's full explanation of the situation, Officer Allen had little to offer in the way of help. He explained that 'without evidence of foul play' a twenty-four hour waiting period was required in order to file a missing person report. Her truthful account revealed that it had only been six or so hours since had Laney last heard from Gabe. His tip for them was to go to the downtown station on Travis and see if Gabe had shown up there and, if not, leave an informal note in case he happened to show up there later.

Inbound on Highway 290, they called the Filas home to check in. Joker finally picked up and they explained the situation, he promised to keep the phone line free and not go back online.

Chapter 25

Back in underground downtown, Smith and Crawford were gracious hosts. Jay was offered a bite to eat, his choice of either saltine crackers and an apple or Ramen noodles. He declined.

Smith asked Crawford to show Jay around. First he was shown a large open area full of foam pallets, around twenty of them, equally spaced and uniformly appointed. "This is where we all sleep…well all of us who prefer to sleep indoors, that is," explained Crawford.

Crawford then pointed to a private room in the corner and offered, "The restroom is over there, it's nothing fancy, actually very basic, but we keep it nice and clean." The walls appeared to be corrugated metal and a navy blue shower liner acted as makeshift door. He then asked Jay, "Do you need to use the facilities?" Jay took him up on the offer.

These 'facilities' were bare bones, but mildly impressive considering the location. To the right stood a large, industrial sink and a huge improvised drying rack with towels and sheets neatly hanging. Another smaller rack held multiple pairs of black boxer shorts and socks. Jay's eyes followed an exposed PVC pipe up from the sink to the ceiling, where two additional pipes entered the room. One pipe had electrical wires branching in multiple directions along the ceiling. The other pipe was empty. He theorized that it might be for ventilation, or even communication, purposes.

Jay noticed and then traced a tee fitting of the water pipe back down the rear wall to a shower valve and eventually a toilet supply line at the floor. The shower floor and the toilet were both metal and raised with large drain pipes connecting at an exterior wall. As Crawford had stated, it was extremely clean and actually smelled fresh, mainly because most of the Subjects preferred to do their business outdoors. Jay finished up quickly and washed his face with a mini, hotel style bar of soap. He checked himself out in a round mirror above the sink and looked better than he expected. Perhaps it was the poor lighting.

Crawford greeted him as he exited the bathroom and said, "Follow me, I'll show you the rest."

They made their way to the kitchen and Jay was somewhat impressed. Like the bathroom, it was extremely clean. Bowls were out with an assortment of snacks, mostly candy with some cookies and crackers mixed in. A series of plastic milk and bread crates made for cabinets with foam board acting as a countertop. There was even a refrigerator and a microwave, but no other appliances and no sink. They apparently used mainly plastic ware. The walls were bare except for some sort of chore schedule and a calendar with days marked out as they passed.

Crawford once again offered Jay a bite to eat, and once again he refused.

Next, they checked out a dining and meeting room with a hodge podge of wooden tables and chairs. Again, the furniture appeared to be from a seventies era high school library. A few much older subjects were sitting around playing cards. Crawford introduced Jay to the group as 'Provisional McKinney'; he was indifferent at this point. In the corner a television was connected to a VCR playing older TV shows, Jay took a closer look and realized that it was an episode of *Thirtysomething*.

Now that Jay was somewhat oriented, Smith emerged and requested that he join him to visit in what he called 'The Green Room'. Walker, still smarting after the altercation with Gabe, exited the room as they entered. This room was appointed with much higher quality furnishings, mostly Edwardian reproductions. High end club chairs surrounded a round table with leather inlays and ball and claw feet. Smith and Crawford allowed Jay to select a seat before seating themselves. An elder subject soon joined them and introduced himself. He went by the name of Allen. Allen was very clean cut and articulate, much like Smith. After exchanging pleasantries, they moved on to business.

Crawford spoke first, "McKinney, what's your first impression of our layout here?"

Jay was exhausted and wanted to express his consternations, while keeping the scene calm, "I didn't choose to be here, but I appreciate that you guys are being civil towards me."

Allen spoke next, "You have most certainly chosen to be here, perhaps it was subconscious, but you chose to return to The District on multiple occasions. Sometimes things work out a particular way for a reason."

Smith chimed in, "It is our duty to treat Subjects with care and, quite frankly, human decency. Your appreciation of this fact is duly noted."

Backtracking some, Jay replied, "'Appreciate' was probably a strong word on my part, especially since I have repeatedly expressed my objection to being held against my will."

Remaining calm, Smith went on, "Whether you object or not, it is necessary that you remain here for the good of The District, and, in turn, yourself."

Allen then elaborated, "It is not personal, clearly not anything against you based upon who you are. It is about your behavior, your decision making and what harm it could cause to the overall good of The District, and its Subjects."

"This is truly exasperating," said Jay, "What do you people want from me?"

Crawford remained silent, aloof even. Jay noticed this and wondered why his host wasn't participatory.

Smith was content to remain subtle, but ready to start digging, "Allen mentioned potential harm you might cause and, likewise, by your behavior you can choose to aid The District. McKinney, you have had multiple encounters in and around The District with a seemingly kind younger man, an office worker. We know that he helped you and your family."

"Yes, it seems that we all know this. Are you spies?" was Jay's snippy retort.

Allen fielded this one, "Your query is appreciated, we are observant when it comes to The District. This allows us to continue to provide for our Subjects, and, hence, them to provide for themselves."

Smith added, "He, the office worker, also seemed to be curious about the happenings in and around The District and, at the very least, casting a judgmental eye on our loyal Subjects."

Crawford, not wanting to be overly conspicuous in his silence, joined in, "So you acknowledge meeting with this gentleman. By what name does he go?"

Jay decided that he had nothing to hide and that his answer would not affect Gabe, especially since Walker had already confiscated Gabe's business card earlier in the day. He gave an honest answer, "He goes by 'Gabe' and his last name escapes me. I know that it starts with a 'W', but that's it, all I know."

Next up was Allen who pressed for more, "It cannot be that difficult to recall the last name of someone with whom you met repeatedly, now can it? Was he good to you?"

Seeing no problem in a candid reply, Jay said, "Yes, he was, or is, generous - probably helped as much as he could without putting himself out."

"He noticed your child and wanted to help. Some would consider that noble," said Smith, before getting to the root of the matter. "Did you ever speak with him outside of The District and its broad perimeter?"

Though already weary and becoming weak, Jay immediately picked up on the backhanded compliment. He had disclosed enough and scaled back his answers, "We spoke on the phone, very briefly."

Crawford then asked, "What was the nature of your conversations? Logistics, advice, or just someone to listen…a shoulder to cry on if you will?"

Jay remained curt, "It was brief, he was busy at work. We set up to meet and then your thug took the money he gave me – all of it."

Suspecting there may be more, Allen inquired, "Did he ever speak about himself, his family or his home, where he lives, or hangs out?"

At this point Jay was done talking about Gabe, though he knew very little about him anyway. He wondered if he was dealing with some kind of a cult here. Though he didn't necessarily want to be physically tortured, their nice guy routine was really starting to wear thin. Still, Jay just answered honestly, "He mostly asked about me, and my family. I never asked and he never offered much of anything about himself."

Smith asked the final question, "So you don't know where he lives or where he would go in this general area?"

Jay quickly responded, "I do not. I know he works downtown and takes the bus, Park & Ride, but I don't even know where his office is, nor his home."

Smith believed him and then concluded, "We should all get some rest," before turning to Jay and stating, "Thank you for visiting with us. We appreciate your time. Feel free to come to any of us if you recall anything further about our mutual friend Gabe."

They all stood and walked out in unison.

Crawford led Jay back to the sleeping area. A few older men were sleeping in the back row, but most of the spots were empty. Jay wondered where everyone else might be at this hour.

All of the pallets appeared to be the same in size, shape and comfort, though the blankets came in a variety of colors. Also, a few had rugs which were mainly used to keep clothes and towels off of the bare concrete floor. Folded burlap acted as pillows. It was all so rustic but seemed to be fairly clean.

What a whirlwind this day had been for Jay. He attempted to process this place and these odd, genteel captors. Jay began to consider all of the events that had swept through his life after being laid off. How had it come to this? These freakishly polite tormentors were actually trying to change his name, his identity, and why 'McKinney'? He felt for the outline of his ID inside of his shoe; it was still there under the insole. In a way he was safe, at least relatively, and relieved to have a place to rest, and maybe even sleep.

Jay thought about Garrett and then Gabe before recalling a prayer from his youth. It was the *Glory Be*, a short and simple all encompassing statement of faith. He quickly faded into a deep slumber.

Chapter 26

Power Tools was an iconic industrial dance club at the very northern edge of downtown, with its heyday in the late eighties and early nineties. Both Gabe and Laney knew the location well, which made for a logical meeting place. Shuttered and reincarnated and then shuttered again, Gabe was now glad that he had chosen this place off the top of his head for multiple reasons. Its extensive back balcony area would make for a great vantage point from which to wait and watch. The darkness there would provide for some welcome cover and temporary invisibility. It was definitely outside The District and Laney wouldn't have to traverse The District to get there.

He just had to get there.

Gabe also had to consider the note from Crawford. The mysterious old timer was certainly to be trusted somewhat after enabling Gabe's escape. But what was his motive?

The area around the Hyatt felt safe and comfortable. Gabe walked slowly, especially as he moved under some good lighting. He decided to take another look at the cryptic note. This time he realized that there was writing on the back side: 'code word: "exile" & avoid police'. As rough as he knew he looked and not having an ID on him, Gabe had no thoughts of going to the police anyway. Regarding the code word, it was definitely simple enough to remember. But when and why would he need it? Which led him back to the main message: 'find defector lamar at north foley'.

The 'defector' part seemed pretty simple, since The District lunatics seemed to think they were governing their own little nation. Walker had labeled several types of people within The District, but had carefully chosen not to acknowledge the existence or possibility of 'defectors'.

So now he just had to decipher 'lamar at north foley'. He knew of Lamar Street, it ran east to west bisecting downtown. In fact, he'd have to cross Lamar to get to Power Tools.

The 'foley' part had to refer to the department store. Foley's flagship store was a ten story behemoth right in the middle of downtown, on Main Street. Though it had a basement, which was very rare in Houston, Foley's was not connected to the downtown tunnel system. Gabe knew of it well and wondered what the evening street scene would bring in that area. Since it was somewhat on the way, and he could come up with no other conceivable meaning, he would go to Foley's and figure out the 'north' part from there.

Though home seemed so far away and work the next week even farther, Gabe considered the gravity of The District. Would he be able to just stroll back into downtown on Monday and go back to business as usual? Of course not, Walker may have been injured but he and his crew would still have to be reckoned with. The extended weekend ahead would offer ample time to work on a solution, but the 'avoid police' warning was highly disconcerting.

Foley's was only a couple of blocks away and, as he approached, he sure wished that he knew the name of the man who'd penned the note.

The landscape quickly changed as Gabe moved from the relative sanctity of The Neutral Zone into the smaller area known on the streets as 'Foley Main'. The marquis on the mammoth store came into view as he reached Travis Street and started north. The shoppers and employees were long gone at this hour.

Homeless here were much more visible. A few were strewn along the sidewalk against buildings, their paper bag lined bottles close at hand. Gabe was actually encountering skid row in real life, though this stretch was somehow clean and clear and open for business each morning. This area was full of Independents and essentially lawless. It was pretty much every man for himself in these parts - though occasional alliances were forged, few were formal or lasting.

The next cross street was Lamar and Gabe wondered what encounters were possibly to be had amongst this wasteland. He was ready to bolt at any second if the need arose, but also prepared to stay calm and transact business as long as conditions allowed. So far, these seemingly lifeless bodies were oblivious to his presence.

Now arriving at the Lamar Street intersection, Gabe glanced to the right for any signs of activity. This section was desolate. The full city block across Lamar from the store was virtually devoid of structures, with a couple of surface parking lots and an unkempt green space. The note clearly listed 'lamar' and 'north foley', this would have to be that location.

Gabe looked over at Foley's and surveyed a wide entry alcove nestled between large Christmas display windows. There he spotted a man huddled upright. He approached and realized that the stranger was standing facing a corner and not moving. Gabe then called out the code word 'exile' to which he received a gravelly reply 'not me, not here, not now'. After thanking him for the courtesy of a reply, Gabe moved on to the empty block across the street.

Passing through a row of small trees outlining the vacuous square of land, Gabe soon saw a dim glow in the distance. He stepped carefully in the dark toward the light and came upon a parking lot attendant booth. Through the window he saw a man seated and realized that he was reading a book, the pages illuminated by the amber beams of a space heater. Looking closer Gabe could see that the man had a neatly trimmed full beard and shoulder length hair. The book was held at a distance seemingly compensating for a lack of reading glasses. Next to the farsighted gentleman laid a pistol in a holster.

Gabe raised both of his hands up high where they could be seen and then brought his right hand down to quickly, but softly, tap on the glass before raising it again. The man rose up right away, taking a peek at the gun but not reaching for it. This guy was definitely older, with a fit, medium build.

Upon making eye contact, Gabe yelled through the glass, "Exile!", upon which the attendant immediately dropped his book and picked up the gun. It was a SIG Sauer P226. He didn't point it at Gabe, but called out, "Who sent you?"

Feeling his heart thumping away, Gabe shouted, "Very old man, underground – I have a note!"

Now aiming the pistol at Gabe, the mysterious stranger slowly slid open a window with his free hand. Then in a normal tone, he demanded, "Put your right hand on the building and give me the note with your left hand." Gabe complied even though it meant reaching awkwardly around his body.

As the elder read the note a huge grin emerged and the gun was lowered, next he shook his head and sighed, "Crawford". A sparkle came across his eyes as he looked back at Gabe and said, "Finally."

"May I lower my hands now?" said Gabe, feeling a slight sense of relief.

The old-timer responded, "Sure, come around to the other side and join me."

Gabe gave a half smile and nodded before cautiously entering the tiny shack. Vintage country music played in the background, a Conway Twitty track completely unfamiliar to Gabe was the current tune.

A stool was offered for Gabe to have a seat, but he declined. "So you obviously know who sent me and why."

The senior gentleman stated, "Oh, we have plenty to discuss. We'll have to move soon, though. But first, please tell me your name."

"I am Gabe and I trust you," was the succinct reply.

"Greetings, Gabe. I am Lamar. 'Lamar' as stated on your note, and you can trust me. I know most of what you need to know now and hope to know the rest soon, as we visit," quipped the new friend.

Lamar then pulled out a full bottle of Jack Daniels and opened it, breaking the seal as he twisted the cap.

"This used to be my poison. I self healed years ago, well maybe some divine intervention helped me along the way," said Lamar before declaring, "Anyhow, I have been waiting a long time for this day to arrive."

Gabe was mainly trying to figure out this character and where this all was headed. He noticed that the book on the floor was *Great Expectations*.

A dispenser of conical paper cups was attached to a water cooler and Lamar poured Gabe a serving of the whiskey before filling the tiny bottle cap for himself and raising it, "Cheers to our new friendship, to our mutual friend Crawford and to the journey ahead."

Chapter 27

Laney and her supportive visitors were exiting the freeway into downtown; it was silent except for the whistle of a slightly cracked rear window and the occasional low hum of the radio in the background.

Each of them scanned the barren landscape for any sign of people out and about. As they unknowingly cruised through The District, subjects were mobilizing and then fanning out to search for Gabe. Seeing random vagabonds with walkie talkies randomly scattering, Jane and Dion exchanged puzzled looks.

Quickly coasting down Smith to Dallas Street, they soon arrived at HPD headquarters. To their surprise plenty of open parking spots were available on the street. Officer Regis Daniels greeted the group as they entered the building, "Can I help you?"

Laney spoke up, "Yes, sir. My fiancé is missing. The last time I talked to him he was downtown."

Officer Daniels responded, "OK, we'll see what we can do. Let's get some information from you. Right this way." He pulled a form from a tray labeled 'Missing Persons' and led them to a nearby desk. "Please fill out this form. I'll take it when you're done."

"Thank you, Sir," said Laney as she immediately began filling out the form. Jane wandered around checking out various mug shots of wanted fugitives, while Dion chatted up Officer Daniels attempting to make a new friend.

The requested information was very straightforward and only the final couple of questions required any real thought. 'Has the individual exhibited erratic behavior or have recent changes in behavior been noticed? If so, please elaborate'. Gabe was almost freakishly normal and she had not noticed any changes in him or how he acted. That answer was 'No'.

The next and final question gave her pause 'Does the individual have any known motive to voluntarily withdraw from or elude interpersonal or public contact? If so please give details'. She paused for a few seconds as various scenarios raced through her mind ranging from job related issues to any possible family or relationship issues. Despite her careful consideration, nothing came to mind. He was so stable in her eyes; once again the answer was 'No'.

The exercise in paperwork had Laney now convinced that his disappearance was either the result of a surprise health issue or a case of foul play. She handed the form to Officer Daniels and declared, "This is all I know please help us."

After initially being warm and friendly, the officer became more serious as he examined the listed responses, "Ma'am, according to the information listed here, your friend has been missing for all of about seven or so hours". Returning the paper back to her he said, "OK, hold on to this. If he doesn't turn up by tomorrow afternoon, once twenty-four hours have passed, then we'll accept the report and open an investigation."

"Really, do we have to wait for something bad to happen before you all can officially start looking for him?" said Laney, trying to remain calm.

It was obvious that Officer Daniels dealt with such situations all of the time, "Miss, we simply cannot get on this now without evidence of foul play – our policy is simply based upon matters of probabilities and resources."

Laney was exasperated and rolled her eyes, "So it's dead quiet around here and you can't help at all. 'Probabilities', really…how about priorities?"

The officer understood and attempted to console her, "The vast majority of the time these cases resolve themselves the next morning with positive outcomes, at least as far as matters of personal safety, injury and such go. We are low risk at this point." He then continued, "So what are his last known whereabouts, that is, as far as you know?"

Feeling slight relief that he was taking a little more time with them, Laney gathered her thoughts and then responded, "Well, I last spoke to him at his office, in The Houston Club Building. He was going to meet one of his coworkers at the oyster bar, there in the building, and then take the Park & Ride to his car. He never made it to his car, we checked."

Officer Daniels considered the information and asserted, "Y'all should go by The Houston Club building, assuming you haven't already. The next place I would check would be the Metro Transit Police, they deal with the busses. Go to 1900 Main."

Laney expressed some appreciation, "Thanks, we'll try. That's all we can do," and they were on their way.

***

Lamar finished his miniscule serving of bourbon quickly while Gabe sipped and pondered the implications of the 'journey' awaiting him.

"Alright, let's get this going. You picked the perfect night to arrive - the parking business seems to be quite done for the night," Lamar mused as he showed Gabe a sign before putting it against the window: 'No Attendant - Pay Slot for Numbered Space at Station'. He chuckled, "They call it the 'Honor Box'; most people just act like they don't see it."

Gabe smiled and nodded as they both noticed shadowy figures moving toward them in the distance.

Now with a heightened sense of urgency, Lamar grabbed a single key off a hook on the low ceiling and commanded, "Let's be honorable and get the hell out of here right now, seriously," before tucking the liquor bottle in his jacket and pulling Gabe's arm leading him out of the booth. Gabe assumed that the pistol was already somewhere on Lamar's person. As Lamar popped back in to pull down the shades, it started to storm. He locked the door and yelled to Gabe, "I know where we're going," before motioning, "This way".

The two new friends took off and then trotted along through the torrential rain; Gabe could only tell that they were moving in an easterly direction. Anyone attempting to trail them lost visual immediately as the new friends disappeared into the stormy night. Besides scattered lost souls tucked away in random alcoves, they had the streets to themselves and Gabe soon recognized the area as the rain started to lighten up. The towering First Interstate Bank building approached on the left. Lamar slowed his pace and they soon stopped at the entrance of The Park Shoppes, an upscale lunch hour mall.

Gabe had been here a few times and he recalled that there was a Brooks Brothers and that, except for the food court, this place always seemed to be virtually empty. Lamar immediately produced a key from his back pocket and opened up a side door adjacent to The Sharper Image, before entering an access code on a panel just inside.

"In like Flynn, whatever that means," uttered Lamar before turning to Gabe, "One never knows how called-in favors will be answered."

Gabe pursed his lips together and raised his eyebrows, "OK. It sure feels good to be in here."

They had entered some sort of break room. Lamar immediately located a couple of large cocktail glasses, which he filled with ice. He poured Gabe some Jack Daniels before filling his own cup with water from the tap.

Handing Gabe his drink, Lamar politely demanded, "Walk with me, Gabe," and they trekked down a long narrow hallway to the back of a floor-to-ceiling one way mirror. Lamar slid the glass to the side, and they stepped through a thick wooden frame into some sort of executive conference room.

Lamar pulled a CD from a case. It was the *Requiem by Hanz Werner Henze,* and he inserted the disc into a Bang & Olufsen CD player located on a credenza on the far side of the room. It started to play, and each of them took a seat at a small round table in a dimly lit corner. Lamar placed the square bottle in the middle of the table.

Chapter 28

An intense stare by Lamar into Gabe's eyes, a stare that would ordinarily be downright creepy, actually brought him great calm.

Lamar opened the conversation, "It is great to have you here – though, without a doubt, it is not the calling of your choice." Gabe rubbed his eyes and Lamar continued, "You must know something of The District. The source of your note confirms that. I will educate you fully on that place and what your involvement entails for you, and for others."

"Wow, Lamar, I guess I have to listen to what you have to say. Though I may like you, I'd rather not be involved - but I am involved. This fact has already been made clear," conceded Gabe.

Without changing his demeanor Lamar responded calmly, "I know that you will listen and be ready. You grasp the gravity of the matters and you know that some solving on your part will be to your benefit. Otherwise you wouldn't have come to find me." He then concluded, "I too am involved and look forward to helping some good people, friends of mine who deserve better."

Lamar pulled a fine tipped sharpie from a drawer in an adjacent end table and handed it to Gabe, "You will need to make a few notes; I will let you know when. Pull up your left sleeve and write on your lower arm, write small."

"OK, let's get this going," offered Gabe as he took a sip of his drink. "Let's hear about this 'District' and your take on those characters."

"Fair enough. In fact, let's start with the characters," agreed Lamar. "They will dictate your play as much as the game itself. I know the main characters and you let me know if I fail to mention anyone, since I haven't received any concrete communiqués in the past few months. I will start with Crawford, you know, the guy who gave you the note that led you to me. You've already met him, and I consider him to be a dear friend."

Gabe nodded with growing disdain, "So you are calling this a game, it pretty much feels like some sort of nightmare."

"It's a situation that we all need to make the best of - you can and will. Have a sip and let's get back to the business at hand," stated Lamar. "Starting with Crawford, his real name is 'Winfield Matthews', we were brokers together at E.F. Hutton. He left the firm in the early eighties and eventually ended up on the streets. He has grown children, and when his wife passed away he just lost it - by 'it', I mean his will to be productive within traditional society."

"Alright, so you two obviously either kept up with each other or just reconnected?" Gabe quizzed.

"Crawford is a fine man and was good to me as I was coming up in the business. We remained friends, and I was obviously concerned about his well being as he went through hard times." Lamar further elaborated, "I left E.F. Hutton in late 1987, after the Black Monday crash, to help form The District. Crawford eventually joined, or shall I say 'was absorbed', into the fold. He is a very good man, with an elevated sense of honor. Crawford saved you, and together, we will save The District."

Now feeling his blood about to boil, Gabe blasted him, "You are admitting that you formed this 'District'? That you are responsible for this atrocious mess! I'd take you out right now, on the spot, but you know I can't because I need you. You wouldn't be such a coy son of a bitch if I didn't."

"Believe it or not, I care about you. Crawford sent you and you were keen enough to find me," a somewhat contrite Lamar replied. "I can tell that you have no interest in being a hero, but can also tell that you're a good guy who will feel good about helping others in the end."

With the most wicked of eyes, Gabe fired back, "You are so manipulative! Trying to help someone is precisely what got me here. I was ambushed and essentially kidnapped because some miscreants deemed me a 'Violator' in their little kingdom. So, Mr. Lamar, since I have no choice, what is this 'District' you helped create really about, and what do you really want from me?"

"Time is of the essence, and it's time for you to start listening and only question items pertinent to the mission," asserted Lamar. "So we have established that you know Crawford. Next you'll need to know of a noble fellow who goes by the name of 'Smith'. His real, well former, name was Connor Ericsson. You may or may not have seen him, Smith only comes out at night. Smith was one of three cofounders of 'The District' and is the de facto leader of the organization. We attempted to go full egalitarian with no defined leader or leaders, but it was soon apparent that our venture would fail in no time under such an arrangement. So we opted for 'soft' leadership by informal committee. Smith, Allen and I became the leaders and we always sought input and consensus, which worked out since we were rarely in a hurry. He rarely leaves 'The Grotto', which is the hidden bunker offering a safe haven to all subjects in good standing."

Gabe concluded that he probably had seen Smith, "I'm pretty sure I saw him at a distance. He seemed to be giving commands to the little brut that took me in and tied me up. Does he wear a mask?"

After taking a deep breath, Lamar continued, "Yeah, Smith would be the only somewhat visible leader with me out of the picture. And, yes, he wears a mask when he goes 'overground' as he jokingly calls it. He was an extremely successful architect and became disillusioned with his life amongst the wealthy and those pretending to be so. Smith felt that there was so much waste in the world, especially seeing outlandish and frivolous spending, while at the same time being exposed to the urban poor and homeless on the streets. His marriage was horrible, mainly because he couldn't stand his pretentious wife and did not like the spoiled children they had raised. Though, as their father, he always loved them. He blamed himself for working so hard and allowing his wife to grossly entitle their brood."

"Now I see you getting to the moral angle and implications…obviously the roots of The District," Gabe concluded.

"Yes, there is some logic behind all of this, but I digress…must get back to Smith. Smith and I go back to our college days at SMU. He grew up in San Antonio - Alamo Heights. After graduation, we remained very close friends and occasionally even did business together. We always saw eye to eye. I was also unhappy, and we considered any and all opportunities that would allow us to start over, with a clean slate in some form of anonymity. We weren't associated with any criminal activity, so the witness protection program was out of the question," he chuckled.

Gabe wondered out loud about Lamar's story, "…and you were unhappy. You're a character in this charade, what's your unhappiness about?"

"Actually I am happy now, content with where my life is and happy that you are hearing this tale," Lamar told as he now poured himself another capful of Jack Daniels.

Chapter 29

As Jay slept away, The District was abuzz with activity.

Inside of The Grotto, only the most feeble of subjects were allowed to stay back. While the able bodied members of the populace were now foot soldiers, conspicuous in their absence to those who remained. With routines firmly entrenched, even the slightest bit of change or unusual activity was met with great excitement within The District.

Outside the tunneled bunker, the great outdoors were inhabited by another breed of subject, 'Outliers'. These subjects were offered refuge in The Grotto, but preferred to be outside, in the quasi wild. Obligations such as cooking and keeping the bathroom uber clean defied the Outliers' collective mindsets. The prohibition of drugs and alcohol inside also kept quite a few out. Still, they were allowed to remain in The District and offered a certain level of protection not ordinarily found on the streets. On this night, any mildly clean, sober and coherent Outlier would be mobilized.

Preston was accompanied by a couple of Subjects as he combed the streets around The Houston Club Building before attempting to enter the lobby. The austere guard was unrelenting in his duty to keep anyone the least bit suspect out, and Preston felt that he was specifically protecting Gabe. Preston radioed across the band his suspicions and the fact that he would hunker down and secure the 'suit chamber entrance', as he put it.

Meanwhile, Walker followed up on a lead that Gabe had been seen in the Foley area. The tipsters, mainly Foley locals, vaguely recalled seeing Gabe pass through by the huge store. When pressed, they wondered whether two figures headed east as the storm hit had been a mirage. Sporadic rumors amongst the Subjects that Lamar frequented Foley furthered the pursuers' suspicions. Walker led Clay in a methodical search of the area and they ransacked the parking guard booth, discovering familiar tropes of Lamar in the process. East they would head.

Smith and Allen were busy preparing for the worst. Their joint decision to delve into the use of force against a reluctant outsider, a Patron turned Violator, could very well doom The District. Jay, now 'McKinney' to them, could possibly be assimilated with lots of grooming and the passage of time, but Gabe was a different story. He was young and aware, with no known chemical dependency or mental instability to slow him down. They had already made the tough call to terminate him, and Walker had failed to execute. Their hope now was that Smith's careless appearances hadn't revealed The Grotto's tunnel access point. Further fortification was necessary, just in case. Smith and Allen mutually agreed that desperate measures were in order.

The possession of firearms by Subjects was prohibited within The District, though blades, blunt force objects and even mace were permitted for the stable. Walker would simply confiscate weapons from the unstable during their slumber. Smith came to accept that outside of guns, small weapons were fine in the hands of those able and aware enough to keep them from Walker. Without firepower of their own and not sure of the type of force Gabe would bring, Allen determined that he would seek outside help.

***

As he nursed and relished his petite serving of whiskey, Lamar was inclined to reminisce, but caught himself and got back to business.

Interrupting Gabe's thoughts of his own life, Lamar continued his narrative, "I feel that you now have an understanding of who Smith is. Please do write his name on your arm."

Gabe considered protesting the request but wanted this escapade to end as soon as possible, so he acquiesced and complied.

Lamar proclaimed, "We are proceeding nicely, very nicely. Let's move on to the third and final founder of The District."

"Go ahead, I'm listening," was Gabe's sharp retort.

On point, Lamar continued, "Allen, the mystery man that you most certainly did not see, or at least I know that you've never seen him in his capacity as a Founder, or Subject, of The District. His former name was Walter Timmons, which is irrelevant for these purposes, and he is a banker, originally from Highland Park, you know, old money Dallas. He is a Vanderbilt alum and 'retired' playboy, never married - always made a concerted effort to stay unattached. I met him through Smith; they were business associates and ran in similar social circles. They also came to hold similar ideals, though for different reasons. Got it so far? Just remember 'Allen – virtually invisible cofounder', okay? Also write down his name."

"Got it, okay. Keep going," nodded Gabe.

"Allen was and is a very active benefactor within the arts community, mainly ballet and opera because that's where the beautiful women are plentiful. He is getting way up there in years now, but still an active donor and theater goer."

Gabe was puzzled, "You mean this guy, Allen, is active outside The District - like in the real world?"

Sensing genuine interest sparked on the part of Gabe, Lamar answered, "Well, we'll get to more about your understanding of The District itself in a minute, but, yes, Allen is a functioning member of society, the 'real world' as you call it. He leads somewhat of a double life, only reports to The Grotto for major matters involving resources and decisions. Your arrival and departure has without a doubt summoned him forth. He is an ally, though his motivation differs from mine, as well as that of Smith."

"Alright, let's hear it. What's he about and what will his role be?" quizzed Gabe.

"As I said, Allen is an ally but the reasons are likely unexpected by you. He actually lives downtown, at the Houston House Apartments to the south and works with Texas Commerce Bank. Besides his role as a founder and decision maker, Allen acts as a liaison. His primary role is to keep our Subjects, or 'street people' as most might call them, off the streets particularly in the evening, when it's dark and theater attendees are shuffling about. People coming downtown to take in dinner and a performance want no part of seeing, much less interacting with, those they view as degenerates. Allen serves on the board of just about every main arts organization and quietly, per a gentleman's agreement, seeks to keep the peace, specifically via the elimination of beggars and their begging. His main directive is to seek money solutions over blood solutions, but ultimately to achieve the end regardless of the means. Allen is basically a good man, but peace of mind trumps altruism in his case, though he has grown to appreciate the value of the lives he's helping."

Gabe interjected, "I think I understand what you're saying and their motivation. This is amazing." He then pointed to his now empty glass and Lamar poured him an extra small portion. Gabe needed to be relaxed but lucid enough and receptive to the details of the knowledge being imparted upon him.

"You're right, it is amazing, all of it. And so good to see you coming around," smiled Lamar, "This motivation on their part allows for the secure funding of The District's operations. As I previously mentioned Allen is a liaison, really *the* liaison. Real cash flowing into The District is delivered by Allen. The cash requirements are actually minimal since the infrastructure is fairly self sustaining with low to no maintenance. The main costs are food, thrift shop clothing and shoes, toiletries - also incidentals such as cleaning supplies and 'tithes' to protectors of the protectors. Chemically dependent subjects, including smokers, are expected to fund their own vices, but strictly prohibited from soliciting theater patrons and harshly punished if caught doing so. Consumption is to be discreet and never inside The Grotto."

"Now I get it. Begging is acceptable; just don't bother people attending plays and such. Is that what you are saying? So The District is really just about a reciprocal relationship which keeps the peace?" quizzed Gabe.

"Sure, I suppose that is a way of looking at it," was Lamar's response.

"Well that explains why no one ever bothers us when we go to see musicals..." Inside, Gabe appreciated The District's efforts in this regard, but didn't dare offer any sort of commendation.

As for Lamar, he had much more to offer in order to properly prepare Gabe for that which was to come. He went on, "Which brings me back to the 'Outliers' I mentioned earlier. They don't want to be housed in The Grotto, but prefer the protection offered by The District. As a compromise, they are allowed to remain under certain conditions. First, they must remain within the known geographic border of The District. Secondly, they are not permitted to carry any form of personal identification. Next, they swear to never speak of The District to non Subjects and keep its very existence completely confidential. Finally, they pay a 50% commission on all funds solicited within The District. We call it a 'guardinar'. Walker came up with the concept and the name. Guardinar collection is based upon the honor system, and the vast majority seem to be extremely forthcoming when it comes to self reporting."

Gabe was overwhelmed by the complexity of The District's structure, but receptive to more details on the various members of The District. "Now you mentioned a 'Walker' - that's a new name. Tell me about him...I assume it's a 'him'."

147

Lamar slowly rocked his chair onto its back legs, "Walker is the main reason that you and I are here now."

Chapter 30

Laney, Jane and Dion located the Metro Traffic Police headquarters on Main Street. Despite the lack of traffic and activity, no parking was available on the street. Laney and Jane would go inside together and Dion slid into the driver's seat to be able to idle at an open corner and, if needed, circle the block.

The ladies entered the station and found the place to be deserted. It was in stark contrast to the frenzy of activity at the HPD station, and they searched to find someone, anyone. Metro cops were mainly concerned with keeping the buses safe and enforcing traffic regulations on the High Occupancy Vehicle lanes. They were the ones who counted passengers as carpoolers entered the HOV, or 'contraflow', lanes and, apparently, also selectively enforced the speed limit.

Finally they found an office with a light on and knocked lightly then harder while calling out, "Hello, Hello…" A female officer emerged and greeted them, "Is there something I can help you with?"

Laney spoke up, "Yes, we are searching for a missing person. This is someone who should have taken a Park & Ride bus home tonight."

The officer responded, "Unfortunately we don't track passengers by name, unless they have an annual pass. But we only do monthly passes for the Park & Rides."

The officer's name tag was covered by a sweater, but Laney noticed an engraved plate on her desk. It read 'A. Kirby Chapman'. She was the one who had stopped the speeding bus for the possible hookup with Alex, the friendly bus driver. This fact of Gabe's detailed retelling of the tale was lost on Laney, though. "Is there any way you can ask the driver about our friend who's missing?" asked Laney politely.

Officer Chapman took the time to give Laney and Jane each a sinister smile before stating, "There's an inquiry form over there. Fill it out and I'll take it here. The Park & Ride buses don't run again until Friday, but the drivers will see the form that morning before they start their routes. Which route number is it?"

Laney paused then answered, "It is the one that takes I-10 out to Beltway 8, the West Belt."

"Ah, that's the 210. I think around five different drivers run that route. It's the least traveled of them all. I will assure you that all of the drivers returning to work on Friday will check your report. Friday is not a holiday for Metro, but some will likely be taking vacation time. Those drivers will see it on Monday."

The prospects of getting real help here seemed even dimmer than over at the HPD. Still Laney felt like she had to do something and filling out this paperwork, which so happened to double as a Lost & Found form, was something. Unturned stones were not an option.

Jane keenly stared out the door at Laney's car with Dion inside, while Laney filled out the half letter sized form.

As Laney handed the form to Officer Chapman, she felt the need to say a little about Gabe, "This man, Gabe, is a great guy and I feel like his disappearance could have something to do with him helping out the homeless. This week he reached out and got directly involved with a father and son needing help. I think he found them by Jones Hall."

The officer affirmed Laney's statement, "Wow, he does sound like a great guy" before downplaying any attempt at correlation between incidents. "I seriously doubt the homeless in these parts are capable of serious malice. Have you seen them? Most are so feeble."

Laney wondered aloud, "I know, you're right, but we went to Party on the Plaza last night and did encounter some real freaks, ones actually familiar to Gabe - and they seemed to know who he was. I just wonder if they had anything to do with this."

"We certainly do have to consider all possibilities, any decent investigator knows this," declared the officer. Now attempting to reassure Laney, Officer Chapman said, "I will put this here for safekeeping," as she tucked the form into an accordion style folder.

***

Back at the plush mall office, Gabe and Lamar discussed a Subject with whom they each were familiar. Reginald Townshend came to The District in 1994, and Lamar knew very little regarding his background except that he was

150

from somewhere in Alabama, and that he had served in the US Army, with time spent in Iraq during Operation Desert Storm.

They both, however, knew the name by which he went now, 'Walker', and that he had the nastiest of mean streaks. Lamar alluded to suspicions of post traumatic stress playing a part in his beastly disposition.

Lamar told Gabe the story of how Walker had come onto the scene as a bully shaking down symphony and musical ticket buyers, instantly disrupting the calm that had permeated The District for years. Complaints poured in to Lamar, mainly from Outlier Subjects, while Allen was briefed by board members from various arts organizations.

In order to avert a full crisis, a meeting was setup at Tranquility Park. As Allen watched through binoculars from atop the federal courthouse, Smith, Lamar and Clay visited with the upstart lowlife. After some back and forth, it was agreed that he would become an official Subject of The District and henceforth be called 'Walker'.

Certain terms of the agreement violated some core tenets upon which The District was founded. Namely, Walker was given the additional title of 'Gatekeeper', while all other non-founders were simply 'Subjects'. This position gave him full autonomy over all security matters and allowed the use of force at his discretion. His motivations had nothing to do with the good of The District, or any sort of greed on his part. Walker was just a sociopathic power monger.

Allen was never comfortable with Walker's special privileges, feeling that the potential violation of personal freedoms went against everything The District stood for. Elevated titles and exceptions set a poor precedent and had no place. Smith, though also reluctant to make such exceptions, was a direct party to the agreement and felt that they simply had no choice. He also felt that new order would reduce the frequency of altercations amongst the Subjects and sure up the borders.

Having been tailed and captured by him, Gabe listened intently to the tale of this scoundrel.

Walker preferred to be a foot soldier. Though sharp and capable enough to become an officer, he intentionally thwarted his military career at every turn to guarantee that he would remain on the front line with the infantry.

Only occasionally venturing into The Grotto for food or to use the restroom, Walker mainly preferred to spend his time roaming and enforcing. He required little sleep and took outdoor cat naps from three AM until dawn and then again after lunch at around two o'clock. The Gatekeeper craved power and rarely operated alone, alternating sidekicks, mainly Clay and Preston, as they slept off cheap souse.

Walker's sole vice was Adderall, as he had participated in the clinical trials and was drawn back to the little pills again and again. It was an expensive habit, especially on the secondary market, which he funded directly out of his guardinar collections. Smith chose to look the other way and Allen was out of the loop on this matter.

Lamar emphasized this point in particular, "The supplier meets up with him daily at Market Square, just a block or so outside The District. Most of the addicted Outliers sleep while he makes his early morning runs and only Clay and Preston have any idea of this daily routine, though Crawford and I eventually figured it out." He continued, "Crawford's note - the one you delivered, made no indication that this arrangement has changed. This will be key for us."

"Point taken," nodded Gabe as he made a note on his arm while remaining fairly quiet.

"He brought evil to The District. Our intention was to operate in a state of grace and harmony, without labels and harsh rules, which inevitably followed upon his arrival," Lamar opined. "To our dismay, he chased off good Subjects, mentally ill folks about whom we worry to this very day."

"Present company included," Gabe simultaneously quipped and wondered.

"Definitely…very astute of you. What else do you need to know of about him?" asked Lamar.

Gabe paused then inquired, "I wondered if he's an American Indian. I mean he has no facial hair and similar features – that was my initial thought at first sight…you know with the cheekbones and deep set eyes?"

"Seriously, of all things that's what you want to know about him? Well, he just plucks the whiskers as they grow in. I guess he feels that it distinguishes him from the other scrubs, or it's a military thing – I really don't know…" Lamar then lectured him further, "Besides, 'American Indians' as you call them actually do have facial hair. Now, is there anything pertinent to the situation at hand that you'd like to know about him?"

"His position and visibility within the organization are apparent, as is your disdain for him. We both know that he's strong and disciplined. You have certainly been thorough in your description. Are there others I need to know about? The clock's ticking and I need to know the mission. What's the plan, for him, for me, for The District?"

Chapter 31

Thursday November 28

At a modest home on North Grace Street in the Goosport section of Lake Charles, Garrett lay awake staring through an open window. It was now past midnight. Despite having healthy foods like fried okra, brown sugar beans and yams forced upon him and the fact that he'd be going back to school, a new school, he loved the comfort and safety of this place. They even had a PlayStation.

In the night sky he searched for the biggest of the stars, knowing that his father back in Houston could see it too, even with the bright lights of the big city surrounding him. His dad was so strong and would be fine, Garrett knew this. But he missed him already.

***

Jay now tossed in his sleep as visions of his captors and this new world with a new name tormented him. The long tunnel seemed to be the only way out, and it surely was closely guarded, no matter how welcoming these gentlemen had acted. Though these glorified squatters had made every possible effort to be extra friendly, they were also very clear about the fact they were completely in control of his situation. It went without saying that 'McKinney', as he was now to be known, was expected to harmonize and assimilate. He had been bold enough not to heed Walker's repeated warnings, and they cared nothing of his former life, including the existence of his son. Walker hated children and the founders were indifferent, Garrett was merely an inconvenience now relegated to a footnote. Only Jay's knowledge of The District's inner workings mattered and they would allow him to live, but only here, and only in secrecy.

Not able to get back to sleep, Jay aka McKinney decided to take a look around. Crawford had vacated The Grotto, and it was understood by all that his feeble self would be of no aid in the search for Gabe. Preferring to sleep under the stars, Crawford found his stash of blankets in a plastic bag along the upper bank of Buffalo Bayou. His bedding was slightly wet from the storm, but not enough to disturb his need for sleep. With the critters gone for the winter, it provided for a warm and quiet nesting spot.

The rest of the elders slept comfortably on their pallets within the confines of The Grotto. Allen had gone for outside help, and Smith was the only other subject to be found awake.

"Hello there, McKinney," was his greeting, attempting to appear calm though his little world was in turmoil. Now realizing that the front gate was virtually unguarded, Smith continued, "I know it's always tough to get some sleep in a new place, even for street urchins such as ourselves."

Jay was not in a joking mood, "You are holding me against my will and have the audacity to try to group me with you 'urchins', as you say. Do you realize this fact?"

"We are here to assist the downtrodden. You are now a part of that class," Smith replied.

"You are. And, I am? Huh! How's that?" snapped Jay back at him.

Smith elaborated, "In this world, which by the way, you chose to enter, we provide a sanctuary - shelter from the elements and perils of what lies above. The District offers food and other necessities for all Subjects."

Hardly convinced, Jay pressed harder, "So it's a sanctuary, but without freedom."

Still remaining patient, Smith gave somewhat of a stock answer, "Once you've been here, inside, it is our duty to provide for you and your fellow Subjects. To ensure continued prosperity, it is sometimes necessary for one to be sequestered during the learning process. You will see the way and secure a fraternal bond with these very fine men."

"It's still basically a prison. That's really what you're so eloquently stating," said Jay. If only he knew that the exit was wide open at this very moment, unfamiliarity was his biggest enemy for now.

Now waxing philosophical, Smith asked, "Do you know what it feels like to have someone give something to you in return for nothing at all? That's 'unconditional' defined, is it not?"

Jay fired back, "Unconditional? I'm pretty sure that 'freedom' goes hand in hand with 'unconditional'."

His ideals and intentions were genuine and Smith, though delusional, affirmed Jay's concerns. He then spoke as an understanding father might, "I realize your concerns, they're normal at this stage. Bear with us, especially since I can guaranty your safety here."

The embedded threat rung through, and Jay figured his best move would not be in the dark of night. "I think I'll go back to my area to rest and consider your ideas - you should consider them as well."

Smith concluded, "Good idea, you get some rest Provisional McKinney," wishing dearly that he too could bed down for the night.

***

In a final effort to potentially assist the Metro Police, Laney pulled a photo from her purse. It was a passport photo of Gabe taken when he was registering for the CPA exam. Officer Chapman made a couple of copies and stuffed them in the file with the report.

Now that everything Laney knew regarding Gabe's disappearance had been shared with this little outfit, the trio was ready to do a little searching of their own.

On the way out of the station, they crossed paths with Walter Timmons as he entered the building. Despite the urgency of his visit, he couldn't help but stop and notice the stunning brunette twins. He knew Officer Chapman well and asked her about the nature of their visit. As one of the few who knew him as both 'Walter' and 'Allen', the officer was a paid ally of The District and quickly filled him in. Allen soon came to realize that his band of roving derelicts weren't the only ones searching for Gabe. Laney had only left her name and phone number, which he copied from the report for later use.

Allen had Officer Chapman make additional copies of Gabe's picture for nefarious use back in The District, before giving her marching orders. As he departed, another Metro employee emerged from a back office where Officer Chapman had been hiding him. It was a driver out of uniform who had heard everything and was curious about the strange visitors to the station. He asked Kirby about the nature of Allen's involvement and his access to police case information. The officer was not at all forthcoming, which only added to his suspicions. Kirby had said that she was a 'dirty cop' and he totally believed her now. An enlargement of the original photo was still on the copier and he immediately recognized the missing person as a regular passenger on his 210 Park & Ride route. The driver was Alex Longoria.

***

Dion remained at the wheel as Laney and Jane peered across the bleak horizon. They slowly crept along scouring the entire downtown area in a matter of twenty minutes, thanks to the synchronized traffic lights. They chose the safety that staying in the vehicle offered and occasional sightings of crossing Subjects were the only signs of life.

The Lancaster Hotel was a familiar landmark, and seemingly the only place with any sort of well lit activity. The girls checked with a doorman and then the front desk clerk; neither had seen anyone matching his description. On their way out, the doorman mentioned that the Hyatt was also "open for business at this hour," and that they might give it a try.

Chapter 32

A mission and plan of action had been demanded by Gabe, and Lamar felt that it was best to now give him the rest of the background information. Specifically, he needed to be aware of the history and, hence, the inner workings of The District. "I have covered the main people of influence. Just don't forget about Walker's enforcers Clay and Preston."

"Yes, I have noted them," confirmed Gabe.

"Great, remember: Clay old, but fit, medium height and Preston middle aged, tall thin pale guy," Lamar reiterated.

"Got it, I've had encounters with each of them and they're here and here," said Gabe as he pointed to his brain and then to the writing on his arm.

"That's most excellent. Let's move on. Listen carefully," stated Lamar. "As I mentioned earlier, Smith and I conceived the idea before being joined soon thereafter by Allen. We wanted to disappear from society, and Allen's backers wanted the paupers to disappear from the byways surrounding their hallowed performance halls and theaters. Somehow we had all found each other, and it was a perfect match, a solid dose of serendipity."

Unable to resist sarcasm, Gabe smugly sniped back, "Yeah, it was destiny. What great fortune, for all of us."

Lamar got back to it, "Enough already. Our concept was and still is philanthropic, this you cannot deny. No one can. The logistical obstacles were threefold. First, we needed stable funding, a source both sufficient and lasting. Allen's involvement solved this one as you know – vital…just so vital. No one would have figured that the money would be the easiest part. Next, we needed a secret locale. It had to be downtown, preferably right in The Theater District, and easily accessible from the ground level at all hours of the day – quite the laundry list of requirements. You'll have to recall that Smith was an architect, and his expertise was crucial in this area. This part's actually pretty damn cool. The solution could not have been any more ideal. You paying attention?"

Gabe responded, "I'm here. I have actually been wondering about this part the whole time."

"You know Houston, right? I mean, you know the geography, right?" asked Lamar.

Nodding confidently Gabe replied, "Sure, I know my way around very well, definitely better than most..."

Lamar interrupted, "No, not the streets. I mean the lay of the land, you know the natural topography – land, lakes and rivers and all that stuff."

"Sure, it's actually more bayous than rivers though, and native pine trees, I guess, plus some oaks," concluded Gabe.

"Yes, you got it, and you made my point," Lamar declared, "By omission, that is. The construction of the Wortham Center was being commissioned at that time, and the usual rudimentary survey work was performed. Typically, in order to save costs, the preliminary survey is simply initialed by the lead architect for the final site work. That works in this town, and your omission speaks to the reason..."

Gabe was genuinely curious, "Enough with the suspense. What is this 'omission' you keep speaking of?"

Lamar further elaborated, "As fate would have it, our friend Smith was the senior site architect on the Wortham Center, working directly with the site engineer. Smith was extremely diligent in his work, not a 'rubber stamper' if you know what I mean, and such a profound thinker. He always walked the project sites, regardless of the scale of the project and certainly wasn't going to take anything for granted on a project of that magnitude."

Gabe chimed in again, "OK, you're rambling."

Lamar got to the point, "Houston's basically flat, right? Well the land bordering Buffalo Bayou actually slopes. Just as you made no mention of 'grade' or 'hills' in your description...of the geography, common assumptions regarding land in these parts opened the door for our operation. Hills, as in primo hillside space along the bayou, were there for the taking, and the 'locale issue' was solved."

"Yep, 'never assume' as my boss always says," was Gabe's statement of affirmation, "I sort of know the 'what' coming next but definitely not the 'how'".

Proud to elaborate, Lamar went on, "Smith is a genius and realized that if enough homeless could be mobilized, then there was a chance worth taking. We basically evangelized, letting them know that their efforts would be rewarded. They would be rewarded with a secure territory and a reliable food source and most of all, a safe haven, a shelter. It worked, they wanted a home."

"And what exactly could they do towards this effort?" wondered Gabe.

Lamar filled him in, "The structure was formed with two-by-fours and plywood, actually pressboard, and foam, lots of foam. Smith brought in a crew, non-union 'wink wink', the evening before the foundation was to be poured. This crew cut out an access hole into the lowest point of the form prepared by the official builders, the spot you know down by Buffalo Bayou. They then proceeded to frame in a tunnel and then a rather large room, though the ceilings had to be limited to six foot six in order to keep the Wortham Center structurally sound."

Gabe was impressed, "I totally agree - that's genius." He then asked again, "What did the homeless do next?"

Boasting a little, Lamar went on, "Oh, this is probably the best part. They all showed up at dusk along with a huge load of foam and old tires. I brought the staple guns and my old friend Winfield Matthews even showed up. He became 'Crawford' that night. Together, he and I brought in the sheets of foam and stapled them all over the framing; Smith genuinely feared that the concrete would seep into the space. Allen then arrived with steel columns cut to spec for placement floor to ceiling throughout the large room. He also brought PVC pipe and made three runs to the surface. Smith checked the prints and ensured that they were stubbed up into a planned janitorial space. An additional PVC line was laid down and out to the bayou for drainage. Of course we duct taped the ends first. The future subjects then stuffed our future home with large chunks of foam until they ran out, this foam was sufficient to fill most of the large room. Then we all filled the remainder of the space, including the tunnel, with tires."

"Foam and tires, huh!" exclaimed Gabe. "Well that's just absolutely amazing, especially since I know the outcome. You guys actually got those sloths to work through the night."

"Most of them, they're not 'sloths' by the way, worked very hard, very late." Lamar remained proud, "A load of fill dirt showed up at midnight, we handed out a few shovels and they covered up our future 'Grotto'. We even covered the entrance with the cutout and then back filled with a huge mound of dirt and branches to cover it, like our own little cocoon or acorn or whatever."

"And then you had to wait a while, and see if it worked…" said Gabe.

"You're a sharp fellow," said Lamar. "I'll round out the story now. Smith realized that multiple commercial grade concrete pumpers would surround the site the day of the big foundation pour. Even on large jobs they pour it all the same day, as close to the same time as possible, to allow the foundation to properly cure as a single form. Smith also knew that most of the attention on what I'll call 'pour day' would be focused on the front right side of the building, while the void, our space, was below grade on the rear left side."

Gabe then asked, "So I get that you are telling me that this void became The Grotto. I just don't get how it came to be on a busy construction site?"

Lamar was glad to further explain, "Everything came together perfectly. We knew that figureheads might be present, you know big money donors and politicians, to take credit and get in their photo ops. Certainly arts board members like Allen, 'Walter Timmons' as he was known then, would be around plus some local media covering the start of construction – surely you've seen golden shovel footage on your nightly news, or photos in the paper. The original plan was for Allen to run interference and just keep all of those folks up at the front area. It didn't hurt that certain Houston Ballet and Houston Grand Opera board members were privy to our plan. In reality none of them would have any interest in venturing around the muddy slope of the bayou in their suits and heels anyway. As it turned out, none of that mattered. It was spring and so the pour actually started in the dark - our handy work was covered up rather quickly, before the sun came up."

Genuinely curious, Gabe questioned, "Sounds like 'handy work' alright. You all basically created a secret cave right under everyone's nose. And what about the supervising engineers. How did you fool them, or keep them at bay?"

"We didn't fool the engineers at all, nor did we try. Smith actually coordinated with the lead on-site engineer to approve the concrete loads and incorporate extra rebar where needed. Since The Grotto was technically never shown on the prints or site plan, and the structural integrity was never compromised. He was comfortable with looking the other way. The funds saved on concrete were diverted to engineering, his engineering – he was comfortable with that financial arrangement as well," Lamar explained.

"Bribes and kickbacks: you all were off to such an honorable start," said Gabe sarcastically.

Lamar attempted to justify the means, "It was a great accomplishment, simply unprecedented. Even you with your smug persona cannot deny this fact. Besides, the finished west elevation of the Wortham Center matches the architectural drawings to a tee and no one was harmed in the process."

Gabe shook his head, "What a great rationalization, except for the fact that I'm feeling more than a little harm."

Chapter 33

The modern steel and glass structures of the Houston skyline were traditionally topped in white lights for the holiday season. With the grand lighting set for the day after Thanksgiving, the peaks of random buildings illuminated as test runs flickered all around. The Hyatt Regency participated in these testing exercises, and Englebert Breaux was busy moving back and forth between the roof and the street. The lighting was a source of great pride for him, his competency on full display for all to see. He was extremely thorough, confirming not only that all of the lights were working, but that the bulb color and intensity were consistent all the way around the mammoth hotel.

As Mr. Breaux moved through the empty lobby to perform yet another inspection from the street, he couldn't help but notice Laney and her buddies headed toward the concierge station. He would normally stop and offer help but at the moment, he was preoccupied with the grand lighting project.

Instead, a desk clerk oblivious to the note in the shirt pocket of Mr. Breaux approached and listened to Laney's description of Gabe and his disappearance. Laney gave her contact information, and the group left the hotel.

Having exhausted their options and energy, they made one last pass through downtown before entering I-10 in the direction of home. Dion was the driver and totally focused on the road ahead and staying awake. He failed to notice the white unmarked Caprice Classic tailing them from afar. It was Officer Chapman. They were soon home and seemingly safe inside, where Laney plugged her phone into the charger and laid back in a recliner to get some rest. Jane and Dion immediately crashed on a sofa and the floor respectively. The officer out front decided to keep a close and constant watch on the house.

***

The education of Gabe continued and, though fascinated, Lamar's story had grown long, "You mentioned three obstacles, and you've covered cash flow and venue. What was the last? Secrecy?" Gabe then took his empty glass to a wet bar, where he filled it to the brim with tap water.

Lamar then became noticeably somber, "Secrecy you ask? You're close, but not exactly. Our perfect location, along with the relationships we forged with our Subjects, would naturally provide for secrecy. The final obstacle was more along the lines of anonymity or alibis or whatever else you'd call it."

Gabe wondered about his sudden change in mood and what his answer meant, "Anonymity, alibis? What do you mean? Sort of sounds like secrecy…"

"You have to remember the lives of the three founders. Allen was single and free and not taking up permanent residence, so his situation was simple. He could just come and go as he chose." Lamar then lamented, "Smith and I, on the other hand, well we had to disappear from active family and professional lives. The emotions of severing relationships and accepting a simpler, much simpler, life were overwhelming. But beyond that, after we made a little covenant with each other to go through with it, we had to work through the logistics of virtually ceasing to exist in this world up here."

Lamar's sappy emotional account of it all was of no interest to Gabe, "Alright, well let's hear this. How did you guys pull it off?"

Lamar thought back to those times, "I've told you about Smith's situation, at least from my perspective. His pretentious wife disgusted him and his marriage was miserable. Though he still loved her, he couldn't stand her company. Smith determined that once his last child married, he'd disappear into our plan."

"Wow, so how did he disappear?" asked Gabe.

"Remember, after the foundation was poured, we had to wait fifteen months for the building to be finished. We each considered every possibility that would allow us to move in as soon as The Grotto was ready, so that we could establish order immediately. I'll say it one more time 'Smith is a genius'. On the morning of Friday, May 8, he told his wife that he was going fishing in Galveston Bay. This was 1987. He drove out to a space between docks where Buffalo Bayou opens up into the bay and removed the cash from his wallet. He then tossed the wallet into his fishing boat and gave it a strong push into the ship channel. From there Smith drove to Kemah and parked near a familiar launch ramp and tossed the keys into the water just as the sun cracked dawn. He then walked about four miles to the South Shore Harbor Resort where he caught a cab to the Main Post Office in Downtown. Then it was just a short walk to The Grotto and, voila, Connor Ericsson had become 'Smith'."

"He is genius, no argument here," said Gabe before quizzing, "But you both had to disappear at about the same time, and you were known friends. Wouldn't that be extremely suspicious?"

Lamar concurred, "Absolutely, we both agreed that I should disappear at a later time, even though the boat was found and he was presumed drowned. We estimated that a six month lag would be sufficient to get his name out of the daily news. Talk about a long six months…"

An exhausted Gabe responded, "Go ahead, talk about it. I don't know your real name or anything – you were so open about everyone else's real lives. What's your story, Lamar?"

"I was born Baron Michaels, in Memphis, an only child in a lower middle class family. My father was a longshoreman and my mother died when I was in high school. I was a very good student and graduated from Vanderbilt and then came to Houston during the seventies oil boom. My career was in securities, I think I already told you that, right?"

Gabe nodded, "Yep, I remember that you and Crawford were stockbrokers…"

Lamar continued his long winded recollections, "Yes, here it goes. I came to this town with one goal and that was to not be poor. My goal was achieved quickly and, regardless of the price of oil or the fluctuations in the Dow, my book of business was solid and the commissions always flowed well. Not everyone at our brokerage did so well, and I was sensitive to their failures, actually felt terrible guilt that tore me up. I got married in 1979 and my wife wanted children immediately, but we were never able to have any. She became melancholy and blamed me. I became disillusioned with success and wondered what this crazy game of life was all about. We grew apart and eventually divorced in 1985."

Gabe made a faint attempt to console him, "Sorry to hear that."

Acknowledging Gabe's words, Lamar went on, "Hey, I was free and clear of a burden. Of course I had loved that woman, or at least I fell in love with who I thought she was. It was time to move on though. First off I wanted to get rid of most of my things, the luxuries, only essential items were kept…you know, the necessities. Most of all I wanted help those less fortunate, which seemed to be just about everyone. I was no longer interested in just writing a check or spending a little time doing charity work here and there. I wished to provide permanent, lasting help. Smith and I had both discussed the waste we saw in the charities we supported, the overhead such as management and marketing expenses, and how little of what we gave actually made it to the cause."

"So this was your grand manifesto: 'Bring the charity directly to the people' or something like that, right?" Gabe mockingly concluded.

Lamar sensed the overt sarcasm and launched into a diatribe, "Don't let your individual situation cloud your judgment of a noble cause! Are you so selfish as to downplay the charitable efforts of others, others willing to give up everything they had and put their lives on the line? The front line!"

Gabe fired back, "You just don't get it - you and your fellow 'Founders' became the new layer of management, the overhead, did you not?"

"Well, we placed ourselves on the same level as those whom we were serving," was Lamar's defense. After a pause he concluded, "Of course there had to be some order, and we worked to provide structure."

"You tell yourself what you want to hear," was Gabe's snarky response. He then commented, "You sure have spent a lot of time on your self-righteous dissertations about the good old days and your old cronies. The ideals you espouse are worthless, once innocent lives are hurt. Now I am starting to repeat myself. Don't you appreciate it? Back to the history lesson, how did you disappear?"

It was a rather somber tale told by Lamar, "Once I was divorced it was rather easy. I lost half of my assets in those proceedings and then sold off whatever was left. I had no spouse, offspring or siblings. Most of our couple friends just went away; those who remained ostracized me, since I took most of the blame for the breakup. My only living family member was my father who was in the early stages of Alzheimer's. I went up to Memphis to bid him farewell. I think he realized and understood that one of us was going away. That was the only tough part on a personal level. I did leave him enough money to live out the rest of his life in comfort and peace. That left only professional contacts with whom to part ways. I began transitioning my accounts to another broker right at the time Smith went 'missing'. This other broker was a young guy, very young with a large family and needing a kick start - mostly because he was simply new to the game and struggling to get out of the blocks. But I saw certain qualities in him I liked. I called it early retirement and declined any sort of fanfare; just a modest sendoff was sufficient. As I told you earlier, I quit my job a few days after Black Monday. I consider it my 'Black Thursday' since I personally went into the black and never owed anyone anything again…"

"You mean you never owed anyone money again," an unrelenting Gabe responded. He showed no pity. "Even a loner like you owes something to someone; surely you've realized this by now. It's an unavoidable part of the human experience."

Chapter 34

Allen returned to The Grotto and updated Smith on his findings, mainly the fact that Laney and the others were also searching for Gabe. He also boasted that he had her name and number, plus a photo of Gabe, and that the Metro police were unofficially on the case.

Walker also returned, with news that Gabe had definitely been seen at North Foley. Furthermore, those present were positive that Lamar accompanied Gabe as he made his stormy getaway into no man's land.

Jay had gone back to sleep, and Smith informed the group of his doubts regarding the upcoming indoctrination process and surmised that 'He's likely seen his final light of day'.

The consensus amongst the group was that they had done all they could for the evening, and that they should all get some sleep, in shifts. Allen would spend a rare overnight in The Grotto and take the first sleep shift, as would Crawford. Preston had already crashed right outside the entrance. Smith took a seat right where the entrance tunnel met the large room and read The Houston Chronicle, as he typically did, front to back every single word of every single page. Walker headed to the Bank One parking lot, his usual spot. Clay joined Walker, and they worked out their own sleeping rotation. The nocturnal regulars, mostly subjects with untreated bipolar disorders, would roam freely and were given special dispensations to leave The District and cover the entire downtown area in order to possibly locate Gabe.

The instructions to all were simple: stay in pairs, in the event of a sighting do an all channel walkie talkie callout of 'Violator G' while identifying the nearest intersection or cross street and, contrary to all past directives, use force without question or warning, a blade to the ribs was the preference. They were reminded of Gabe's description and assured that help from fellow subjects or Metro Police, or both, would arrive within minutes of their radio call.

***

Lamar's extensive narrative was finally nearing its end. He knew that the detailed histories and explanations were somewhat cathartic on his part. Living in exile for over two years, Lamar knew that Gabe's appearance meant he'd be returning to The District, either as a heroic Subject or a fallen patriot.

Tired himself from all of the lecturing, Lamar declared, "Just a final bit of background info to help set up our plan. I left The District in the spring of 1994. I would have left sooner but chose not to set out during the dead of winter."

Gabe mocked him, "You're literally a fair weather friend. I love it how you were the last one in and the first one out."

Lamar was quick to defend himself, "It was a group determination that I would be the best one to observe from afar and send in help to remove Walker, if and when such help was ever needed. I was the first to object to his special privileges and heavy handed tactics. Crawford, as an Outlier would be the point man on sending word my way at Smith or Allen's direction. I seriously doubt Allen is aware that you have been sent to seek my help. That was either Crawford acting at Smith's request, or, quite possibly, Crawford acting alone."

"Walker became the chink in the armor that needs to be expunged," said Gabe before proclaiming, "You so eloquently enumerated three obstacles to the establishment of your little utopian society. I have to contend that there is a fourth obstacle, an eternal one: the people problem. You know what is said about the problem with managing people: it's not the managing, it's the people. Within any group of two or more there will be ranges of selflessness and selfishness. This fact cannot be denied. You all weren't the first society to strive for such equality; you were just really small, so you were able to last longer without force. Then force came and you bailed, and now that force has to be met with more force. Security is a need that you all overlooked, or at the very least miscalculated. If Walker were to somehow vanish or falter, then a power vacuum would be created. Security needs are real in all associations of two or more. Now my future is tied to such needs."

"So I'm not the only verbose louse in the room, very thoughtful," stated Lamar, "Now back to the task at hand. You just acknowledged our success and longevity. The peace we enjoyed shall return. Walker simply needs to go away. Whatever it takes to eradicate him must be done. We have a common enemy, Gabe. Notice that while you were held, they made zero attempt to rename you. Normally they would give you some sort of single name like mine, as a Subject. Did they?"

169

Gabe had no reply.

"Everyone there understood that Walker intended to terminate you."

***

Back on the home front, Laney finally dozed off and the Filas house was quiet for the night. Out front, Officer Chapman kept a close watch for signs of Gabe or any sort of movement. She also repeatedly attempted calls to Allen, at both his home and mobile numbers. His slumber and poor cellular signal deep within The Grotto prevented a connection. Kirby was a lone wolf and had no other options for backup.

Meanwhile, Alex Longoria was questioning his allegiances as he searched Officer Chapman's desk at the station for any further signs of malfeasance on her part. The strictly cash arrangement she had with The District left nothing to be found. He did however find lewd Polaroids of Officer Chapman and other coworkers stacked neatly in a bottom drawer. Alex stashed a few of the photos, near duplicates less likely to be missed, in his coat pocket.

He then reviewed the 'Lost & Found' report filed by Laney, jotting down her phone number on back of one of the pictures. Early shift and overtime officers began arriving at the station; a downtown parade was happening later that same morning. Alex exchanged pleasantries and then excused himself to leave the station. He drove home in his old Jeep Comanche pickup truck as the *Heaven Tonight* album by Cheap Trick played at a very low volume in the background, so low that he could hear the spinning of the cassette click along in the player. Along the way, he wondered how he could help with minimal involvement. Alex wanted to do the right thing without compromising the simple job and lifestyle he loved.

Chapter 35

Although still safe and warm, Gabe was stuck in a seemingly endless description of people and places he'd grown to detest. He lashed out, "Why are you stalling with all of this useless drivel?" He stood up and leaned over the table towards Lamar, "Aren't we supposed to be in a hurry here. Isn't time of the essence?"

Lamar's calmness was unrelenting, a trait apparently synonymous with leadership within The District, though it was more innate than learned. He leaned up in his chair towards Gabe and issued a measured retort, "Time is of the essence, I do agree. Does that necessarily demand that we rush in our preparations?" His original intention had been to quickly brief Gabe and get him into a liquor induced sleep by midnight, so that he'd be well rested. As it turned out, he rather enjoyed visiting with Gabe, who, by the way, was too much of a sipper anyway. Lamar now felt that the mission would go equally well after pulling an all-nighter.

Gabe walked over to a window on the far side of the room. It was still raining some, though down to just a drizzle. Turning back towards Lamar, he noticed a clock. The time was just past 12:30.

"You're not ready to go out into that yet anyway, are you?" asked Lamar. "I am down to the last few background items."

Gabe snapped back at him, "I just need to stand for a little while. Go ahead."

"As I told you earlier, I orchestrated a gradual and less dramatic disappearance, a withdrawal if you will. I sometimes wonder if anyone ever misses me, you know like a 'whatever happened to that guy?' sort of thing. Anyhow, I arrived at The Grotto a liberated self…body and soul. Though I had walked by many times, I had never set foot inside the finished product; it wasn't allowed until I had officially 'disassociated'. With the exception of Allen, anyone entering The Grotto is forbidden from leaving The District. Those who do are 'Defectors'; you learned that today, right? - though a bunch of them are surely pushing those boundaries tonight looking for you," said Lamar with a smile.

Gabe nodded with zero appreciation for any attempt at humor.

"The tunnel in is lower, the ceiling I mean, lower than the ceiling in the big main room. Remember we used old tires there, and they hadn't held up as well as the foam during the concrete pour - or maybe the framing was just weaker there..? It's fine though because the room seems that much larger when you finally reach it, and, also, pitch dark tunnels are long as heck."

Despite his strong desire to keep the story moving, Gabe was incredibly curious about the construction and felt compelled to interrupt, "You never mentioned anything about the removal of the foam and tires. How was that accomplished?"

"Unfortunately I was still, shall we say, 'associated' when that was taking place. I wasn't yet fully free to enter The District as a full Subject and, therefore, wasn't able to assist with 'The Big Dig' as it came to be called. Thus, my knowledge is second hand. But they were always up for proudly retelling the story, and there was plenty of time for storytelling. Needless to say, it was definitely a huge undertaking."

Gabe kept his reply succinct, "Yep, no doubt - who did it?"

Lamar gave the details, "I do know that Allen brought in chainsaws and a large truck to haul the filler away. The tires were extremely difficult to get out since they were tightly crushed by the concrete. A couple of chainsaws working in tight quarters, along with poor lighting, meant that their removal was most tedious. Crawford and a man who came to be known as 'Preston' handled this work. Allen and Smith acted as lookouts and kept checking to see if the chainsaws could be heard by theater patrons or the firefighters at the station across the street. Obviously, the farther into the tunnel the chainsaws got, the quieter it got…though full of exhaust fumes. This part, removing the tires, took most of the night, and the tire debris filled up multiple box trucks. Once the tunnel was clear, a mass of new subjects with pick axes and crowbars streamed in and out with chunks of hard foam and scrap wood. Fortunately Allen had the foresight to bring in a bunch of those cave lights you wear on your head. The wood was stacked in piles along the brushy bank of the bayou and the foam was tossed in the water to drift away."

"That's pretty much how I pictured it - a chain gang of sorts," said Gabe.

Lamar completed his description of the construction, "Yeah, they moved in as the sun came up. It was a quiet Sunday morning. Eventually the ceiling of the tunnel was raised with a little chisel action; I actually got to help with that, plus the wiring and the plumbing. The power and water pipes, actually conduit for the wires, had been roughed in as the theater above was trimmed out and just had to be patched into the dome below."

"So you did get to help out a little," replied Gabe as he retook his seat and looked down saying, "I cannot deny the fact that this project, this whole story is simply unbelievable – whether it's true or not. Is this all true? Is this real? Are these people real, and did you all truly build a homeless shelter within the deepest recesses of the Wortham Center?"

"Doubt is totally understandable. It is all too incredible to fathom tonight. I was able to take it in over the course of years," stated Lamar. He then questioned, "Allow me to ask: Are your encounters with Crawford and Walker not real? These events happened. We are here, I am real, and so is The District."

Gabe rolled his eyes up and then down to the floor, really wanting to keep them closed and make this all go away. It had been less than a couple of hours, but felt to him like he'd been there listening to Lamar all night. He began to speculate internally as to the purpose for which he was being groomed. Gabe thought of Laney, picturing her beautiful face and where she might be at this very moment. He considered life itself.

Finally, Gabe spoke, "Our reality is here. Please proceed." Lamar wasn't sure whether to read resignation or resolve into his stoic demeanor. He looked into Gabe's eyes and nothing was revealed.

Lamar poured then took another sip of bourbon before continuing, "I think that covers the creation of The Grotto. Let's not wander any further. We were discussing my journey to escape from the only version of the world known to most. At that moment of my entry into The District, Baron Michaels ceased to exist as an entity in that world. I became 'Lamar', a name collectively chosen by Allen, Smith and Crawford. We also came up with the term 'Grotto' then."

The term 'full blown cult' immediately came to Gabe's mind, but he bit his tongue so that Lamar wouldn't have to stop and start again.

Lamar rocked back in his chair and put his hands, fingers interlaced, behind his head recalling fondly, "We had pulled it off and been reunited, and our great idea was in action, functional. The Subjects were so glad to have a home, a safe home with life's necessities provided for. They had helped build it, for all to use. And as for the theater board people…they were absolutely thrilled with the arrangement. Their customers were able to move comfortably within The District without being harassed, at a relatively small cost to them."

Gabe couldn't ignore the magnitude of their feat and consciously chose to give a subdued acknowledgement, "Despite my cynicism, you made it happen, brought your vision to fruition - Kudos to your effort."

Telling the story brought Lamar joy; Gabe's half-hearted approval meant that much more, "Yes we did, and we celebrated. And to think I actually broke the rules right away. I brought in some Scotch, single malt, pretty much my last personal possession outside of clothing and this gun." He laid the gun on the table, stating, "And this shall be yours. I t is not registered anywhere - virtually untraceable."

Raising his eyebrows, Gabe stared at the pistol and spoke, "I assume it's loaded?"

"Yes indeed, fifteen rounds," he answered.

"And the plan..?" asked Gabe.

Lamar flashed a sly smile, "The plan for now was to get that gun out of my pocket. The blasted hunk of metal's been digging into my leg all night. But, ultimately, it will be yours and for your use."

Chapter 36

Smith kept vigil at The Grotto's entrance, pondering the fate of their shared experiment. Had the decision to accept Walker, warts and all, ultimately doomed The District? Should they have used force against him back then, rather than use force with him now?

Over at the Bank One parking lot, Clay and Walker made pallets from boxes and sheets of velvet fabric stashed in a traffic signal controller box. They used a torn sheet of plastic tarpaulin hung across hedges to shelter themselves from the light rain. Walker anticipated that Clay would sleep late as usual, typically until the bank employees started showing up for work. The first flicker of natural light would awaken Walker and he would make his daily visit to Market Square, allowing him to be back in The District before the sun, or Clay, had arisen.

***

Alex Longoria lived just off Navigation Street a few miles southeast of downtown. Alex, one of six kids, was still living with his parents and had just about saved up enough for a down payment on a home in the same Second Ward neighborhood. He grew up in a rental home and his pledge to himself was that he'd never be a renter, or a landlord for that matter. His contemplation regarding the fate of Gabe, and now Laney, cycled through his mind over and over, but ultimately came down to simple empathy. He finally asked himself 'what would I want someone in my situation to do if my brother or sister were facing a similar situation?' An initial inclination on his part to go out and attempt to find Gabe was soon replaced by the more practical decision to call Laney.

It would be a call best made from a pay phone and there was one in the parking lot of Ninfa's Mexican Restaurant, a Houston institution located on a nearby corner. Alex mentally prepared himself to carefully choose his words. He slid a quarter into the coin slot and dialed the ten digits of Laney's mobile phone.

After a couple of rings, a soft, yet slightly dopey, voice answered, "Hello"; it was Laney awakening from her slumber.

Alex took a quick breath and then spoke, "Hello is this Laney?"

Suddenly wide awake, she replied, "Yes, this is Laney, it's me."

"Very good. I am an acquaintance of your friend Gabe," said Alex, attempting to remain as monotone as possible. "Please listen for a moment. I am calling to help."

She considered his words and expressed her wonder, "You know something about Gabe – and want to help? How do I know that you are really trying to help?" The emotion of Laney's response woke up Jane, who quickly sat up and listened intently.

Alex remained steady in his cadence, "Gabe has encountered evil, but is safe to the best of my knowledge. However certain people want to harm him. You know though, I think he is sharp enough to stay a step ahead of them."

She attempted to process what the stranger was saying, "Where is he. Do you have him?"

"No, I do not have him; I want him to find safety. But I do know that he's been in the downtown area and seems to have found a safe place or even a getaway. Those who would do him harm are searching high and low. Unfortunately the police are among those after him."

Laney was so very puzzled, "The police? Did he break the law? Is he hurt?"

Alex remained cool, "He is not hurt and they are not after him for breaking the law. Dirty cops really do exist. Do not trust any of them for now."

Now completely mystified, Laney teared up, "I am sorry. This is so much to process. You are telling me that Gabe is on the run, and that I cannot go to the police. Is this correct?"

"Yes, that is correct," said Alex. "Also, you gave them, the police, your name and phone number. It will be easy for them to find your home. If you are at home, please get away to a safe place soon. Are you home, and do you know of such a place…a safe one?"

She cried out, "Yes I'm home. Oh my God! Will they try to hurt my family?" Everyone in the house was now awake and listening. Joker picked up a receiver in an attempt to listen before realizing that Laney was on her mobile phone.

Still playing it very cool, surprisingly so to himself, Alex tried to calm Laney down. "They would attempt to capture you in order to get at Gabe. Your family might be safe, but you need to get out of there before they show up – pack enough for at least a few days. Check for suspicious vehicles out front and watch your rear view mirror as you go."

She gathered herself and asked, "Who are you? Why should I believe you?"

He remained on track, "I must remain anonymous, but I really do know Gabe and that he's a good guy. I would not be saying the things I'm saying if I weren't trying to help you. You'll realize this shortly. Give me a number to reach you at later and I will update you the best I can. I promise, Laney."

"You can call me back at this number. It's my new cell phone, and I'll keep it charged," she said before deeply sighing.

Alex then said, "I am calling from a pay phone now and will call you from another as soon I learn more, especially about the police's involvement. I have an angle I think I can work on this…the police part I mean – I will get right on it. Seriously though, avoid them for now. You do have a place to go, correct?"

"Yes, I have a place to go. I will be careful and bring someone with me." Laney then asked Alex one final question, "Please let me know. Does any of this have to do with him helping the homeless - a guy and his son?"

His answer was as she'd suspected, "Yes, it is directly related."

Chapter 37

Gabe was now ready to move into action, and he demanded concrete details of Lamar's ever evolving plan; the twisted mind of his aspiring mentor had certainly changed as the night progressed from late evening to early morning.

Gabe excused himself and went to the executive restroom within the suite. Meanwhile, Lamar paced and considered the options, none of which were simple or easy.

He had originally intended to have Gabe track and kill Walker in his sleep. Lamar would tip off the Metro Police, who would arrest Gabe on the spot. Gabe's story would be so absurd that he'd be declared insane and institutionalized, allowing order to be restored to The District and himself to return as a savior.

He now felt that Gabe was intrigued by The District and sympathetic to its subjects. An amiable guy like Gabe, who was young and fit, could fill the security void that Walker's demise would surely bring. A nice guy on patrol would rebuild and strengthen The District's image. Had Gabe mentioned the power vacuum because he saw himself filling that role potentially? He had said nothing about his life - though he actually hadn't had an opportunity to do so. How happy was he with his life, his work? He didn't seem like a particularly materialistic type of guy. No wedding ring - what were his personal attachments?

Crawford's intentions were not revealed by the note Gabe had brought. He obviously saw Gabe as an asset to be utilized against Walker, but what after that?

Gabe found a plush lobby area with a scale model of the mall. He solemnly lifted his eyes upward looking past the ceiling above. It was a reverent roll, if there could ever be such a thing. In this moment he lamented the fact that his prayers of petition were far outnumbering those of thanks. He knew that Walker had to be eliminated from the scene; this fact was simply a given. The real question for Gabe was the fate of Lamar, and ultimately, The District. Knowing what they knew about each other, was it possible for him to coexist with them in downtown Houston?

Lamar called out, "Gabe, are you in there?"

"Yes, I am here. Be there in a second," he replied.

Gabe had determined that he would continue on and go with the flow of Lamar's plan, while mapping out a plan of his own. Lamar was an isolated coward whose value was in information and a handgun, both of which he had essentially conveyed to Gabe at this point.

Lamar envisioned his glorious return to The District. The life he'd come to know these past years was comfortable but so lonely. Sure he had interaction with customers at the parking lot, but they were always rushing in and rushing out. He was just a cash collector to them, providing a fleeting service. Most of them considered a parking space to be a necessary evil and, generally, a cost wasting their hard earned wages.

His meager physical existence was fine by Lamar. Though he had shed his full name and had no form of identification, he had been able to make a barter arrangement with the owner of the parking lot. In exchange for a light evening shift, basically eight PM until whenever, he was provided with an access card to the Downtown YMCA. It simply read 'Lamar', with the address listed as 'North Foley'. He had unlimited access, which included an extra large locker, an occasional bed and, most importantly, clean restrooms with showers. Every time he opened the locker there was some sort of non-perishable meal awaiting him and it would always be replenished by the time he next returned. Occasionally fresh sets of clothes would appear as well, always with cash in the pockets. He was welcome to spend nights in the parking attendant booth as well, and this was typically his preference. This bare bones lifestyle suited him fine, but he sure missed his old buddies.

A rejuvenated Gabe retook his seat at the table saying, "I am ready. Look at this," as he showed the notes on his arm to Lamar.

Lamar was proud, "Very good. Just think of all that you've learned. It looks like you've got everything covered. Walker will obviously be your main focus, along with his fellow enforcers Clay and Preston. Eliminate Walker, and the other two become fair game when they get in your way or resist…though both are followers and will likely fall in line behind you." Lamar then nudged the 9MM further towards Gabe. His gun safety protocol was in order, as he kept the barrel pointed to the side, away from both he and Gabe.

Gabe smirked, "I love how you assume that I am ready to deliver a bullet from this gun to another man on command. That's quite a leap, especially since you've given me plenty of filler but nothing in the way of a plan."

Lamar attempted to wax poetic, "What a wonderful word 'leap'. It fits with your spirit. Leaps move us quickly in this world; certain times call for them. Let's plan and leap."

"Let's hear it, and please stay on track."

Lamar complied with Gabe's request and got right to it, "If you'll recall, Walker is extremely disciplined, but has a pill habit to feed. His supplier meets him in Market Square every morning at the crack of dawn, which allows him to slip back into The District before any other subjects wake up. In order to be as close as possible to Market Square while remaining in The District proper, he almost always sleeps in the Bank One parking lot amongst a row of tall hedges. Unless it's below freezing or storming, he will be there."

Gabe asked, "You've been away for years. How do you know that's still his routine?"

Ready with an answer, Lamar replied, "Crawford's note gave nothing to indicate changes in his pattern," before adding, "Plus, I keep an ear to the ground. Really, he hasn't changed."

"OK, makes sense," said Gabe.

Remaining on point, Lamar proceeded, "The bank's at the corner of Congress and Louisiana, and you need to be there by six-thirty to ensure that he's fast asleep. His spot is along Louisiana under the small oak trees. Look along the space between a short concrete wall and some hedges. Preston will probably be there too, or maybe Clay. Remember, Walker prefers not to be alone."

From his jacket Lamar, produced a round light and battery pack with a headband. "You'll need to bring this along and be prepared to wear it. Also, we need something to cover your face." He then checked the top drawers of a nearby Bombay chest and found a large black tablecloth, which he tore into the shape and size of a mask. Handing the makeshift mask to Gabe, he said, "You will need to wear this. Approach quietly and fire at close range, head or heart – your choice." He then produced a stainless steel cylinder, seemingly out of nowhere, which he rolled across the table. Gabe noticed that one end was threaded as Lamar spoke again, "Attach this to the barrel at the appropriate time. It screws on," he said as he pointed to the gun. "Loud bangs tend to echo off of tall buildings; let's aim for small bangs."

The request was somewhat as Gabe had expected. He was already mentally prepared to kill, if necessary, to protect himself and, ultimately, Laney. He spoke, "I get it, you expect me to kill this man, and you know that I don't have much choice in this matter. You make it sound so simple, like pushing a button. What about his partner you say is sure to be there? And what about the police? After the trigger is pulled…what do I do from there?"

"I've got that covered. First of all, the partner will almost certainly be hung over and react slowly to the shot. Make it a single shot. If he does react quickly, take him out too. Might save you trouble down the line anyway." Pointing at the gun he reiterated, "Don't forget, fifteen rounds in there, but you should be able to easily outrun an old drunk."

"OK, I am now potentially a double murderer. What about the police? That's a heavily patrolled area, is it not?"

"Actually that area is not policed as you would think," declared Lamar. "The District watches itself and reported crime is extremely low, especially for an urban area. The HPD mounted patrol rolls in every morning at dawn, but you'll be in and out of there before then. The Metro Police has a presence, but they are closely aligned with The District. They will be elsewhere during your mission."

Gabe scoffed at Lamar's nonchalant response. "Oh you make it sound so easy. What do you mean by Metro Police? You're not talking about the traffic patrol are you? Don't they just write speeding tickets and count carpoolers?"

"You call them what you want, 'traffic patrol' or whatever, but they have vehicles and uniforms and guns. Their jurisdiction actually extends across county lines, so they wield some power and operate as accessories of The District."

"OK, they have power and are crooked; I never really thought much about them. It's good to know that they'll be elsewhere. Now tell me, where do I go after I take out Walker and whoever? What's next for me, Lamar?"

"First off, head towards the county courthouse and jail on the north side of downtown. You can blend in there, and it's a good spot to chunk your weapon into the bayou, far away from your noble task."

Gabe questioned, "That's a rough area, crawling with police isn't it?"

"Listen to yourself - that makes no sense," Lamar lectured. "Trust me, I have thought this out. Just keep moving and you will blend in. Ditch your weapon before the sun comes up and make a loop around to the east side – by the convention center. Scores of unaffiliated homeless roam that area, and the Cameos will be showing up right about then."

Gabe sighed, "OK, I'll bite. What are 'Cameos'?"

The old codger explained, "They are those who choose to make an annual appearance to help the underclass. Cameos show up Thanksgiving morning and pass out some turkey and biscuits, before patting each other on the back and disappearing for another year. You would hope people operate out of love or kindness; it seems to me that most charitable do gooders are driven by guilt. But I think the Cameos are the worst! Pride and vanity motivate them – with a hint of convenience sprinkled in for good measure."

Not interested in debating motivations, or any heavy topics for that matter, Gabe understood and nodded, "I will head east and mix in with the crowd."

"Yeah, they'll even feed you a nice big meal." Lamar then rounded out the plan, "You will need to hang out in that area for the day, you know, to let things calm down."

"Sounds like a suicide mission - that's a no man's land. And then what? Assuming I survive…" Gabe wondered aloud.

"You see this shirt?" said Lamar, pointing to the blue oxford he was wearing. "As soon as the coast is clear it, will be under the big decorative ball in front of The Wortham Center…you know on the corner of Smith and Texas."

In this moment, Lamar's very being moved to a point of diminishing returns in Gabe's mind; though he kept up the act with another contentious reply, "So you'll just leave your shirt there?"

"It'll be there tonight, late – just check at midnight. Then you're in. I will have paved the way, and you will be welcomed into The Grotto."

However daunting and unappealing it may have been, Gabe seemed to accept Lamar's plan, "I'll go with it. I'm ready."

Chapter 38

Careful to coil up and pocket her phone's wall charger first, Laney gathered her crew for a briefing. None of them could believe what they were hearing; it was just so surreal. They brainstormed and considered a few evacuation plans.

Initially they were inclined to venture to West Texas and stay at the large family spread near Roosevelt in Sutton County. Laney's great aunt and uncle on Shelly's side were always more than hospitable and looking for visitors. This gang would be most welcome. Swilling Ranch was remote and expansive, with multiple living quarters scattered across the various sections. Strangers about the area would be conspicuous and could literally be spotted from a mile away. Also, an extensive arsenal was in place should there be a war of attrition, not to mention ranch hands in place to defend the acreage.

The plan quickly evolved, and just the ladies would head to the ranch, while the men held down the fort at home. Dion and Joker would be armed and ready to respond, plus Joker had to report back to work in a few days. But driving six hours to the ranch in the dark and questionable cellular service once they got there ultimately ruled out that option for everyone.

In the end, they decided to stay in town and go with the friendliest of secure locations. The Shell Refinery in Deer Park offered a massive, active site with gated security friendly to Joker and, presumably, his kinfolk.

Jane and Dion hadn't unpacked upon arrival from Nashville, so they were ready to go and were tasked with gathering up some blankets, towels and food, including the Thanksgiving fixings. Shelly's Chevy Tahoe was parked in the attached garage, and they loaded it up while the others packed.

Joker secured the lock on his six foot gun safe, before reaching up top for a couple of loaded pistols, one a forty-five and the other a revolver. He also retrieved a loaded Remington shotgun from behind the safe, informing everyone that it was "ready to fire" and then leaning it up against where the wall met a door jamb. Next he instructed Dion to stash the two handguns under the driver's seat of the Tahoe, while he gave Jane plastic bags of dry ice for the cooler.

It was just after two o'clock when the garage door slowly opened. Joker backed the Tahoe out, coming to a stop parallel to his old Mazda pickup truck.

Next, Dion and Shelly walked out of the garage and got into the front seats of the pickup. Dion would be the driver. They were followed closely behind by the twins, both with their hair down and dressed similarly. Jane and Laney got into the back seats of the pickup and Tahoe respectively, figuring a little confusion wouldn't hurt their cause, with anyone possibly observing this exodus.

The pair of vehicles formed a lonely caravan down the Northwest Freeway; everyone soon realized that they were indeed being followed. As they approached Loop 610, they separated according to plan. The Tahoe exited towards the North Loop, while the Mazda pickup merged onto the West Loop headed south.

Their pursuer chose to stay right behind Dion driving the pickup, and he just poked along as Joker had instructed, completely counter to his lead footed instincts. He looked over at Shelly and then turned back to Jane in the back seat. Each of them were only up to slight eyebrow raises, nary a word was spoken. Though he'd quit smoking, a single 'emergency' cigarette awaited him within the inside pocket of his jacket. This was as good a time as any to keep it from going to waste, especially since they were about to visit a refinery. He opened the window ever so slightly and gave Jane one more look before reaching into his pocket. Approval actually mattered little to all parties at this point. The ride remained silent except for the whistling wind sucking out the visible puffs of white smoke. The unseen, yet odiferous remains of the smoke billowing from the driver's seat filled the cab.

Over on the North Loop Joker, raced at full throttle along his familiar route to work, easing slightly up the usual speed trap overpasses, all the while checking and tapping the Passport radar detector on his visor. His best case scenario had played out so far, and he knew that he and Laney would arrive at Shell first. In silence he worried, hoping that the others were also finding safe travels.

Laney held her phone close and kept flipping it open to check the battery charge indicator - three of three black squares still appeared indicating a full charge. Joker gave her a reassuring smile and said, "If you keep opening it, the battery will go down. Let's get to safety and take care of things from there." Laney fawned a weak smile and blinked softly so as not to spill tears. They were not far from Deer Park.

***

The Longoria family was extremely close knit and resting up for a big Thanksgiving together.

Following the call to Laney, Alex's resolve to help the young couple grew, and he awaited the arrival of a special visitor. His older brother Martin was coming in from Corpus Christi, where he had worked himself up to a Plant Operator position at the Valero Energy refinery. Martin was Alex's only older sibling, and also the only one not living in Houston. Alex greatly cherished time together with the brother he'd always admired, and he always waited up for his arrival. The younger brother settled in on the front porch, knowing this reunion would be particularly special.

A loaded and lifted Ford Explorer screeched around the corner, bringing a smile to Alex's face. His brother was home. As always, Martin pulled all the way back in the driveway and parked in the grass beside an old carport. Pulling the chain link gates together behind him, Alex ran back to meet him. Their handshake quickly became a tight hug; neither could lift the other off the ground, though they each tried. The brothers spoke on the phone regularly, so there was little catching up to do. Alex immediately let Martin know that he needed his advice and, possibly, some help.

Martin listened intently as Alex informed him of the sordid details from his fling with the policewoman to the bribes and imminent threat to Gabe and Laney. For once, Martin was actually engrossed by the happenings in his younger sibling's life. Besides the excitement of the events and situation, he really couldn't wait to see the photos. Alex had snatched four of the racy shots of Officer Chapman, all of which clearly showed her face. Other familiar Metro employees also appeared in the pictures. Alex now realized that these were mostly folks up the ladder from him in these compromising positions. Martin was most impressed with what he saw.

Sly grins appeared and Alex asked, "Which one do you want? Go ahead, pick your favorite."

"I'll take this," replied Martin as he stuffed the one he was already holding into the pocket of his jacket.

"You have to safeguard that, with your life if necessary," said Alex. "If anything happens to me, it needs to be copied and plastered all over Downtown Houston, especially around the Metro Police headquarters on Main Street."

"Sure, I will keep it safe and sound." Martin then shook his head, "Alex, let's just not get in too deep on this."

Alex fanned out the remaining three pictures, "These here will protect us. We can save a good man and still keep our distance."

Martin could see that he was determined, "If you say so. You are the good man."

They went inside the dark house, and everyone was asleep. Alex waved one of the photos high in the air before sticking it in a white envelope and sealing it up. He wrote 'Metro Police Officer Kirby Chapman pictures. Copy and share this with media if I am harmed –A. Longoria' before sticking it atop a tall kitchen cabinet. "Another backup copy," he quietly chuckled as he pointed in the general direction of the newly stashed evidence.

Martin raised his eyebrows, "Hopefully none of the young ones find it."

"I'll eventually move it, once we get everything settled," Alex concluded before digging into his pocket to confirm the presence of a quarter. "Now let's go for a drive. We should take your sweet ride. I'll drive."

"This better be quick, and safe," demanded Martin.

They drove a few short blocks over to Harrisburg Boulevard, where Alex knew of a drive up pay phone. He positioned Martin to make a call from his shotgun seat and rolled down the window. Martin's voice was much softer than his with virtually no accent, ensuring anonymity. Handing his big brother a coin and a slip of paper, Alex was very clear and kept it simple, "I am ready for a quick getaway if needed. Here is a quarter. Keep your gloves on. Dial this number. Say this: 'I am with the Homeless Command. Discontinue any pursuit of Gabe Wagner immediately', listen for the reply and then hang up."

Martin didn't at all protest and immediately rehearsed his line a few times, while building up the courage to dial.

Officer Kirby Chapman was still following the little old pickup truck, as Dion remained true to the plan and stuck the speedometer on '55'. The snail-like pace was painfully slow for everyone, especially since they were seemingly the only vehicles on the South Loop freeway at this hour. As the broad thoroughfare occasionally narrowed down to three and then widened back to five lanes, it couldn't be more apparent that the unmarked cop car was tailing them.

Though completely unsure if she had the right twin in her sights, Kirby determined that the capture of either girl would garner Gabe's full attention. Without backup or cause, she'd have to act quickly. Focused on the end game, recapturing Gabe, and taking the stark landscape of the early morning hours into account, it was time to make a move.

The officer turned on her flashing lights in silent mode, no blaring sirens.

Dion instantly noticed the grill flashers in his rear view mirror and exclaimed, "Dad gummit! I knew that was coming."

Jane buried her face in her hands, and Shelly began to speak, "You keep driving to a place with more people around…"

Just then, Kirby's mobile phone lit up and started to ring. She immediately flipped off the bright blue and red lights but continued to follow. The incoming call was from an unfamiliar number. She figured that it was either a wrong number or Allen trying to reach her.

Officer Chapman answered with a simple 'Yes' and could hear light breathing followed by a quick statement. 'I am with the Homeless Command. Discontinue any pursuit of Gabe Wagner immediately'.

Startled by the poignancy and relevance of the words she'd just heard, Kirby paused while her mind raced. She didn't recognize the voice at all and cautiously replied, "Who is this, are you watching me?" There was no reply from the other end. She heard a train horn in the distance, and then it went silent as Martin hung up with his left index finger before returning the receiver to the cradle. The Longoria brothers made a quick getaway, as if they'd pulled off some sort of heist. Martin's open window allowed in a flow of cool, fresh air, offsetting their shared adrenaline rush, and they were quickly parked safely at home once again.

Chapter 39

After a final review of Gabe's knowledge of the names and descriptions of The District's main subjects, Lamar proclaimed him ready to commence his quest.

They shared a final sampling of Jack. This time Gabe drank from the bottle and encouraged Lamar to do the same. He willfully obliged in a big way. Gabe carefully tucked the gun into his rear waistband and reclaimed the half full liquor bottle for the road. A new state law passed earlier in the year allowed for concealed weapon carry by Texans who had passed a course and background check, but Gabe had not yet obtained such a license.

It was time to move into action, and they turned off the lights and music before heading for the same mysterious door through which they had entered. Lamar commented, "My father always said to exit the same way you came in."

Having carefully paced his drinking in order to preserve brain function, Gabe's thought process was lucid, and his plan was clear as they emerged back onto the street. According to Lamar, he would accompany the omniscient elder to the YMCA and rest up for a predawn departure.

The night was eerily quiet, and Gabe once again offered Lamar a swig of the bourbon. Its golden hue shimmered against the glow of yellowish street lights. After so many years of abstaining and then finally reacquainting himself with the flavor of on an old favorite, the Jack Daniels proved to be sweet nectar, which Lamar simply could not resist. His anticipation of the glory to come further fueled his frenzy, and the old soul that had been so calm throughout his dissertation lost control, inevitably, just as Gabe had expected. Occasional outbursts and stumbles revealed Lamar's state. Gabe's only surprise was that true inebriation had taken so long, but this timing actually worked out for the best.

A swift pace brought fresh blood pumping into Gabe's brain, and he concluded that Lamar would not be a part of the long game.

The pair repeatedly traversed massive ventilation grates which were seamlessly recessed into the ground. As the next grate, a smaller one, approached, Gabe adjusted his gloves and allowed his tipsy partner to move slightly ahead. Once they were back on solid ground, Gabe noisily plunked the bottle of Jack Daniels down onto the concrete sidewalk bordering the steel grate.

Lamar turned back and loudly objected, "What are you crazy? You can't leave that there."

"Sure, why not? I can't just carry this through downtown. I've got business to handle," was Gabe's calm response.

Lamar stopped and headed for the bottle. Butterflies filled Gabe's stomach as everything suddenly became so real, and he pulled the gun from behind his back. As Lamar bent over and reached for the bottle, Gabe popped him in the back of the head with the butt of the stock. Lamar fell to his knees, and Gabe hit him one more time, this time bottle to skull. Surprisingly, the glass did not shatter as his old new friend went down hard. Next, Gabe lifted the end of the grate where Lamar was laid out; it took all of his strength to bring it up to shoulder level. With his right foot, Gabe slowly rolled Lamar's midsection towards the opening. His head and feet followed. A low hum buzzed below, and Gabe wondered what fate awaited Lamar's limp body as it began to go over the edge. A snort followed by a grunt echoed throughout the dark expanse below as the man originally known as Baron Michaels disappeared in super slow motion. Gabe listened for the sound of the body's arrival at its final destination. He cringed as he wondered if some sort of massive fan would chop it to shreds. Instead there was a loud thud followed by a secondary muted thud, possibly indicating a tumbling roll. Moved by the nudge of a heel, the square, black labeled bottle soon followed into the void, quietly shattering within Gabe's earshot only. The metal grate was lowered back into place and crashed loudly, as Gabe released and pulled back his fingers so as not to be crushed. He checked for blood and found none.

Lamar was either dead or would be by the time he was found.

Gabe regretted that this person had to meet such a sudden and gruesome demise, but he also had no doubt regarding the additional harm that the continuation of Lamar's life would bring. Though their intentions were more than noble, the grandiose plans of he and his cohorts were wreaking havoc with Gabe's life. Their attempts to reign in chaos had wrought suppression of free will and had begun to leave a path of destruction in its wake. Gabe's mild buzz dissipated, as blurry tears formed, and dread filled his soul.

***

Joker carefully guided the Tahoe over the Houston Ship Channel bridge and prepared to depart the Loop for the final leg of their journey. He turned to

Laney and prepped her for their entry and interaction at the Shell Refinery. She listened closely to his instructions. As the burly SUV veered right to make the exit onto 225 towards Deer Park, Laney reviewed her father's directives over and over in her head. The scene turned full-on industrial with rail yards and chemical plants now dominating the landscape.

Soon enough, the freeway exit approached and Laney unbuckled, before climbing into the cargo area at the very back of the vehicle. She curled up amongst the bags they'd packed and covered herself up with a dark navy blanket.

The refinery's main entrance approached, and they came to a stop at the guard gate. The guard was accustomed to quick wave-throughs, but didn't recognize this vehicle. He immediately realized that it was Joker and asked with a smile, "What's up Joker? Why are you coming in at this odd hour?"

Joker was relieved to see a familiar face and quipped, "Happy Thanksgiving, Professor. I have family in town and need to ask a favor of you."

The guard, Hanson Rogers, responded without hesitation, "Anything for you Joker…as long as it's legal. Whatcha got?"

Joker knew he'd help and stated with a straight face, "Our oven is broken. We realized last night when we went to cook dinner. We already had the turkey, fixins' and desserts and all for a huge Thanksgiving meal today. Of course it'd be a shame if all of that food went to waste. No way could I get it repaired or get a new one on a holiday. So I am here to use the kitchen."

Hanson saw no trouble in such a request, "Joker, you're a longtime employee – an upstanding, card carrying OCAW guy. You don't need my permission to use the kitchen."

"Well, that's not really the favor. I am here so early because the oven's small. I tried to sneak out so everyone could sleep. But my wife insisted that she come and help - she just called me on this," pointing to Laney's phone. "She's just a few miles back. My daughter's betrothed is driving her in my silver truck. Will you please wave them in when they arrive?"

"Sure, your truck has a permit. That's no problem at all," said Hanson before noticing something in the vehicle. "Oh, I see all of the food in the back seat. Go ahead Joker; of course I'll let them through. Have a Happy Thanksgiving."

The vehicle didn't move and Joker wasn't quite done. He took a deep breath and looked squarely at the guard before speaking, "Officer Rogers, I have something additional to ask."

The lonely guard was not at all put off. In fact he was just glad to have someone with whom to converse at this odd hour, "You haven't really asked for anything, Joker. I've known you for so long and am sure that your request will be reasonable."

"I appreciate your faith in me," replied Joker. "Here's the deal. Our neighbor is a cop and tends to be overzealous, usually towards outsiders – about meaningless, petty stuff. The rest of us neighbors usually blow off the quirkiness. It's partly why we want to cook here rather than borrow a neighbor's oven."

"Yeah, so what's up?" wondered Hanson.

"This cop neighbor watches our street at night and sometimes meddles, just gets into our personal business," answered Joker.

Hanson pressed for more, "Meddles, how…for example..?"

Joker elaborated, "Sometimes by knocking on the door at all hours of the night and waking everyone up because of 'suspicious' sounds or lights, or other times following us in a patrol car and showing up at our destination. No one really wants to report a cop, and we all pretty much guess that it helps keep our block safe."

"So how does this relate to a favor?" asked Hanson.

"Well, since I left in the middle of the night, and then Shelly left soon thereafter, we wouldn't be surprised at all if one of us were followed here tonight," said Joker. "This rogue cop could show up here and start asking questions, wanting to get into the plant just because one of us left the house at a different time than usual."

"You know I can't keep a cop out if they want in," Hanson asserted.

"But, you can be difficult to a point. Technically, a warrant would be required to visit me at my workplace, correct?" countered Joker. "You don't typically have cops showing up here do you? Especially in the middle of the night, right?"

Hanson thought for a second before responding, "Come to think of it - practically never, pretty much only when there's been an accident."

"Hanson, I'd just prefer not to be bothered by this strange neighbor of mine. Please at least stall, and give me a heads up if someone comes looking for me here. That's all I ask." Joker then handed him a slip of paper with Laney's mobile number, "Call this number if they do come inside the gates. Of course, this little matter will be kept just between you and me."

Joker's straight-laced old friend considered the request. It was minor, and he relented, "Oh, I'll do what I can for you, Joker."

Thanking him with a smile, Joker reached out and shook this hand, "It's a real favor, I know. But you know I appreciate it. It likely won't be a thing at all. Oh, and thanks for working on the holiday."

Hanson nodded slowly, "I'm out of here at six AM. It'll be a turkey and nap day around our house. I hope your meal turns out good, Joker, and I'll be on the lookout for your wife coming through – and maybe a cop…"

Joker nodded back and drove in. He chose to go to the left, pretty much because everyone always tends to go right. Laney asked for the all-clear before moving to the middle seat and calling her mother with instructions for their arrival at Shell.

Chapter 40

As he bolted and left this former stranger of a man for dead, Gabe contemplated his role. It was so simply direct. The events leading up to this action on his part ceased to matter for a moment. This blip in time was such a horrible deed, one that would forever be a part of who he was. Had anyone he knew ever chosen to take the life of another human being? He considered the veterans in his family as well as the older guys with the firm who had served, but none of them had ever made it to combat, as far as he knew…maybe Ralph Farnsworth in World War II?

What a creature he'd become in the moment, with a secret that he could not even share with Laney. Could he tell her one day, since their lives were on the line? Indeed, circumstance had brought him to such a rare place.

Still, he wanted no part in the potential enablement of the reliving of Lamar's glory days in The District. It was time to head back north, towards Power Tools and, hopefully, a saving meet-up with Laney. Unbeknownst to him, Gabe was once again passing through The Neutral Zone. It seemed to be a fairly safe area, as long as he kept moving, which he did at a steady, brisk pace.

A movie scene came to mind, which Gabe related to his mindset regarding Lamar's fateful end. Though westerns were not necessarily his genre of choice, *The Unforgiven* had resonated with him. Particularly profound to Gabe was the scene where Clint Eastwood's character, a seasoned bounty hunter, describes the emotions of taking another's life for whatever reason. Eastwood's character attempts to temper the regret-fueled enthusiasm of a young shooter who has just killed someone for the first time. The elder outlaw enlightens the young killer on the magnitude of such an act, and how it demands some level of separation and numbness each and every time, no matter how many times. Gabe's stomach turned.

***

Alex and Martin Longoria were sons of immigrants who had each forged their own path to second generation success. After securing a couple of cans of Busch, Alex coaxed his tired big brother to join him on the screened porch for a beverage.

They recalled being younger boys, and how their parents worked so hard to put a roof over their heads and food on the table. Each of them remembered seeing their father's daily struggles from a language barrier to slow periods with little to no work, or injuries, not to mention reliance upon less than stellar public transportation. Day to day, their mother kept the house in order, and the children were fairly well behaved, all of them. It was as if they somehow sensed the strain life bestowed upon the adults to which they were entrusted and fell in line. Friends and neighbors were always astounded at how well the Longoria kids behaved, at home, school, church, wherever. Somehow, even with six children, year in and year out, each of them had new shoes for the first day of school and new toys under the tree at Christmas. Their mother taught them about faith and honor through discipline, and their father modeled the same, laced with a serious dose of work ethic.

These young adult men hadn't gotten where they were by being reckless. Martin did what he could to not let this notion be lost on his younger brother. The relative success they were enjoying in their lives could be gone in a flash if carelessness prevailed. Alex was quick to remind his older brother of the virtue of kindness, including the protection of the innocent, elevating his stance in this case, since kind justice could be gained without risking peril.

Alex considered the next step and spoke, "We need to make another phone call, well at least I do. It just so happens to be what's needed now." He knew that his older brother would feel the need to come along and watch out for his safety, which is what Alex really wanted.

Martin lightly protested, "Oh Alex, I am ready to get some sleep," while following Alex out and away from the house.

"Man, it would only take a few minutes," replied Alex. "Besides you can sleep late, it's a holiday. Take a nap in the afternoon after we eat turkey. You and dad always do that during the ball games anyway."

Martin acquiesced, "OK, but let's make it quick", then saying, "I suppose you want to use my ride again," as he reached in and patted the dashboard.

"Yep, everyone in the hood knows mine too well. Thanks, Bro," responded Alex gratefully. He then opened the center console and successfully located a quarter before proclaiming, "Let's ride."

***

Shelly directed Dion off the freeway, and they were soon at the main entrance to Shell where Hanson waved the familiar truck through. This was Dion's first visit to the refinery, and he was taken aback by the sheer scale of the place. The expanse of early morning lights made the sprawling plant look like some sort of futuristic city. Shelly called Laney who guided them around to the far left corner of the parking lot, where they found a spot tucked amongst a multitude of larger pickups. The little grey truck had virtually disappeared in the massive parking lot.

Officer Kirby Chapman's unmarked car slowly eased up the drive to the guard shack, as Alex's attempt to call her off had been in vain. She knew nothing of the 'Homeless Command' and certainly wasn't heeding directives from some random caller.

The guard gate arm was down and she approached as though it would automatically go up because a police officer was driving, as if there was some sort of law enforcement privilege to magically raise it. At the last possible second she slammed on the brakes, stopping an inch and a half from the reflective orange control arm. Fully perturbed, she immediately threw the car into reverse and sped to another screeching stop, this time, lined up with the guard shack window. Kirby reached out and rapped on the window.

Hanson Rogers slowly slid the glass and poked his face out. "May I help you?" he asked.

"I need to get through - open the gate," she rudely commanded as she flashed her badge.

The guard remained calm and answered, "I'm sorry Ma'am, but what's the issue? I have not been notified of a call for outside police help."

She had no time for this, "You're so polite, now let me in. I'm here on important business and need to get through."

"I monitor all channels on my scanner and there haven't been any calls from this campus." He then asked, "Are you here to execute a warrant?"

Remaining defiant, Kirby began to fume, "Listen here, I am not going to let a rent-a-cop interfere with my business. Now raise that gate, or I'll just have to go through it."

The loyal guard was not at all fazed and chose to follow protocol, "I am sorry. What department are you with? You're not Deer Park or county are you? I wasn't able to make out your badge."

Her bluff was being called, and she decided to fall back, "Your failure to cooperate ain't gonna be forgotten." She pulled a u turn around the guard gate and stationed her patrol car onto the shoulder to monitor the exit.

Hanson immediately called Joker on Laney's phone and updated him on the exchange with the maniacal cop and the fact that she was now watching the exit.

Joker thanked him as he and his visitors scurried around to the rear of a smaller building labeled 'Operations Control: Olefins'. The pungent air was a shock to the eyes and nostrils of the newcomers. As the group rounded a final turn with overnight bags and a raw holiday meal in tow, they entered a tight, dark alley. The corridor narrowed, and they descended a few stairs before arriving at a hatched door. Joker punched in a code on a number pad which flashed green as the lock clicked. He nodded to Dion and said, "You do the honors," as he started to turn a wheel handle. Dion spun it quickly until the heavy door opened, and they entered a sixties era fallout shelter full of control knobs and large buttons. "Welcome to the 'Shellter' as we call it around here, get it 'Shell-ter'..." said Joker with a smile, attempting to provide some levity. The creature comforts included multiple utilitarian dine in kitchen areas, fully tiled bathrooms adorned with simple metal fixtures, and numerous bunk rooms.

After twenty plus years with Shell, these were Joker's first visitors. Most of the employees never had visitors. The smell and inherent danger of the environment were not particularly welcoming, nor was the supposedly tight security. But, in Joker's case, it was more of a case of location. Shelly had insisted that they live nowhere near this foul air, regardless of the commute. Still, this refinery provided for a stable living, and, on this strange night, a secure locale for a family holiday.

Being the proud husband and father, Joker regretted that he had to take his guests into a secluded Cold War era hideout, rather than showing them off to his coworkers. On the other hand, he was not ashamed to show his family this most impressive complex where he spent half his waking hours.

This shelter was one of four onsite and featured backup power, air and water supplies, plus enough non-perishable food for fifty people to survive six months. The concrete walls were six feet thick. Joker was all too aware of this fact since he had been part of group of five who secretly hand chiseled an access tunnel from the main control room up above. These five worked night shifts together during the eighties and figured they'd pass time while ensuring that they'd be included in the protected group if the 'big one' ever came. The tunnel took five years to complete and was three feet across at the top tapering down to two at the bottom. Rebar brought in from home was cut to fit nicely and make for five ladder rungs spaced a foot apart. The entrance from above was located under a compressed air tank, and the opening below into the bunker was above a pantry shelf with jumbo sized cans of cling peaches stacked tightly to the ceiling.

The guests marveled at such an oddly modern, yet dated space, as Joker and Laney remained focused on the task at hand. While the others were figuring out how to heat up the oversized stainless steel oven, the two of them worked on finding cellular service for Laney's phone. Joker showed her to the pantry, and they began moving the peaches. Laney then donned a headlamp and climbed up the shelving and into the overhead tunnel. As she reached the top rung, the phone's display showed three signal bars, much better than they had expected and more than sufficient. They then connected the charger to an extra long, super thick extension cord. It was rigged up to allow the phone to hang within view of a plush chair situated below the opening.

Next they made a couple of test calls and checked her response times as she attempted to scurry up the chute and flip the phone open within four rings. She comfortably made it each time, as the others counted off the rings and seconds. Jane and Dion watched closely, since it was possible that they'd need to take shifts on call duty.

Chapter 41

Attempting to refocus on his mission and having lost all track of time, Gabe swiftly covered one short, empty block of pavement after another. A strange realization came. This would be his first major holiday not spent with his family, who were all in New Orleans by now. Thankfully his mother knew nothing of his current situation. He skirted The District and before long could see Power Tools up ahead.

This venue was the iconic industrial dance club of the late eighties, which had drawn the post punk crowd to the northern edge of downtown. After closing and then reincarnating before fading once again in the early nineties, the building had been abandoned for years. Gabe recalled a balcony that he'd be able to reach from the outside as a great spot from which to wait and watch the street for any sign of Laney. Of course this rescue option was only viable if her search for him had found the Hyatt and its gracious manager, Mr. Breaux.

Her car was nowhere in sight, in fact the entire scene appeared to be devoid of life. Gabe kept moving without pause, as if this arrival was part of his normal routine. He climbed onto a decorative concrete barrier along the street and leapt to grab the base of a balcony before pulling himself up and over the railing. Coming to a seated position, he was amazed at the adrenaline reserves fueling him. He had broken a slight sweat and now noticed the cold, still air which the dead of night had brought.

Gabe was alone in occupying the balcony, but intuitively also knew that his movement had to have been seen by some random lost soul, perhaps along the banks of Buffalo Bayou below. Tales of the vacated Donnellan Crypt came to mind. It had contained the bodies of a family of early settlers, but the corpses were moved in the early 1900s to accommodate development. Those daring enough to go down below the bridge and enter the site were supposedly met with paranormal experiences.

Thoughts of ghostly visions gave way to total exhaustion while he watched for Laney, pondering his next step. Jay and Garrett were likely asleep somewhere, hopefully comfortable and dreaming well. For Gabe, sleep was not an option, since he didn't have an alarm by which to awaken.

***

Alex racked his brain to come up with another drive thru pay phone not located in or near downtown. Nothing came to mind in the area. So he expanded his range and they headed to *Brady's Landing*, a finer restaurant on the Houston Ship Channel where his family sometimes celebrated special occasions.

This call would be made by Alex, so Martin did the driving. They arrived in no time and didn't see any signs of others loitering or lurking. It was now 3:00 AM.

Martin edged up to the phone, and Alex dialed.

On the other end, a thud followed by the low hum of a compressor motor masked the sound of the ringing. However, a focused young lady awaited any signs of life from her still new phone. As soon as it began to flash, Laney noticed the dark tunnel lighting up. She burst up the improvised ladder in a flash and, against her normal instinct to check the caller ID, immediately flipped open the phone. Interrupting the third ring, she anxiously answered, "Hello".

Alex spoke with a heightened sense of comfort, as if she were an old friend from their prior conversation. "Laney, it's me again, same guy, different phone. Are you able to talk now?"

"Yes, I can speak where I am." Her shelter mates quickly gathered below and attempted to listen.

"Are you in a safe place?" he asked next.

Laney considered the question for quick second, "Yes, we are safe, but only to a point."

Her answer puzzled Alex, "What do you mean safe 'to a point'?"

She looked down the dark tunnel to the light below and responded, "Well, in a way it's a safe spot. But we were followed by a white police car, and it's waiting out front for us."

The latter was surprising to Alex, "Did you see the driver of the car? Do you have a description?"

"No, I didn't, but my family did see her," she answered before elaborating, "And someone else here, where we're staying, got a very good look. It's a lady officer, sort of pretty with long, dark hair."

It was certainly Kirby, and he hoped that she was alone, "Just one officer?"

Laney confirmed his presumption, "Yes, definitely just one – as far as we know, or were told."

"OK, I know who it is. How long ago did you arrive at your safe place?"

She estimated, "Maybe forty-five minutes, definitely less than an hour. We left right after of your first call."

Alex gave her new hope, "I will get the officer off of the case. She will be forced to leave Gabe, and you, alone. Based upon my knowledge, she is the only cop on the side of the bad guys."

Mystified, Laney had to question, "I obviously have to wonder how you know this, and how you would have such power. Who are you really?"

Measuring his words carefully, Alex paused then responded, "I know Gabe through his work downtown. He has mentioned you a few times, and I wanted to help you both by what I know about those attempting to cause him harm. I also know that you two are recently engaged. That's all I can say."

"Alright, fair enough…if anything about this is fair," she conceded. "So what's next?" As the compressor above finally cycled off, four sets of ears below listened carefully to glean any possible bits of information from Laney's side of the conversation.

Martin couldn't help but become enthralled with what he was hearing on the other end. His little brother was handling some heavy drama.

Alex thought through his next instructions for her, looking over to his curious brother and shaking his head. "Laney, as soon as I hang up, I am going to make another call to get that cop out of there and totally removed from this situation, period. She will pull away from the scene and leave you all alone. This should happen within minutes."

She liked what she was hearing, "That would be very good. You sure seem confident."

"That part I can handle. I will call you back if I run into trouble with the officer. No call back from me means that it's handled, completely," he replied. "The rest is going to be up to you."

Laney was reenergized, "OK, I'm ready – what do I do?"

His directions were simple, "First, confirm that the officer has left – again, should be no issue there. Stay where you are until daybreak; get some rest. Gabe is probably in a fixed location for now; it's just too dangerous to make any sort of move in the dead of night. At the crack of dawn, head downtown and comb the streets. Check his office."

She sighed, "We've pretty much already done that, but I'll trust you - especially if that cop goes away. So you think he's safe?"

Alex attempted to reassure her, "From what I heard, he is a step ahead of the bad guys."

"Who are these 'bad guys'?" she now spoke more quietly against the sound of workers' footsteps and voices up above.

"Actually, I am not exactly sure who all is involved." He added, "Hopefully he'll be able to tell you all about them."

"Yes, hopefully…What if I can't find him downtown?"

Alex recalled how scraggly his normally clean cut passenger had appeared the prior morning. He pictured him again after factoring in a night on the streets. He was on the run and it had stormed. Finally, after considering Gabe's likely options, he said, "Have someone check at home…his home, your home. He may just walk there, even if it took all day. Gabe's a runner, right?"

Her emotions swung, "That's it, needle in a haystack, huh? Any other ideas? Should I go to the police now?"

"No police just yet; wait on that. Keep your phone on and charged, in case I hear anything else soon. I would call again from a different number. Regardless, I will check in with you again this afternoon." He was really ready to wrap this ordeal up. Now, yet another forced pay phone call awaited.

Laney realized that it was time to wrap up, "Well, I appreciate the help, and some hope. I guess that's it for now? Thank you."

"Yeah, that's all I've got at the moment…and you are most welcome. Good luck to you Laney." Click.

After checking to confirm that the area was still clear, Alex jumped out of the vehicle and ran around to Martin's door. Martin locked the doors, and Alex reached in the window, attempting to find the button. He yelled, "Don't mess with me right now, we are just about done. I have an obligation, and we are just about done."

Martin's comeback was swift, "You sure are mixing up your 'I's and 'We's aren't you? You're trying to get me involved in your hero duty, and you really want me to call that cop again, don't you?"

With his brows now fully furrowed, Alex attempted to call him out, "We are already here. It'll just take you a second. Then our obligation will have been fulfilled. Why can't we help these people?"

Knowing that Alex wouldn't give up, Martin relented, "Let's get this over with. I didn't come home for this, Alex! What do I say this time?"

Alex was ready, "Very simple: Tell her that you are disappointed in her for not backing off, and that you have pictures of her doing despicable things with her coworkers that will be distributed to everyone, if she or any other cop pursues Gabe or Laney – stop now, final warning."

Martin jotted down his main talking points and rehearsed in his head a few times. He was ready, "Got it. Give me a quarter."

This time, he put an old shop rag over the receiver before dialing, reducing the chance that his voice would sound like a brother of Alex.

He dialed and Officer Chapman picked up on the first ring, "Hello, who's calling?"

With his eyes closed, Martin spoke, "Hello Officer Chapman. I am so disappointed that you failed to follow the earlier instructions. Stay away from Gabe Wagner and his friends and family starting now, immediately. We have nude photos of you and your coworkers engaged in acts that would ruin your life if shared, which will happen if you do not back off immediately. Leave now and go home."

She was rattled, "Who is this - are you watching me?"

Martin could sense her weakness and got into the role, "I am the one with the photos, and I know where you are. It's Thanksgiving. Back off or copies of your candid escapades will be floating around downtown faster than you can say 'Kwik Kopy'. We know what you're about Kirby."

Kirby's voice quivered, "OK, I'm off it. All of it, for good. Are you still there?"

It was time to quit while he was way ahead, "I'm here and glad that you understand the situation. You and any other cops, yes all cops, are to remove yourself, themselves, from this matter immediately. Remove yourself for good or flyers will go up."

Feeling completely helpless, she started her engine and spoke, "I am off the case and leaving the scene. I have been working alone, no other cops..." Though she was defeated, Officer Chapman remained somewhat defiant, "If any of those pictures do happen to get out, Gabe and his girlfriend are history. Oh, and I will find you too."

Totally relieved that his role was successfully ending, Martin finished, "Good deal and good bye."

He slammed the phone down and turned to Alex, "You and I have both come a long way in this world, and it would be quite a shame for us to lose it all over some unfortunate people I don't even know? You don't really know them, either. Alex, you do realize this, correct?"

Alex remained serious, "I do realize this and will not ask anything more of you. That was awesome! You know I still brag about you, don't you?"

Their beer buzzes waned and the *Brady's Landing* sign triggered hunger. Typically they would stop by a twenty-four hour taqueria, but home beckoned on this most odd of nights.

Chapter 42

Thanksgiving dinner remained in limbo. Shelly debated moving the food from the coolers to the refrigerator and firing up the oversized oven to start the turkey.

The others had caught most of Laney's conversation with Alex, and she filled in the gaps regarding what she knew about her informant, the rogue cop and their plan. The root source of this malice remained a mystery to all.

They all agreed that it was time to get some rest, but that rest would be more easily achieved if they knew the stakeout in their honor had ended.

Joker would make a call to the guard gate up front, using Laney's phone, since the number was in the call history. Their patriarch waited in the tunnel for the compressor to kick back on, his deeper voice required full cover. Just above him, he could hear the familiar tones of his coworkers chatting along, with intermittent beeping of the control equipment. Suddenly the compressor clicked loudly as its motor fired up.

The guard's number was already queued up, and Joker immediately hit the 'Send' button, hoping that Hanson Rogers would answer.

As expected, Hanson picked up, and Joker inquired right away as to the status of their unwelcome visitor.

He confirmed her departure, "Oh yeah, she just took off – in a big hurry, tires screeching and all..."

Joker thanked him and gave the latest on their plans.

Laney's phone remained in the tunnel, charging and ready for calls. Shelly's phone was rigged up as well. They all took turns watching the phones and napping, except for Laney who mostly watched the clock.

***

Allen had slept a few hours before he began to toss, turn and rollover; too much was on his mind to just go right back to sleep. Additionally he was unaccustomed to the assortment of noises made by a dozen men sleeping in the same room. Still, he was somewhat recharged and wanted to get out of The Grotto before daybreak.

Up front at the tunnel entrance he found Smith still on guard and finishing up the daily crossword puzzle.

Allen asked him for an update, "What's the latest? Any word on our fugitive?"

Smith stayed optimistic, "Not yet, but we'll get him. Where's he going to go? We literally left him with nothing more than the clothes on his back."

"Really, Smith? He left us, and that man has a home and a life. If he's gotten out of downtown, we won't get him back."

Maintaining hope, Smith countered, "Well, then good riddance. He knows not to mess with us, and we are back to business as usual."

After a quick glance at the clock, Allen remained realistic, "His livelihood is here, and I'm sure he'll not be giving that up. Besides, we kidnapped him, and were prepared to go further – he knows that."

Smith could sense a certain level of resignation on Allen's part, but he remained defiant, "We built something great; we've maintained something great. I am not letting some yuppie scumbag ruin our creation."

Allen became nostalgic, "Think about everyone we've been able to help here. Only our vision and clever execution could make such a solution possible. Still though, we're already on borrowed time, probably always were…"

It was clear that Smith wasn't giving up. "Now don't go all past tense on me here. Allen, my dear friend, we need to keep this going. We'll get this guy back. You said he has a career here – he'll be back and we'll get him back, eventually. Time may well be on our side this time."

After a long pause, Allen responded, "I am not ready to give up hope. I just feel that we have an obligation to be prepared for different outcomes."

"I live here, this is my home. This is where I'm preparing to be," said Smith.

Allen pressed him to broach the hard option, "I know your plan if this guy's recaptured. But what's your plan if this place goes away?"

Such prospects horrified Smith; he preferred not to dig so deep, "I'll deal with whatever happens. We all know that you'll be totally fine. Your little arrangement has to provide for a certain level of comfort."

"I realize this - there's no denying that I have the least to lose," Allen lamented. "But you know the depth of my emotional commitment here, even if I only kept one foot in the door."

"There you go with that past tense crap again. You know I'm here for the duration, perhaps even long enough for Lamar to return." Smith's determination never ceased to amaze his old friend.

The mention of the third founder did nothing to excite Allen, "Now you're really dreaming. Lamar bailed on us because we took Walker in – without Walker, I doubt we would have lasted this long."

Smith was quick to defend his old friend, "Perhaps Lamar was correct, though. We could have terminated Walker and still be in full control. Walker is the one who brought in 'Violator GW', which, as you have stated, may bring our undoing."

Allen responded, "We had no means to cleanly rid ourselves of the Walker problem. Any investigation would have most certainly led to me and us. Remember we had no police protection back then."

The realization that The District could be exposed soon shook Smith greatly. He knew such an outcome was possible the moment they'd captured Gabe, but the escape, and now Allen's sobering words brought him slightly away from full denial. Smith then snapped back into full defensive mode asking, "We have the Metro Police on our side, and HPD and the county patrols are happy with our arrangement. They will surely ignore any claims he makes. He'll come off as a lunatic."

Attempting to reign him back in, Allen replied, "Don't exaggerate; a single Metro cop on our dole doesn't give us full police protection. That's for sure. He can clean up, and then get a lawyer or private investigator on it."

Smith proudly boasted, "No one wants to come down here without police protection. I can guarantee that our young fugitive wants no part of this dark and well hidden place."

Allen was growing weary of Smith's fantasy scenarios and decided it was time to speak frankly on the situation, "Smith, listen to me. This place is on the endangered list. The Grotto could be found and shuttered. This may all just go away, so you need to be prepared to move on if need be. Would you want me to help you repatriate into the world up there? You know I will. Just say so."

Smith looked up and placed both hands on the low ceiling. "This is where I belong. If The District goes down I'm going with it."

"I understand," was Allen's reply upon receiving the expected answer. He gave Smith a promise before exiting via the tunnel, "The sun will rise soon, and I will pursue Gabriel Wagner to all ends."

"I know that you will. You're too good a man not to," said Smith, wondering if this was a farewell.

Beyond a curtained partition, Jay had awoken from a creepily blissful nightmare and listened carefully to most of the founders' conversation. Their turmoil and hints of dissention reinvigorated him. He would play along, learn the routine and wait for the perfect chance to make a break for the free world.

Chapter 43

Drifting and swaying, Gabe fought to stay awake while repeating the past hours' events over and over in his mind. Images of Lamar's demise were by far the most vivid, inducing renewed alertness every time he needed a recharge.

The slightest crack of sunlight emerged to the east, and the longest night of this young man's life was finally coming to an end. A rejuvenated Gabe popped up and sprung into action, leaping the railing and bounding back over to the sidewalk. His next move involved venturing back into The District as desperation overcame trepidation.

To his surprise, the target of this morning's mission lay just across the street from where he now stood. A Bank One light came to life, and Gabe quickly realized that the stress and fatigue had thrown off his normally impeccable bearings. According to Lamar, Walker and one of his cronies would be found in or around the bank's parking lot.

Sure enough, the outline of the burly bully emerged as he arose from his slumber nearby. Just as Lamar had anticipated, Walker stretched and then began a short walk toward Market Square, disappearing from Gabe's line of sight.

Gabe reached around to confirm that the pistol was still present and properly situated in his rear waistband. Having somehow become accustomed to the full racing of his heart, he actually relished its presence and began to circle the block. In a controlled pursuit, he periodically checked the general area where Walker had awoken, ready to bolt if spotted by an observant sidekick. Skirting Market Square, Gabe spotted Walker once again. The sun began to emerge as Walker not so subtly brought his cupped right hand to his mouth and tilted his head back before swallowing. The addict's daily business had already been transacted, and Gabe could see the pill pusher, clad in an all white sweat suit, disappear at the far end of the square.

Walker was now ready for a new day and swung back by the bank to gather his partner, who had just awoken as a van pulled in to service the ATM. Gabe immediately recognized him as Clay and watched while the two subjects exchanged morning greetings and packed up their sleeping gear. The clock on the bank sign read '6:52', it was 48 degrees. The familiar pair next walked casually in the direction of the Wortham Center, and Gabe followed from a distance, scouting out their routine and the overall scene. Lamar's credibility skyrocketed as the whole scene unfolded exactly as he had described.

As Gabe followed their trek from afar, he found himself under the cover of a temporary construction walkway. The signs on the old building above read 'Avail. Soon: Hogg Lofts – Theater District Residential'. He noted the directions on each of the one way streets along the journey, as well as the traffic volume. The scenario was shaking out perfectly, and he'd have a clean shot and quick getaway when they reached the next intersection.

Would he go after them both or just a couple of rounds for Walker from behind – head then body, or vice versa? After all, he was the real culprit, directly responsible for Gabe's current misery. Clay was a pawn and pretty much a non-entity upon Walker's demise. But would Gabe live to regret not taking out an eyewitness to the bullets he was about to send their way?

Gabe grasped for and found the gun, first feeling the cool side of the handle away from his body. As he grabbed the handle and began to pull his weapon, the steely warmth of the barrel moved up his lower back. The silencer was tightly secured into place within a matter of seconds. The villains were held up from crossing the street by sporadic but speeding traffic. The range and time were right. He had fully readied himself to kill, once again, when a startling yet familiar fixture suddenly altered his plan of action. He alertly slid the now longer barrel of the gun back into its safe hiding place, taking in the morning scene.

Just like any other day, the HPD's mounted patrol had arrived at the corner of Preston and Smith Streets. Gabe was familiar with their routine. Every day at sunrise a double police horse trailer arrived and parked under the Interstate 45 overpass, with the two officers and their mounts splitting up from there. One of them was always stationed at this very spot, conspicuously guarding the safety of arriving commuters in this southern city bordering the West.

The plan was quickly voided and relief beset with dread kicked in. Gabe watched closely as the traffic stopped, and Walker and Clay crossed the street, fully honoring the crosswalk. The two passed much closer to the horse than he would ever be comfortable, especially after a certain Mardi Gras incident when he thought petting without permission was no big deal. Police do not take kindly to anyone touching their animals, their fellow officers, without full and expressed permission. He gathered that the officer and his steed were familiar with this pair of street walkers, bearing a certain level of tolerant coexistence, bordering on contempt.

The path to Walker's demise was forced to evolve, as Gabe noted the angles, lighting and backdrop of the panorama, particularly focusing on access to cover and escape. Overgrown kudzu and trumpet vines lined Buffalo Bayou and flanked the officer to his left, Gabe's right. He noticed the rays of the sun between the skyscrapers to the east as they shimmered off the glass of the windows and parked cars. Despite a foggy haze, even the light grey concrete streets intensified the glare between the long shadows. The horse bore blinders, and the cop sported mirrored shades.

The targeted subjects had now faded into the distance, presumably down into the depths of The District. Both were completely oblivious to Gabe's trailing and targeting.

Slowly the streets above came to life as yellow school busses full of marching bands arrived for a parade. A line of recycled floats streamed into town, pulled by late model white pickup trucks prominently displaying sponsor logos. Numerous packs of colorful horseback riders also streamed into town, complete with fancy costumes adorned by ample fringe and sequins.

Gabe noticed but disregarded the preparations for the parade. Rather he focused on processing the earlier movement of his pursuit and the habits of the various players. He suspected and then observed that codependent ruffians and payrolled civil servants were better about maintaining their respective routines than even he, especially on a holiday. He would in fact bank his very future on this theory.

***

Thin clouds veiled the morning sky above Deer Park. Steam and carbon waste from the mass of industrial sites melded into this dull white canopy. Though muted, the light from the rising sun was more than sufficient to blind eyes emerging from a deep bunker.

The clan had chosen to keep separate pairings. Both vehicles needed gas, and Dion made a dig at Joker as he raised his hands and looked all around, "Isn't there a factory outlet somewhere around here?" Joker and Laney would take the Tahoe, as Dion and Jane stuck with the Mazda pickup, while Shelly would shelter in place to stay safe and prepare the feast. They had successfully tested a land line in the shelter which would allow Shelly to keep in touch. The mobile phones were fully charged and primed to receive full open air coverage once again.

Joker and Laney would focus their search on the downtown area. Her natural inclination was to go to the police, but Alex hadn't given her the all clear just yet. Anyway, it still hadn't been twenty-four hours, which just did not seem possible to her. Besides her immediate stress, another concern lingered. A group decision had been made to notify Gabe's family when the police report was filed. They were in New Orleans for the holidays, and Laney prayed that a resolution was near, and that it would be Gabe calling his family, not her.

Dion and Jane's mission was to check Gabe's apartment and car, then return to the Filas home. Dion drove, and they followed the Tahoe past the guard gate and onto the freeway before going their separate ways.

***

The final preparations for the Foley's parade moved into full swing. Allen arrived at viewing stands jointly controlled by the Houston Ballet and Houston Grand Opera. Here, he was obliged to glad hand and air kiss various donors and VIPs. He knew most of these people very well, and a few were insiders familiar with The District and its role. Allen had realized long ago that these high society types were just like any social group, with an assortment of the real and the pretenders, both angels and hellions.

With his appearance made, Allen considered getting back on the search for Gabe, though he had never actually seen him and had only a single photo by which to go.

Then his phone rang. It was a somewhat familiar number. He excused himself to answer and was greeted on the other end of the line by a frantic Kirby Chapman, "Hey Allen, game over for me."

Allen wondered to what extent she was 'over', asking, "What's up, Officer? Were you not able to locate our friend?"

Kirby quickly declared, "I'm out! Someone's on to me – like a stalker calling and threatening me if I don't back off. And, no, I did not find him. I tailed his girlfriend for a while, but she found a guarded safe spot, and I'm no longer there."

"So, you're done for the day?" replied Allen, "Any clues for me?"

The officer concluded, "I'm done with our little arrangement for good – I'm out, totally out, and wish you and your people the best going forward. I have no idea where he is."

Allen realized how big a blow this latest news was to the search for Gabe and the longevity of The District, though both were already closely tied to one another. His last words conveyed a certain sense of finality, "You take care, and let me know if you change your mind. Happy Thanksgiving!" There was no reply, and the line went silent. He ended the call and considered words he'd quite possibly have to share with the arts boards in the upcoming days or weeks. Allen returned to his apartment to watch the rest of the parade from his balcony above.

Chapter 44

Gabe made his way through the gathering parade crowd, soon realizing that people were avoiding eye contact with him. Most feared that such a ragged fellow would ask for something, or, at the very least, do something strange enough to make them feel uncomfortable. They also wanted no part of the odor he was sure to emit. Though the streets were so familiar, the light of day and fresh faces created a truly surreal world around him.

The focus of Gabe's attention had shifted from targeting Walker to a mission of somehow getting home, the sort of home he'd feel at the sight of Laney's sweet face.

He came to realize that his best chance to get somewhere would be to connect with Nelson Bosch, who had volunteered to feed the needy this Thanksgiving morning. The route over to the convention center brought Gabe to retrace the steps he'd taken with Lamar for their meeting at the mall. He cringed as he stepped around the ventilation grate where Lamar had met his end. What would become of the body? A cold winter would impede decomposition, but also reduce the smell and delay its discovery. Regardless, the lost life would be unidentifiable and cause of death unknown, not traceable to Gabe.

The nature of street traffic changed; not the pattern but rather the types and condition of the vehicles. Older, rickety cars and trucks filled the streets and parking spots, populating space usually occupied by luxury sedans and, as of late, SUVs. Houston's less fortunate were trickling into downtown to receive a full meal, plus blankets and winter clothing. Gabe's disheveled self was herded into the 'Guest w/o Children' line. He willingly accepted the assignment, potentially bringing him to Nelson and, at the very least, providing sustenance for the day's journey.

The quality and scale of the event was most impressive, truly a matter of thousands feeding thousands. The massive George R. Brown Convention Center was teaming with activity, as well organized lines snaked around the building. Though the food was appetizing and brought movement to his stomach, Gabe focused on the faces of those prepping and serving. Nelson was nowhere to be found, as the sheer number of volunteers soon became overwhelming.

His most recent revelations and experiences had left Gabe somewhat jaded. He mused that this whole production might just be a scheme to keep the undesirables gathered in one place, while the shiny parade happened on the other side of downtown.

Gabe's queries as to Nelson's possible whereabouts, as well as requests to see a volunteer list, were summarily dismissed by those in charge. Though they seemed to be extremely busy, he wondered if those in charge would have had time for someone less unkempt than he.

Everyone got a serving of each item on the menu, no choices a la the grade school cafeteria line. At this point everything looked very good, even the canned cranberry sauce, and he was glad to see that the turkey was mainly dark meat.

Gabe stood as he ate in order to watch the comings and goings of the volunteers. His positioning and staring clearly made those around him uneasy, and he was asked to clear the aisle and find a 'comfortable seat'. In exchange for complying with the request, Gabe was able to convince someone to lend him their mobile phone for a single call. It was another fruitless effort, as no one answered at the Filas residence, which he found absolutely astounding. After all it was Thanksgiving morning. After leaving a message, Gabe returned the phone with a forced yet genuine 'Thanks' followed by a quiet expletive to himself as he stomped his foot. In his mind he acknowledged that his own creepiness strongly overrode any bit of pride which might remain.

The food lines kept moving smoothly, even as another shift of volunteers took their posts. Still, there was no sign of Nelson, or the wife who had signed him up for this.

***

Thanksgiving morning was always special in The District, since it signaled the beginning of their holiday season. The holidays were celebrated vicariously in this existential realm. Seeing others dress up and dine finely to attend performances of *The Nutcracker* and *A Christmas Carol* was the closest most of them came to actually experiencing a festive break from their mundane lives.

Most of the Subjects were night people, but arose early on Thanksgiving, the first of The District's three true holidays. Each holiday was marked by a parade, the other two being the Martin Luther King holiday in January and the Houston Rodeo kickoff in February. All three of these parades ran through The District and their processions provided rare times to truly feel a part of something beyond their immediate anonymity.

Besides being the first holiday in this little season of theirs, Thanksgiving meant that Allen would bring in a special meal with sides way beyond the usual. Also holiday decorations, mostly Christmas trees and lights, would now appear throughout The District. Rooflines would be crowned with white halos, from the wide, low rise theaters on up to the tallest of soaring skyscrapers. Even dulled senses required occasional stimulation.

The fugitive Violator remained the main focus of their attention, but an hour or so of respite from the chase was acceptable to all. Smith and Walker were most keenly concerned about the threat that his escape brought. Crawford feigned similar concern, while this awareness actually brought inner hope to him. He so yearned for a return of free will.

Jay's eyes opened slowly and he remained on his sleeping pallet, calmly taking in the sounds of his first morning in The Grotto. He knew better than to ask for permission to go out and up to the parade. Anyway, his real longing was to be reunited with the family he missed so much. It was Thanksgiving morning, and his son was in a good place with good people. This solace was short lived, as thoughts turned to Garrett's mother; he had failed to keep her safe and was now plunged into a world another step farther away from hers.

***

Simultaneous major events gridlocked downtown. The people, vehicles and closed streets related to the charity feast to the east and the parade to the west made Joker and Laney's search extra difficult. Open parking spots were non-existent and splitting up to allow either to search by foot was simply not an option. So they moved along slowly and watched carefully for any sign of Gabe, who would presumably be moving about.

They soon came to within a block of Gabe's office. Joker found a good place to stop and Laney jumped out. Though the guard was adamant about the fact that the twelfth story was clear and vacant, she was able to get him to allow her to go up. After jotting down her drivers license number, he accompanied her and even let her in to look around. Everything was cleanly buttoned up for the holiday weekend, except for a few random ceiling tiles atop step ladders. All of the lights were out, and there was no sign of life about. The restrooms were also checked to no avail. The guard had been correct, and she thanked him.

Though Laney was a native Houstonian, this was her first glimpse of the Thanksgiving parade, yet its sights and sounds were completely lost on her. Joker had always been cooking or working Thanksgiving morning and was quite impressed with what he could see of the tops of floats moving along. Laney focused on the faces in the crowd, and Joker saw only the despair in her eyes. It was futile, but really their only option. Joker was willing to keep up the search as long as his daughter could last.

    ***

After passing through Shipley's for donuts and kolaches, Dion and Jane stopped by Gabe's apartment. They parked outside the gate and did not have to wait long for someone to follow in. After a few hard knocks, Jane turned the key with great apprehension, a large part of her hoping not to find Gabe there. Closure at this point would likely be tragic for her dear twin sister. Only Brittany greeted them at the door - still no sign of Gabe. The pup was in desperate need of a walk, so they decided to grab her food and walk her towards the pickup to go home with them. She was willing to go along for the ride, though not with her usual vigor.

Along the way home, they passed through the Park & Ride upon seeing that Gabe's Audi was still there. Brittany recognized the car and her nub of a tail wagged furiously, anticipating that Gabe would emerge. But he was nowhere to be found and, once again, Jane was relieved as hope survived.

They left for home with great wonder as to what may await them. Dion switched the radio to a country station and *Carried Away* by George Strait was playing. Jane promptly turned down the volume. Alex's assurance that dirty cops were no longer involved only provided a certain level of comfort as they made their way around Beltway 8. Upon reaching the neighborhood and then their street, a couple of slow laps around the block revealed nothing obviously out of the norm. As they could best determine, the duo found Brookstone Street to be clear of suspicious vehicles following them or watching the house.

Entering the garage with trepidation, Dion pulled the revolver from under the driver's seat, exactly where Joker said it would be found. To their relief, the alarm was still set as they entered. Jane quickly disarmed it and then immediately reset it in 'Stay' mode, even though they had no intentions of staying long. Once again, there was no sign of Gabe. This time, Jane was genuinely disappointed – here was where she had hoped that they would find him. Now Gabe would have to find them.

They gathered a couple of items from the kitchen and disarmed the alarm once again, before putting Brittany in the backyard and preparing to leave. Jane remembered one last item with which they had been tasked. In the side hallway, an answering machine blinked and indicated a single message waiting to be heard. She pressed the button and crossed her fingers while the tape rewound. Sure enough it was a message from Gabe: "Hello Laney – I love you…Everyone, I am stuck downtown without money but am working on getting to your house. A night from hell - my keys are gone. I don't have a callback number to leave and cannot stay where I am, but I will get there."

Chapter 45

Morning was slowly giving way to midday, and the final shift of volunteers served the last of the needy guests. Second helpings of all courses were offered, and most doubled up on desserts. Gabe chose turkey and mashed potatoes, since the pies hadn't quite measured up to the quality main courses, and certainly not to the ones he'd become accustomed to at the Filas house.

A skeleton crew of volunteers began to clean up the serving line and take out trash, signaling the beginning of the event's end. For the most part, the diners cleared their own tables as they made their way out. Gabe held out hope and would be last to leave. Still Nelson Bosch was nowhere in sight, nor did anyone recognize his name. As the venue emptied out Gabe began to accept the fact that, aside from the much needed meal, his efforts to find Nelson here had been in vain.

Back out on the streets, simultaneous event conclusions created human gridlock. Gabe squeezed through, as the charity meal crowd met the larger crush of parade goers. He had a destination in mind; it was just blocks away and would allow him to get out of downtown. His route took him down Rusk to Travis, once again to the border of The District. He scooped up a crushed turkey hat to provide some cover, should he encounter his pursuers.

At Travis, the crowd was most dense, and Gabe was barely able to move, when he caught a glimmer of hope. He was forced up a high curb bordering a large planter and spotted a familiar vehicle. Across the parade route, and a couple of blocks to the south, Joker's silver Mazda pickup truck moved through the intersection. Its rack and striping were unique. Its driver was unmistakably Joker. Forced back down to the ground level by the crush of the crowd, he lost his line of sight just as he noticed that someone was in the passenger seat. It was physically impossible for him to make his way through the sea of humanity between him, and his future father-in-law and Gabe let out a deep growling sigh. The buzz of the crowd and music in the distance muted his outburst. Only those directly next to him noticed.

As he desperately pushed through toward the intersection where he'd spotted Joker's truck, Gabe wondered if they had heard the message he'd left at the house and how long they'd been downtown. How much longer would the two of them remain in the area? Despite the density of the crowd and endless sets of eyes, he felt a now familiar feeling. Across the street and a couple of sets of barricades, exactly in the direction Gabe was heading, a couple of The District's Subjects appeared and clearly had Gabe in their collective sights. Down the way, more such scoundrels notice Gabe just as he noticed them. As a regular bus rider and a former captive of theirs, he was quick to recognize them, where others would only see shaggy, stubbly faces, tattered clothing and red noses. Now his only option was a full retreat to his originally planned destination, the place where he was headed before the random appearance of Joker.

The crowd thinned quickly, as Gabe ventured away from the parade route down Travis to Walker Street. In no time, he arrived at the Houston Chronicle building. After passing a huge printing press behind a wall of windows, Gabe ducked into an oversized garage doorway. This was the staging area for street corner newspaper distribution. A constant flow of trucks carrying bundled papers and vendors passed through this bustling passageway. These 'red light hawkers' were familiar to all Houston drivers, and Gabe was relieved to find that a major holiday brought no stop to this operation. Numerous white box trucks were lined up with a crowd of haggard characters gathered alongside of them, all donning blue t-shirts. A crew leader and uniformed drivers stood at a counter motioning for Gabe to come over to the motley crew of vendors checking routes on clipboards. Gabe complied and joined them, watching as they secured assorted ad buttons to their matching shirts.

A few familiar faces dotted the vendor lineup, scraggly guys who regularly appeared on busy intersections in west Houston. One of the leaders tossed Gabe a t-shirt, and he got in line with a particular guy he recognized from the Highway 290 and Bingle area near the Filas house. He perused the various clipboards and signed up for a corner out beyond his intended destination. Next, he grabbed a 'Final Edition' button and a bundle of papers before jumping into the back of the truck with around fifteen others. The driver came around and confirmed '290 – Northwest Freeway, departing now' before pulling the door down more than halfway and tying it into place with a frayed rope.

The opening was enough to allow in fresh air and see the ground behind them. It was also large enough for someone to bounce on out. The veterans had secured the spots closest to the front and showed little concern as the engine fired up. The greenhorns, which certainly included Gabe, found and tightly grabbed straps along the walls as they rolled out of the garage.

Though relieved to be somewhat secure and headed in the right direction, Gabe kept his wits about him. His present company was not specifically out to get him like the villains of The District, but their desire to earn didn't fully camouflage the rough edges. Lawlessness was just below the surface. Too soon, the truck stopped for a red light and diesel exhaust flowed in. In accordance with his luck of late, it was of little surprise to Gabe when a pair of subjects from The District approached on the adjacent sidewalk. But of course, it was Walker and Clay. Fortunately they could not immediately make out the shadowy figures in the dark truck. Gabe realized the cover he had been afforded and resisted the urge to yell out to them as the light changed and they accelerated, freeway bound.

***

At the opposite end of downtown, Joker navigated bumper to bumper event traffic, as Laney began to fade. All of the faces dotting the dense foot traffic began to look the same; it became overwhelming and exhausting. Just as tears began to roll down Laney's face, her phone rang. This time the number on the caller id could not have been more recognizable - it was her home phone.

With a hint of hope, Laney answered, "Hello".

Jane replied with guarded optimism, "Hi Laney, we are home and have some news, not bad news."

"So is he there?" asked Laney.

"No, he is not here. But he left a message and is trying to get here from downtown, trying to get a ride."

Laney wanted more details, "OK, that's good, at least he's alive. Did he say where he is? We are still downtown."

"No, he said that he couldn't stay, or maybe 'say', where he was – it was a little unclear. I think he was calling on a cell phone," replied Jane. "He said he was working on getting here."

"Did he leave any explanation?" wondered Laney, "I mean what exactly happened to him?"

Jane covered the receiver to conceal her sigh and responded, "Laney, there was no explanation. He sounded tired and rushed, not like himself."

Laney considered what Alex had told him about the situation, "Yeah, we'll have to see what Mr. Gabe's story is…When did he leave the message?"

"It was about an hour ago, according to the machine," said Jane.

"Wow, an allnighter," Laney sniffled a little and cried to her sister, "I miss him so much."

Jane consoled her, "I know, Girl. He's trying to get here. What do you want us to do now?"

After considering the options and not wanting to chance missing him, Laney instructed her, "Please just stay there. We'll get Mom and come home now."

"You got it. We have Brittany here. It's very quiet."

Laney expressed her appreciation to her sister, "Thanks for being there. I'll call Mom now. Why don't you go ahead and preheat the oven for her, to 350 or something like that. We'll be there in about an hour."

"OK, bye – love you."

***

The Longoria home had come to life hours earlier and Thanksgiving feast preparations were in full swing. Martin had been awoken by the clicking of a squeaky door knob, turned repeatedly by his younger siblings anxious to see him. The youngsters had gone to the parade downtown and were now either gathering in the kitchen or getting ready to watch some football.

Alex was able to peacefully sleep late, mainly because he was more used to the commotion. Eventually Martin sent in a little brother to wake him up. Alex didn't jump right out of bed but laid there and considered the events of the previous evening and early morning hours. His thoughts moved from the pay phone calls, then to Gabe and Laney's collective states of well being, and finally back to Kirby. Alex realized that he needed to call her and feign a minimal level of interest in order to maintain his cover.

He dialed her up and she answered, "Hello".

"Happy Thanksgiving, Kirby!" was his greeting.

She was less enthusiastic, "Hi Alex, Happy Thanksgiving".

Alex responded, "What are you up to?"

Kirby was somewhat guarded in her response, "At home laying around. I worked some overtime last night, actually that private gig I told you about."

Pretty sure that she wasn't at all on to him, he played dumb, "Oh, how'd that go? Busy?"

"It was a little strange, turned out to be the last of my work with them."

His comfort grew and Alex played along, "Oh, any particular reason?"

She'd shared enough, "It's just time to move on. They're on their own now."

He was relieved that she didn't seem to suspect him at all, "OK, I understand. Will I see you today? Can I see you today?"

Kirby was obtuse, "I don't know. You said family first, right?" She had really wanted him to be open and welcoming.

Alex was really not anxious to get together and was fine with her resistance. "Yes, actually family always does come first, in my family anyway."

She got the message, "OK, family man. Maybe we can get together later."

He followed up with an aloof retort, "Sure, I'll give you a call."

"Sure, sounds good – Bye"

"Good bye, Kirby"

He grinned and then gave a mini fist pump. She seemed to be totally unaware of his role in the forced termination of her involvement with Gabe and Laney and, ultimately, The District. They were all safe, at least from the law. Additionally, he was off the hook and free to chill with his family. Turkey and football awaited. His lone regret was the occasional awkwardness to come when paths crossed with Kirby at work, but two degrees of separation there afforded him some level of comfort.

Chapter 46

Back at the Grotto, the less active Subjects were returning from the parade while Clay and the rest were still out perusing the thinning crowd. Someone mentioned that Gabe was possibly spotted in the parade crowd near the end. As the various reports came in, Smith realized that Gabe had either gotten to safety inside a building or slipped out of downtown in the light of day. Yet, they had everything to lose and would maintain full surveillance mode until Gabe resurfaced in any form.

Still, it was Thanksgiving, and Allen would have typically brought in a huge spread by now. The Outliers would even venture inside for this feast of turkey, sides and desserts.

But this Thanksgiving was different. Allen was just arriving, and the meal was clearly far from homemade, not exactly the solace they'd anticipated. A couple of pre-packaged turkey breasts, some canned yams and small individually wrapped pies were all he had to offer. It wasn't for a lack of care. More so, he had been preoccupied with the pursuit of Gabe and the future of The District. Everyone soon realized that the pickings would be slim. Though most felt entitled to better and more, nary a single word of discontent was uttered.

***

Isuzu commercial trucks boasted ample power but poor acceleration. Being new to the traveling newsy game, Gabe felt every bump and turn. He couldn't help but notice that they were moving along with the flow of wide open Houston freeway traffic - seventy, seventy-five..? Whatever the speed, it was clearly apparent that someone up front was mission driven, like perhaps to catch a holiday meal or a football game. The cargo was less than precious or fragile, for the most part.

Gabe only raised his eyebrows at the sudden jerks, while those around him appeared bored and near sleep. He soon became comfortable with this docile crew and the lack of eye contact.

As his comfort grew, Gabe's mind wandered to trivial matters outside of Laney, Thanksgiving and The District. Facing backwards, this road was all too familiar, but this new perspective was curious, like his daily grind in reverse.

He reminisced about the times just a few years back, before The Houston Chronicle had acquired The Houston Post, and envisioned the competing vendors on each corner. This was now a one paper town, and this new breed of vendor had no competition, with higher prices to pocket. This afforded his present company a new level of comfort. How long would it last?

And how did the money work? Did these vendors have to give a cut of their sales back to The Chronicle on each paper sold? These guys surely didn't seem up to such accounting, or trust. Pops had told Gabe that the newspapers just wanted the additional distribution in order to boost their advertising rates and, somehow, newspaper sales revenue dwarfed that of ads.

Gabe noticed that they were slowing up in relation to the surrounding traffic, as the truck veered to the right and exited. The freeway portion of this journey had ended, and they had made significant progress in the right direction, halfway there. If he jumped off here it would be a two hour walk, but knowing, hopefully, the upcoming stops held him in place. It was a turbulent thirty minute zig-zag of a ride with stops every few minutes to dispatch his fellow drifters to their appointed corners, corners which were usually much busier on regular weekdays.

Finally they approached the intersection of Bingle and Highway 290, within three miles of his destination. Though the next stop may have been closer, he couldn't chance a turn to come pulling him farther away. Gabe quickly ditched his Chronicle t-shirt at the feet of a sleeping vendor and exited the truck as it came to a slow roll, never looking back. He heard the truck moving away in low gear. Once at a comfortable distance, he took a quick peek back and realized that he'd made the right move, as this spot was apparently as close as this free ride would bring him.

The walk would traverse a bit of a dicey area, but it was broad daylight, and he was numb to slight danger by now. Besides, he looked pretty rough himself at this point.

***

Once out of the heavy downtown traffic, Joker made great time in getting back to Shell. Hanson Rogers was gone for the day, and a less familiar guard was there to greet them. After checking Joker's corporate ID, he wished them a "Happy Thanksgiving" with a smile, and up went the control arm.

Shelly had packed the food back into the coolers where plenty of dry ice remained. The bags were packed and at the entrance, so that Joker could just pull around to the back and load up everything fast. She ensured that everything in the bunker had been left exactly as they'd found it. Within three minutes they were on their way home for a later than usual Thanksgiving meal. The turkey was not done, but just to the point where it started to smell good. Hunger set in as Joker's inbound pace matched that of the outbound journey they had taken just twelve hours earlier.

Shelly dwelled on her concerns about the meal to mask her concerns for her daughter and the possible crushing of her younger twin's dreams. Worry even showed on the usually stoic face of Joker. They had just started to really get to know Gabe since the engagement. Hopefully he was en route as he'd hoped according to the phone message. Perhaps this awful holiday would end well.

***

At the house, Jane and Dion were chilling with Brittany and the loaded shotgun. Dogs weren't usually allowed in this house, but these circumstances were special, and Shelly wasn't home. Football was on the tube, and Dion snacked on coffee table candy corn, while waiting for the Dallas game to kickoff. He was a diehard fan of the Cowboys, since there was no NFL team in Tennessee.

Jane was paranoid, so Dion kept moving the gun closer and closer to them; ultimately it was leaning up against the sofa. She then kept asking him to check the safety. Did red indicate 'fire' or 'safety'? Her constant pestering had him second guessing himself.

Dion anxiously awaited the game and the arrival of the rest of the family. His luggage contained a special weapon, which he couldn't wait to show to Gabe. They had an appointment to keep, which involved his new prized possession. He had wondered if the security screening would detect it in his checked baggage, or if they'd even care. But he surely knew that Jane would care plenty, if she ever found out how much it cost, despite bargained pawn shop pricing.

They heard the garage door opening and jumped up to confirm that it was the Tahoe. Dion held the twelve gauge, while Jane peeked and then unlocked the door for warm embraces. First the food and then the luggage was brought in.

Dion was sure to personally get his own bag, so that he could feel the outline of his new toy and gently place it down.

Laney and Jane set the table. Shelly insisted that they go with the Corelle dinnerware to save them the time and trouble of hand washing china. Regardless of this constraint, they were determined to make the table beautiful and succeeded in doing so.

Joker immediately got busy, first sticking the turkey in the oven and locating the electric knife. He then pulled another pistol from the safe, confirmed that it was loaded, and laid it on an end table. Brittany nuzzled up against his leg. Both parents noticed that she was inside and didn't object.

***

It was just a couple of miles up Bingle and then left for another half mile to the Filas' neighborhood and house. Gabe was so ready and mustered up the strength to run the entire way. If there was still no one there, he figured he'd just end up in the backyard hammock until someone came home.

The familiar route went quickly as he considered how much he'd share about his ordeal. He figured they'd doubt his story and wasn't up to giving all of the sordid details, especially to the whole family.

Rarely did he and Laney go a whole day without seeing each other, and Wednesday had been such a day. Gabe anticipated the sight of her beautiful face, her round lashy eyes, dark and warm. And it would be a joy to see her family, soon to be her side of their family.

He also relished the simple comforts of home, any home. His mind wandered to Brittany, his incredibly disciplined and sweet pup. It would be shocking if someone hadn't gone over to his apartment for a feeding and walk. Maybe this was why no one was there when he'd called. But wait. Someone would have stayed home to watch the oven. His thoughts became scattered and incoherent, exhaustion peppered with a tinge of runner's high.

After rounding the final corner, he walked the last half block to catch his breath and wipe away sweat. He gasped with a brief sigh of relief at the sight of Laney's car and Joker's truck both in the driveway. Everything appeared normal, but these people weren't about not answering phone calls. Maybe they had a story to tell as well.

Chapter 47

Brittany's ears perked up and she began a mild whine, which soon morphed into a full blown whimper. Laney looked at her eyes and tail before saying, "What's wrong girl?" Everyone noted a slight hint of hope in her voice. Joker and Dion grabbed their pistol and shotgun respectively, before waving everyone toward the back of the house.

The doorbell rang, and Brittany went into a frenzy. Joker checked the peephole before turning back to the group with a smile, "It's him - Laney, it's your groom". Though mild by most standards, this expression of raw emotion was downright enthusiastic for Joker.

Laney sprinted past everyone to fling open the front door and screen. Their eyes met just before their lips, and a long, tight embrace ensued. He smelled of sweat, old and new, with a hint of street gutter splash. She'd never seen him look so ragged. Even after mountain biking, spots of clean would remain on his clothes and face amongst the fresh mud. This was pure grime.

With her eyes welling up Laney spoke, "I knew you'd get here. Come in, come in."

Gabe followed her into the front hallway, "So you got my message right? I love you."

"I love you. Look at you all scruffy," she responded as a few tiny tears flowed. "Yes, we got your message. I guess you got a ride…" The others gave them room but listened intently.

With a smile, Gabe replied, "Yeah, I pretty much got a ride – most of the way."

Joker chimed in, "You weren't followed, were you?"

After some real hugs with the ladies and handshake elbow hugs with the guys, Gabe answered, "I am not an easy follow – otherwise, I wouldn't be standing right here."

Laney then spoke, "Sounds like you got into some really deep stuff. Anonymous calls came in to me with information and threats and help. All of this had to do with the homeless, helping them I mean, right?"

Gabe was shocked to hear this. He noticed the guns out and teared up, "Oh, I am so sorry – I had no idea that you all got drawn into this. But how? They were just after me…I will fix it."

"We are pretty sure that everything's fine now…with the help of a kind stranger, who proved to be credible," said Laney, attempting to calm everyone.

He had unfinished business, but still attempted to reassure everyone, "This stuff is not quite done, yet…but good enough for now, for the weekend. I just need to make the right calls, and it will be handled."

Laney grabbed his hand and led him into the family room, "I am sure that you will fill us in on everything. Sounds like evil stuff out there…"

He looked into her eyes and shook his head, "I have seen all sorts of evil, from simple greed to evil masked as pride…and some just purely for the sake of evil." The familiar smell of a meal in the oven was so welcoming. Being too exhausted to retell or piecemeal the story, he decided to share with everyone at once, immediately.

His description of the events was full, save for a couple of omissions, both of which involved Lamar: the pistol he'd gifted Gabe and his timely demise by ventilation duct.

The whole situation seemed so convoluted that everyone would have doubted its validity. Did the anonymous phone calls make it real? But there was no question about the existence of the cop tailing them across town, bookended by stake outs at home and at Shell. It was all undeniably real, as Laney told their tale of worry, search, evacuation and return. She was fully convinced that the dirty cop was out of the picture. Gabe took special note of this final part of her story. Gabe was floored at what they'd experienced and searched for connections, external forces both to harm and help his fiancé and her family. Deep down inside, he wondered if he would have had the clarity to make it out had he been aware that Laney was being subjected to such torment. He'd found just barely enough focus, as it was.

Just as Laney was wrapping up, the doorbell rang. Joker jumped up, again with pistol in hand, and answered the door. It was a pair of newlyweds,

230

Laney and Jane's brother D. John and his wife May. Gabe ducked into the bathroom for a shower and shave, borrowing an oversized sorority mixer shirt from Laney and some elastic waisted sweatpants from Dion. The young couple couldn't help but notice all of the guns out, and Joker just explained that he was showing the guys some of his collection. D. John and May lived on the outskirts of town, and he found no need to get them involved at this point.

It was time for the meal, eight courses strong. Apparently the intermittent method of baking provided for extra tender, falling off the bones turkey and easy carving. Joker said the blessing and oddly vague words of thanks went around the table. The side dishes were passed around and normal conversations ensued. Dion kept an eye on the ballgame and joined in between plays.

With May's doing, the conversation turned to Black Friday shopping. Though still in a slight state of shock and insomnia induced delirium, Laney perked up at such talk. It wasn't necessarily the shopping that got her attention, but more of a return to normalcy and salvaging the rest of her sister's visit. While the guys would normally ridicule the ladies over getting up super early to save a few bucks, Dion was preoccupied with his Dallas Cowboys and D. John was apathetic. Joker was back to his usual hush self, and Gabe, who would normally chime in, had other plans for that next morning, a twist on a holiday tradition.

***

Though his family prepared a traditional 'Pilgrim Thanksgiving' meal with turkey and sides, Alex Longoria's current stuffed condition was a result of tamale overindulgence followed by a huge serving of flan. His parents truly cherished the company of all of their children together, and that they were now mature enough to get along so well. Moments such as these were few and far between.

Alex also relished this togetherness but was a man of his word. As a diehard fan of the Houston Oilers, he also hated the Dallas Cowboys, especially since they were winning once again. When the Redskins fell behind, he figured he'd seen enough and that it was promise keeping time. This time he would fly solo.

An alibi would be offered only if one was warranted. Sure enough, his father demanded to know where he was going, and they all joked about 'his special lady friend'. Alex went along with it and his mother insisted that he bring her, Kirby in this case, back to the house with him. That wasn't an option, so he assured them that it would be a quick outing.

It was time for a new direction. This time he went south to a Shell station on Loop 610. He was less nervous this time, but realized that each of his phone encounters increased the risk of blown cover or other such failure. At least his calls were friendly ones, unlike the threatening calls he had coaxed Martin into making. He found the pay phone at the far corner of the parking and dialed the ten digits.

For a new phone and number, Laney's mobile phone sure was active. She jumped up from the table to take the call, and everyone in the know gave each other looks of wonder, while remaining calm, so as not to spark curiosity on the part of D. John and May. Laney thanked Alex again and let him know that the cops seemed to be gone and leaving them alone. Alex let her know that he had been guaranteed that the dirty cops were indeed done with all matters related to Gabe. Laney then let him know that they were now home, and that Gabe had made it there too. As Alex expressed his joy at the news, Gabe excused himself from the table and walked up close to Laney. She turned the phone slightly, so that he could listen. Gabe found the friendly stranger's voice somewhat familiar, but just could not place it. He considered everyone at RPG, at the Houston Club and even The District. He concluded that it had to be someone operating from the inside via Crawford. Laney thanked him profusely, for both his help and keeping his promise to call one final time.

Alex was free to go and drove for a while to burn some time. He came upon a Stop-N-Go convenience store and grabbed a couple of twelve packs of *Bohemia* for Martin, one to be shared that evening and one for him to take back to Corpus Christi.

With still more time to burn, he popped open a bottle and continued to cruise around the outskirts of downtown. His thoughts naturally focused on Gabe and Laney and their odyssey. Had he saved a life? He also thought about Kirby. Though led by the physical, his feelings for her were real, even after he figured out she was moonlighting for the underworld. But the shocking Polaroids revealed her as common to the Metro police force, ending any possibility that he would ever bring her home to mom.

Alex didn't know The District by name, only of a downtown underworld with Kirby Chapman formerly on the payroll. She'd never called it by name and only stated that they were helping the homeless but needed an occasional show of force. Only Kirby's intuition could reveal he and his to be behind the mystery pay phone calls. Could she figure him out?

Such limited understanding dictated his thoughts going forward. He considered the older man who had stopped by the station searching for Gabe, and his possible motives. Maybe Gabe had gained just the right amount of exposure to this underworld and survived their pursuit with what he would need to end them. Would Gabe ever again show up on the Park & Ride?

A single drink gave him ample comfort with his decision to get involved and the outcome. Alex finally pulled in the driveway of his parents' house ready to enjoy the rest of a great holiday weekend with his family.

***

Pecan and pumpkin pie were the staple desserts at the Filas house during the holidays, with Dion and Gabe being the main connoisseurs. To Dion's delight, the Cowboys were winning comfortably, while everyone sat around in a post feast stupor. With D. John and May still around, everyone just rested quietly and pondered the new details they had learned regarding events of the past twenty-four hours. Based upon Gabe's description, they all pretty much figured that his safe return to his job downtown required further measures to kill or neuter The District.

Despite Laney's reassurances, based on the phone calls from Alex, Gabe still did not trust the police. He played along but had a self-determined idea in mind.

Just as dusk set in, Gabe let Brittany into the backyard and commented on how nice it was out. Unaware that Dion had quit smoking, Gabe invited him to come out and join them. Dion knew something was up and went out back. A matter of a certain holiday ritual was to be addressed, and Gabe wove it into his plan. They had originally intended to include D. John, but the circumstances altered their plans.

Dion was proud of his new toy but unable to show it off just yet. Jane would certainly get on him for sneaking it onto the plane from Nashville.

As Gabe entrusted Dion with the details of his mission, Dion quickly realized that a second man was needed and that he was that man. Without hesitation Dion said "I'm in, all in - count me in" with a wink and a big hug.

Gabe knew that Dion was always up for adventure, but getting to use his brand new weapon of choice sealed the deal.

***

Thanksgiving without his family wore on Jay, and he was ready to lash out at his captors, when something caught his attention. While everyone was wrapped up in eating the store-bought holiday fare and watching VHS replays of old football games, Allen was sneaking around. Jay noticed that Allen was particularly wary of Smith and resumed his odd behavior every time Smith looked or walked away. His main focus seemed to be pulling sealed envelopes, receipts and other paperwork hidden in various nooks of The Green Room, which he discretely stashed deep within the pockets of his loden overcoat. At one point, Jay felt that Allen had spied him watching but seemed to care very little, so long as Smith remained unaware.

Jay ultimately decided to accept the fact that he'd be spending another night in this dungeon. Simply too many of these degenerates were scattered about the place to allow for an escape. His hitchhiking venture required daylight for success, and he scoped out the area for possible weapons. He then noticed Allen entering the tunnel, inconspicuously exiting with his personal effects tucked under his left arm. Jay washed up and found his sleeping pallet to settle in for the night.

With the day winding down and the crowd thinning some, Walker and Clay's unusual presence inside The Grotto was obviously unnerving to the rest of the Subjects. The creepy enforcers weren't particularly comfortable themselves, either, remaining inside only for the sake of the holiday festivities at Smith's request. Wandering was their way, and they were soon off into the night to patrol the perimeter of The District. Clay scored a quarter bottle of *Dobra*, cheap potent vodka left behind by teen drinkers seen scurrying away as the shadowy pair approached. While in Tranquility Park, Walker solicited a few bucks from visitors, completely within The District's anti-begging guidelines. No scheduled performances meant that no theater goers had been harassed. The two of them then covered the perimeter of The District before settling into their usual spots in the bank parking lot. Gabe had proven to be most elusive, leaving them to contemplate their little utopia's future viability as a going concern.

***

234

The emotion and corresponding lack of sleep slowly sapped the energy out of the Filas home. D. John and May exchanged looks of consternation as the rest dozed off one by one, apparently moved way beyond regular tryptophan induced fatigue. It was as if they'd pulled a collective all-nighter. The glow of *Home Alone* opening credits lit up the room and early morning shopping plans were finalized before the young newlyweds left.

For the sake of safety and convenience, Gabe and Brittany would stay the night. They barely moved from cozy spots in the family room, as they nuzzled up with a shotgun like hunters in a blind.

Chapter 48

Friday November 29

Everyone in the house slept well with the sole exception of Joker. Shift lag may have played a part, but the protection of his home and growing family were at the forefront.

The ladies woke up first and immediately got moving, as May arrived for some serious shopping. Shelly discretely tucked a loaded derringer into her jacket, making a half awake mental note to exercise special care, especially when trying on clothes. After grabbing some muffins to go, the ladies were out the door and on their way in no time. The Galleria awaited with early bird deals to be had.

Gabe heard the scuttlebutt and laid there gathering his thoughts while wondering about the time. It was a typical dark and cold early morning like any other during hunting season. He rehearsed his plan over and over in his head, finalizing the finer details. He heard the garage door opening, followed by the sound of the Tahoe backing out. The time on the cable box read '5:45'.

Gabe stood up, and Brittany went over to the sofa where Dion was sleeping to give his ear a wet sniff, ending his slumber. While the guys were layering up in desert camo, Dion made a feeble attempt to whisper, as he proudly showed off his new gun. Joker sat back in a recliner, watching and listening between intermittent bits of sleep. He had offered the use of his truck, wisely not asking questions. With keys and weapons in hand, the two of them scooped up some muffins and bananas for the road.

This was a relatively new, but still somewhat established tradition for Dion and Gabe. Some early primal fun, while the girls did their Black Friday morning thing, left ample afternoon time for leftovers and college football. Only, the events of this week had brought major twists to their newfound ritual. Normally fading in the rear view mirror as they left town, the shimmering skyline instead grew, as they made Gabe's all too familiar commute.

Dion soon became amped up for the adventures ahead and began to throw out clichés from action movies. Gabe's recent conditioning allowed him to remain calm inside and out. He felt some relief at having a partner for this next step and attempted to temper Dion's emotions by reviewing the mission's course of action and then some fun plans for the afternoon.

The Smith Street exit approached, and they clutched their weapons before exchanging final looks, both extolling confidence. Light from the array of the sleek towers pierced a ring of fuzzy glow through the pitch black sky. Soon the little truck decelerated, the road noise muted, while the second verse of *Luckenbach, Texas* crackled quietly through a blown dash speaker. Every traffic signal in sight burned of bright emerald green, hopefully a positive omen precluding them from stopping and possible second thoughts.

After a quick right onto Franklin, the vehicle slowed and Gabe pointed to identify certain locations which Dion had heretofore only seen on a map. The volunteer became uncharacteristically serious, and Gabe anticipated another corny movie catchphrase. But his accomplice simply looked over and said, "We got this," before tucking his weapon into his jacket and jumping out.

Gabe proceeded down Franklin past the main post office's ample parking lot which was, unfortunately, surrounded by cameras - 'Federal' cameras. The District loomed to the left. Upon reaching the elevated portion of I-45, he was able to find a less than well-lit parking spot under the overpass. He exited with his weapon comfortably concealed, as he steadily strolled back down Franklin toward his post.

Up ahead, he heard a slight rustling of the brush on the far side of the bayou, one which only someone fully alert and aware would have noticed. According to plan, it was Dion settling into place. Gabe checked his coconspirator's line of sight, and it was as perfect as he'd calculated. This rendezvous was in order. The darkest depths of The District loomed below; its aura was undeniable to Gabe. Now clean shaven with slick backed hair and full camo, Gabe would be much less recognizable to most in The District.

The slightest bit of early sun rays appeared, and Gabe slowed his pace. Just as Lamar had taught, and as he had seen for himself the prior morning, Walker emerged from his slumber in the bank parking lot. Gabe made a fist and twisted his wrist back and forth, confirming to Dion that the plan was a go. Both of them couldn't help but notice that the stout outline of their adversary remained as formidable as ever. Fortunately, none of their scenarios called for hand-to-hand combat, at least not with this beast anyway.

Sure enough, Walker headed to Market Square to take delivery of his choice pill. As the codependent Subject vanished from sight, Gabe quickened his pace, passing across the street from Walker's lair. One listening closely, such as Gabe, could hear Clay's snoring during the breaks in traffic. Again, Gabe gave the twisting fist signal, letting Dion know that Clay was also in place as expected. He then slipped into place at the construction catwalk and waited, hoping this semi-holiday of a Friday would yield just enough normalcy.

**

Over at the Galleria, the ladies took their marks as stores readied for the onslaught. *Casual Corner* was the first choice on this Black Friday, sharp work clothes being the driving factor. They had learned to avoid the discount stores, which had become either bait and switch or just too rough of crowds. An instrumental version of *Gangsta's Paradise* was piped in, as they debated whether or not the lost sleep was worth it. It was their bonding ritual, and plenty of sleep could be had later.

While May made a run for more coffee, the others mused as to Dion and Gabe's whereabouts. Were they catching up on sleep or getting into mischief? Laney felt inside that Gabe might be up to something, hopefully something more worthwhile than vengeance. After the events of the week, she was just glad to know that Dion was around to accompany him, whatever wherever.

Just as May returned, they hushed and changed the subject. Seven o'clock arrived, and the doors opened; everyone entered in an orderly fashion. To their delight, the women's shoulder pad craze had waned, just as the twins were entering the real working world.

**

Market Square was littered with assorted homeless sleepers occupying every square inch of park bench. Walker wondered about them, as he waited to secure his hit of Adderall. Where did the allegiances of these wayward scoundrels stand...ties to criminal gangs? After all, the jail was in the vicinity...were the better groomed ones recent releases? Would any of them be worthy additions to The District? Most of them sure as hell knew to avoid The District, which made him proud. His dealer finally appeared and delivered, on time. Walker now realized that he had awoken just a bit early. He rarely considered the future, but this day felt different. Would Allen abandon his cohorts, launching a new era? Back at the bank he made a sharp whistle, and

Clay arose before promptly stashing their bedding. They were both anxious to get back to The Grotto and get the scoop on the latest news.

Nestled in their respective bits of cover, Dion and Gabe needed one final piece to fall into place. Sure enough, the HPD mounted patrol prepared to take up their posts. Once again, a single officer led a slow trot up Preston Street. Sunrise was on, and Gabe's heart raced, mainly because the mount seemed to be moving at an incredibly slow pace. Gabe rehearsed the bailout signs in his head. If either of them wanted to pause the mission, they were to simply put an open hand on their head for at least five seconds. Another option was a delayed retreat, indicated by tapping the head repeatedly, at least five times. A closed fist double tap to the face followed by a thumbs down was their signal to immediately abort and bolt.

Walker and Clay appeared in the distance, and Gabe pointed their way for Dion's sake. It seemed that they were early and moving with a sense of urgency. Out of nowhere, yellow flashing lights escorting a delivery of construction equipment slowed the two - just in time and just enough. As Gabe's head whipped back around, the police horse found its usual spot. Perched just out of the flow of traffic, the cop had a perfect vantage point to monitor the long shadows of traffic. The glare of dawn, however, favored Gabe. He remained virtually invisible, despite the officer's heavily mirrored shades.

Right on queue, the targets arrived at the intersection. Well aware of the presence of law enforcement, the pair stopped and waited for both the vehicular traffic and the signal light before entering the crosswalk. A repeat of the convergence on which the plan's success hinged was properly occurring.

Dion confidently smiled as he pulled out his Shocker pneumatic gun. This model had just come out and was the first paintball gun with a solenoid rapid fire trigger. His ammo hopper was full of nylon slugs, and he had been assigned two targets.

Across the street, and facing the opposite direction, was Gabe. His weapon was an older, smaller gun known for its accuracy. He was armed with common red paintballs, and his target was perfectly lined up. It was time.

At the very moment Walker stepped off the street and onto the sidewalk, Dion lit him up with two shots across his broad chest. A passing bus masked the sound, and the layers of clothing dulled the points of contact for just a split second. Though regular paintballs certainly stung as they marked victims, these solid slugs impacted with no give, much like mini rubber cannonballs. The morning chill first muted and then amplified his pain, though he had no idea what was happening to him. Walker began to wail, and Clay turned to comfort his partner. Instantaneously, Dion tagged Clay's lean torso. This time it was only a single shot, which cleanly connected, just enough to hurt without major injury. Clay screamed out as well.

The officer noticed their strange behavior right away, as Gabe immediately pelted the chest and shoulders of the horse with red paintballs. It seemed as though the hooligans were attacking the animal, as it reared up and appeared to be bleeding. A billy club came out and then crashing down on the taller man's head, before a strong arm lifted him by the collar. Clay soon found himself pinned against the body of the horse with night stick wedged under his neck. A couple of nudges from the toe of the cop's boot reminded him not to budge, as the equine's unsettled jerking brought intermittent choking.

Walker was all about moving away from the scene and figured he'd let Clay take the fall. He sprinted toward the hidden security of The Grotto but was quickly chased down by another mounted patrol in the area. An officer had been attacked, and a swift reaction demanded a lack of discretion. The order to 'Halt' was ignored, and he was trampled head to toe. The fresh welts on his chest were promptly matched by equestrian footprints on his back, bringing face first whiplash into a white stripe amongst the dark asphalt expanse.

Both Dion and Gabe were able to calmly tuck away their weapons and flee the suddenly active scene. Dion located the truck as planned and picked up Gabe in front of Power Tools. His ride from there had at last arrived. They drove to the Elysian Viaduct, where they ditched their weapons and ammo out the window and into Buffalo Bayou. Dion briefly mourned the sinking of his gun, still so shiny and new. Gabe promised a loaded replacement.

From a distance, the two of them gleefully watched as the crime scene was cleared, and their targets were led away in handcuffs - such shame to be relished. Dion was pumped up by the thrill and success of the paintball onslaught, but remained quiet out of respect. He knew that Gabe's dirty work was not yet quite complete.

***

Word of the incident reached The Grotto in no time. A couple of Subjects reported sighting someone scurrying along the bank of the bayou, possibly with a gun. They had little knowledge of paintball and such guns, suspecting that it been a pellet gun ambush. Someone even suggested that it could have been a flare gun firing blanks.

Smith remained in denial and proclaimed it all to be a case of police brutality. His convoluted theory led to further speculation of a shakedown clearing the streets of the homeless ahead of the arrival of downtown holiday shoppers. A directive was issued ordering all Subjects to avoid any possible contact with police, including security guards and anyone in any sort of uniform. Furthermore, everyone was to remain in or near The Grotto until further notice. Inside, he knew that Allen's absence and Walker's arrest made for heightened vulnerability.

Chapter 49

It was still early this Black Friday and the light of day had not yet reached the cavernous expanse above The Grotto's entrance. The presumptive future brothers-in-law cased the scene as they made a single pass on Bagby Street. It was just as Gabe remembered and expected. He wanted to strike again while the police were preoccupied. He also wanted to clean up this whole mess already.

Dion then drove down Prairie Street where the road passes under The Wortham Center, stopping just at the edge of the building. Gabe reached under one of the back seats and pulled out the pistol, silencer still attached, which he tucked into his jacket pocket. "I'm going in," he proclaimed before nodding and climbing out. Dion was to drive around the block one time, slowly enough to catch each red light, giving Gabe a full three minutes.

Gabe stayed along the upper corridor of the massive theater's western wall before descending at the last set of concrete stairs. Based upon his recollection of the layout while he was captured, plus Lamar's extensive descriptions, Gabe located the hidden opening in short order. He donned a headlamp and began a full speed trek down the long narrow corridor. Where tunnel became dwelling he found and immediately recognized Smith. Lamar's training had truly been most excellent. He pulled his gun and waved Smith up from his seat and over to stand alongside him before confirming, "You are Smith, correct?"

Smith nodded with a response, "Yes I am..."

He started to go on, but Gabe cut him off, "Very good, that's enough" before raising his voice, "Alright, everybody up and at 'em! All you 'Subjects' need to gather up and hear this."

Gabe waved the pistol above his head, grazing the extra low ceiling. The gathering crowd soon grew to about fifteen, it was quite the motley crew assembled before him.

He soon noticed a familiar character standing at the tunnel entrance and realized that he'd been followed in. It was his old friend Crawford. Of those present, Crawford appeared to be the only one fully awake and happy to see Gabe.

Soon, another familiar face peered around a thick curtain acting as a room partition. It was Jay, who was nonchalantly slipping his shoes on.

Thrilled inside, yet remaining stoic, Gabe called for Jay to stand behind him before addressing the crowd: "This place, 'The District' as you know it, ceases to exist as of now, and I mean immediately. Your individual freedom has been restored. So expect nothing further in the way of food, shelter or any sort of protection from this place. Take what you want, roam freely, seek help. You are Subjects no more. Others, people in the real world, want to help…rediscover your faith and treat what ails you. Gather your belongings and prepare to vacate – you all need to be out of here before the concrete trucks arrive to fill it in. They will, very soon. Any questions?"

There were no questions.

From his back pocket, Gabe produced some cards for the Star of Hope, which he'd picked up at his Thanksgiving meal the prior morning. He placed them on Smith's chair, along with some handwritten sheets listing the addresses of the Harris County Psychiatric Center and the Texas State Hospital in the nearby town of Rusk. A single Metro bus pass was placed atop the pile. His hope was that at least one random soul amongst the crowd would be saved.

He then pulled Smith aside and stated kindly, "Thank you for your cooperation. I will work with Allen to ensure that you are taken care of. Consider the options, your options, and we'll be in touch."

Crawford would be fine. He had been the catalyst for change, helping Gabe free himself and setting the wheels in motion by directing him to Lamar. Though it had been almost ten years, Crawford yearned for freedom. A simple life of begging suited him well, and he had no use for mental help. Gabe discreetly patted him on the back, so as not to raise suspicions on the part of Smith.

The exit was clear, and Gabe turned his headlamp back on before telling Jay to go first. Journeying out fit well with Jay's plans for the day; however, he hadn't anticipated such an early start. They whispered as they methodically trudged along through the long, dark tunnel. Finally, flickers of light appeared ahead, and they quickened their pace before emerging into the fresh new morning. Jay savored the sight of the sky above, its hue irrelevant. The coast was completely clear, and only the sound of an opening fire station door right above them broke the silence. Gabe held Jay back from breaking their brisk walk into a full sprint. No need to bring unwanted attention. They scaled the last of the stairways back up to street level and into the sunshine. Sure enough, Dion had the truck running and waiting.

A slight jog was fine for the last few feet, and the former strangers dove into the vehicle for a rapid getaway. "Boo-yah!" exclaimed Dion, recognizing Jay immediately from Gabe's description. Jay gave a quick recap of the events of the escape with Gabe filling in any skipped details. Dion took it all in with silent laughter in the form of long exaggerated nodding bends at the waist. All the while an unlit cigarette dangled precariously from his lips. Jay began to openly weep as informal introductions followed.

    ***

It was only eight o'clock, and Laney and her band of shoppers had just found their groove. Shuffling from store to store they found the bargains to be genuine. The crowd thickened, as elevators brought wealthy Latin Americans down from their rooms within The Galleria's luxury hotels. Everyone was relatively well-mannered, and the ladies found upscale shopping to be quite a pleasure.

With wedding expenses looming, Jane and Shelly were less spendy but enjoyed themselves nonetheless. Retail bliss provided a perfect escape from their heretofore tumultuous holiday. They all took a moment to admire the huge Christmas tree encircled by talented young ice skaters practicing on the rink below. A late breakfast at *La Madeleine* allowed them to rest their feet and gather a second wind for another round of buying, this time on the unchartered third level of the mall. Laney wasn't sure if the guys would be up yet and chose not to call home.

    ***

Though in a collective hurry, Dion realized that extra fast served little purpose now, as he uncharacteristically drove under the speed limit. Eastbound Interstate Ten was less than scenic; only a *Budweiser* brewery and the expansive ship channel broke up this span of flat prairie swamp.

Still, Jay found the ride wondrous, taking in every single mile marker on the route home he'd envisioned. His life had been salvaged, and he continually checked the shoulder for hitchhikers, while measuring the viability of his original plan. The modest interior and cramped backseat of the compact truck seemed downright palatial. He basked in the genuine warmth of his rescuers' company and realized that he would see Garrett again. Jay also felt the need to share.

Though only a few years their elder, Jay spoke as if he was some grizzled old veteran of the cold, hard world. Once again he recounted the story of being laid off from his great job and the fruitless search for similar work. The joy brought on by the events of this day kept his spirits up as he gave the details of household financial collapse. It turned somber, however, when he answered Gabe's remaining questions about the situation.

The front passengers were unable to see the pure sadness in Jay's eyes. But the melancholy resonated as he spoke, "What tears me up is how it destroyed my wife, my beautiful Olivia. I couldn't take care of her - like I should...in accordance with my wedding vows."

Gabe wondered aloud, "How's that, Jay? We know you, and that you would do all that you could."

Jay explained, "Olivia is schizophrenic. Her symptoms were well controlled by *Clozaril*, her medication. For years she did great, but this *Clozaril*, it's not cheap and we lost our health insurance. With a son to take care of, she was willing to sacrifice, like any mother, and thought she could handle skipping her pills."

"And she couldn't..?" chimed in someone from the front.

"Absolutely not! She spiraled out of control within days," said Jay before concluding, "My Olivia was on the verge of becoming a street person. Her sister came and helped me talk her back, well sort of."

The guys up front once again led him to continue, "Sort of? What happened with Olivia?"

Tears flowed as Jay told the rest, "She wasn't going to get herself right in our house. So her family took her back to Louisiana, Lake Charles, where she's from. They committed her, temporarily, to a mental home near there. I haven't seen her since. Neither has Garrett as far as I know - well, maybe he has now…"

Gabe consoled and encouraged him, "I am so sorry Jay. You are strong enough to get her back now. We'll have to stay in touch so that you can keep me updated. I want to meet Olivia one day. You still have that business card I gave you?"

Jay still had a sense of humor, "Gabriel, that card is now property of the area formerly known as 'The District'. Seriously though. Man, you need to give me your number again."

This time, Gabe gave up his home number. Jay had earned such trust. Plus, it would now be a long distance call, unless Jay's path somehow took him back to Houston, which became doubtful as he spoke.

"My priorities are in order now," said Jay. "I am not looking for big success…well success has been redefined for me. I need a steady job with benefits, nothing fancy. Even something in a plant or some sort of government position would work. I want whatever it takes to hold my family together."

Dion chimed in, "I get it, totally. You are strong and will take great care of them."

"You guys have main girls?" asked Jay.

The two guys turned to each other with looks indicating that they would keep it simple. Gabe responded for them both, "Yes, I am engaged, and he will be soon, I suspect. We both have 'main' girls."

Jay lectured again, "When you find the one, her, don't screw it up. Regret is sorrow and stupidity all in one. Remember this now…"

"I think we get that," replied Dion. "Somehow each of us found incredibly beautiful girls. Both of us have really good taste."

After a long deep breath, Jay sighed and mumbled, "Oh, my Olivia is some kind of beautiful. And I see her in my boy. Thanks for getting me closer to them!"

The intense conversation sped up the second half of the drive and hastened their arrival in Port Arthur. Jay directed them into his old neighborhood and to the family home. His brother awaited them on a porch rocker, and Gabe was unsure how, or even if, he'd known they were coming. Everyone hopped out. There was no luggage. Jay and his brother came together for a long embrace before making introductions. By virtue of meeting the brother, Gabe finally learned Jay's last name, which was 'Bourgeois'. A fond farewell followed, and Jay's genuine appreciation for his new friends and their actions was undeniable.

Dion and Gabe had another new tradition calling them back to Houston post haste. It was prime oyster season, and *Christy's* on Westheimer served the largest by the dozen on the half shell. Though excellent seafood was plentiful in the Golden Triangle, the tri-city area defined by points from Port Arthur to Beaumont to Orange, they were going with the sure thing. Gabe craved the familiar and the extra spicy Bloody Marys back in Houston.

Gabe was thoroughly exhausted and let Dion continue driving, even though it meant enduring herky-jerky lane changes and the retelling of his old stories from growing up back in Nashville. Adventure always seemed to find him, and he recounted tales of his exploits ranging from monster trucks to schoolboy fights and near death experiences involving caves and cliffs and rocky creeks.

Afterwards, a buffet of leftovers and college football games would round out the day. LSU vs Arkansas was Gabe's main event and Texas vs Texas A&M was the dessert to follow. He craved the normalcy and was so glad to realize that the games still had something more than a trivial meaning to him.

The shoppers soon arrived back at the house and everyone swapped select versions of stories from the morning's adventures. They all pretty much hunkered down and enjoyed the pleasure of each other's company for the duration of the weekend visit.

Chapter 50

Monday December 2

A new week was starting, and Gabe reveled in the routine it could bring. After spending the balance of the long weekend at the Filas home, he was well rested, while Brittany was totally spent from the oodles of attention she'd soaked up. Joker had become particularly attached to her, and Shelly actually tolerated the well mannered pooch in the house. Little things like dirt and fur didn't matter, at least for these past few days.

Waking up on his own ahead of the alarm, Gabe actually had time to catch the morning weather report and plan accordingly. He also had time to take Brittany for an extra long walk, but, for once, he pulled more than she, and so he cut it short.

Though ahead of schedule, Gabe was ready to get going and peaked in the mirror one last time. He also triple checked his back pocket for his wallet; it was there each time. The pistol Lamar had gifted him adorned his nightstand and would accompany him only as far as the car on this day. His further business required force of a different sort.

Pretty much unfamiliar with the 210 schedule at this early hour, he'd take whatever was in the offing. He approached the Park & Ride lot, and a bus sat waiting, as usual. Perhaps it had just pulled into the station. Or, maybe it had been there a while, now full and ready to go. It didn't really matter. A familiar and friendly face was there to greet him; it was Alex. This sight triggered an image in Gabe's head: one of Alex driving the final bus out of town off into the distance and commencing Gabe's whirlwind odyssey. He took one of the few remaining seats; all were non-window at this point.

The harrowing events starting with his last workday still loomed, but a couple of full days of downtime had allowed him to process and start to move on. Gabe was confident that Walker and Clay would be locked up for some time to come. Assaulting an officer and then resisting arrest did not constitute minor charges. Even if they were bailed out, somehow, the local beat cops would keep them clear of The District and surrounding area. Besides, they wouldn't want to face further disgrace at the hands of their former Subject friends. The shame of a public beat down had surely been enough, as word of their respective whippings bore legendary makings.

Fifty or so commuters, plus a driver, rode along in this bus. Gabe wondered how their weekends went, and if anyone else's day ahead would be as intense as his.

'Walter Timmons: Specialty Funding' was the sole listing Gabe had found under the yellow pages heading 'Banking – Independent'. He was very familiar with the location.

In his mind, Gabe anticipated the possible directions his unscheduled appointment could take, while rehearsing his handling for each.

Soon enough, the freeway exit dumped the bus into downtown. Gabe strategically chose to go one stop further than usual, where he could exit and head right into the tunnel system. He saw no need to tempt fate, with the final phase of his plan lining up fairly well. Despite the extra long walk, he made it to the office in no time. As usual, Lonnie Lesson had already arrived, but that was it. He pretty much had the place to himself.

Gabe pulled a couple of folded papers as well as a floppy disk from the inside pocket of his jacket. The papers were identical letters, and the disk stored a soft copy of the same letter in the form of a WordPerfect file he'd created over the weekend. Dion, now back in Nashville, also had a printed copy. A final hard copy had been stashed in Gabe's bedroom closet, placed to be easily found by anyone conducting a cursory search.

He felt that his bases were covered, as he filed the disk between other floppies in his overhead bin and put one of the printed letters in his bottom desk drawer with the snacks. The remaining printed letter was tucked back into his jacket for delivery.

Ivan Williams soon arrived and immediately sorted through Friday's mail for any checks to be deposited. Thankfully, a couple of very large checks had come in. Ivan and Gabe inquired about each other's holiday weekends, before discussing the need to get the checks deposited in order to 'more comfortably' cover payroll. Aside from the lunch hour, Gabe was looking for as many opportunities as possible to get out of the office, since he had no idea of what kind of office hours his intended target kept. Besides, additional anticipation would do nothing to further his efforts. The bank deposit was prepared in record time.

Upon excusing himself, Gabe bought extra time by mentioning that he may need to visit with bank security for an update on the box cutter attack case.

On the way out, his path crossed with that of Leah Roberts, his best friend in the office. They greeted each other with the usual post weekend chit chat somewhat amplified by the extra days off. Gabe knew that Leah could be trusted more than anyone else within the firm and decided to confide in her. His story told of the details on the bank lobby attack and the pending investigation, everything that would soon become common water cooler knowledge. But he gave her an added tidbit. Evidence to possibly be shared was stored on a disk in his office. Gabe gave the exact location and asked for a favor on her part, if he failed to report back to her by the end of the business day. She was to share the file with everyone in the office, as well as other names listed on the disk.

Without hesitation she replied, "Of course," before asking if he needed the name of a good attorney.

He thanked her and said, "Oh, no, not yet, anyway. I'm sure it will go smoothly," before smiling and leaving.

The elevator, lobby and street scenes were busy, once again as everyone hustled to get back into the last push of productivity before the year wound down. Across the street, Gabe could see the bank manager and a security guard unlocking the main doors to the lobby. He scanned the pedestrian traffic and half expected to see one of the characters from The District lurking, but all was clear.

Things seemed to be back to normal for Vernon Norwood, as he tidied his teller window and the first customer of the new week approached. As always, Gabe was cordial, but careful not to bring up the incident the prior week, mainly because doing so would have lengthened their conversation considerably. He tucked away the receipt and was immediately on his way, definitely on some sort of a mission.

His destination was much like the bank in that it was not tunnel connected. Still, the tunnels would be the safest route, at least for as far as they'd get him. His access was via the Texas Commerce Bank parking garage, and he was extra careful not to be seen by any coworkers just then arriving. The underground route terminated at the Houston Chronicle building, and he ascended through horde of folks he imagined to be reporters, though most were actually in ad sales.

A block and a half towards The District brought him to a white granite clad tower called The Lyric Centre. Gabe entered the lobby and nodded to the guard as if he belonged, before catching an elevator up to the fifth floor. He approached a door marked only by its suite number and let himself in. In the middle of an ample entryway was a Chippendale desk with claw foot legs and a leather top; an equally ornate chair with matching legs and leather sat empty. It appeared as though neither had been used or moved in months. At the far end of the room was a wooden door flanked on either side by frosted sidelights and sconces.

Gabe knocked and there was no answer. He put his ear up to the door and could hear some Dixieland jazz playing; the track was *Kansas City Stomp* by Jelly Roll Morton. He knocked again and could hear movement. Upon grabbing the crystal knob, he felt someone turning it from the other side and heard what sounded like the deadbolt being disengaged.

The door opened, and a distinguished looking older man was there to greet him, "You're Gabe aren't you?"

"Yes, I am," said Gabe, as he matched the figure standing before him to Lamar's detailed description. The full head of salt and pepper hair along with grey eyes confirmed that he was in the right place. "You must be Walter Timmons - nice to meet you, Mr. Timmons."

"You got here before I could get to you. I am glad for that, we need to visit," he extended his arm and directed Gabe, "Have a seat."

Gabe obliged as he noticed one of his RPG business cards, uncrumpled and sticking out of Walter's shirt pocket. Gabe got right into it, "So here we are, finally able to discuss your creation, your other world."

Walter was more receptive than expected and replied, "Maybe you'll make this easy – why not, right?"

Gabe leaned forward somewhat puzzled, "You want this to be easy? Hopefully 'this' means the same thing to both of us."

"I want a resolution. My demands are not unreasonable," the elder stated calmly before showing some fire, "But just don't forget where you are, and I'll be a proper host."

"Yes indeed. I have something for you," said Gabe, as he opened his jacket to show that he was reaching for a single trifolded document and not a weapon. The eager guest placed the paper on the desk and slid it across to Walter.

"Of course - I expected something from you. It appears as though we are going to conduct ourselves in a most civil of manners," said Walter as he unfolded the letter. Gabe noticed the view over the shoulder of his host. Just below the window was an enormous violin sculpture, most familiar to him from street level. Beyond the work of art, a broad panorama of the Theater District provided for a dramatic backdrop, a downright strategic locale from which a founder could observe his fiefdom.

Gabe interjected, "Please note, as you read, that I have placed sealed envelopes containing this document with a couple of my most trustworthy, though unlikely, associates. In the event of any harm to me or those close to me, they will go to the media, who would be sure to run with such a story. I know more than a few folks with the Chronicle and also have established contacts with radio and TV. Anyway, sorry to interrupt – just wanted to provide a little context…"

"Got it, we're fine here Gabriel," stated Walter calmly before continuing his read:

Early December 1996 – Houston, TX

The best of intentions have run afoul. The release of this memo ensures that another victim has been claimed.

A secret lies below Downtown Houston. An underground dwelling and related community was established in the Houston Theater District. 'The District', as it's known by those involved, was originally conceived with the dual purpose of serving the homeless and insulating patrons of the various arts venues from pandering and harassment by said deplorables. These same arts patrons, though without their knowledge in most cases, funded its construction and upkeep through ticket purchases and in-kind donations. The boards of directors of these organizations envisioned such an arrangement, and all serving on these boards were at the very least aware and, in most cases, fully engaged.

Houston banker and philanthropist Walter Timmons is the point man on this covert coalition, and his role as a founder proved key to the operation. He acts as primary liaison between the privileged and the needy, reporting to leaders of both. Also, anyone wanting to know the whereabouts of one Connor Ericsson will find him there.

The hub of this underworld lies at the northwest corner of the Wortham Center in a cave craftily planned and formed within the foundation. Insiders incorporated this clever design when the building was constructed. The secret entrance is camouflaged by brick and ivy and the living space within has been termed 'The Grotto' by its inhabitants. The opening can easily be located in the light of day. All members of the community call themselves 'Subjects' and abide by the strict code of conduct which prohibits begging from arts patrons and venturing beyond boundaries, as outlined by the founders. In return, these 'Subjects' are provided with food and shelter, as well as physical protection.

If anyone doubts these facts, then just consider your personal experiences in the Theater District. When is the last time you were asked for money walking to attend a performance? Big cities typically have beggars in such settings, pestering the well-to-do.

In some cases, law enforcement has directly aided the efforts of the founders or simply been complicit in choosing to look the other way to maintain forced peace. Officer Kirby Chapman with the Metro Police has been an accessory to this arrangement.

Again, the release of this document warrants full exposure and investigation. I, Gabriel J. Wagner, am being held or have been killed in The District.

"Well that pretty much sums it all up now doesn't it?" said Walter. Gabe now noticed some penciled in notes, presumably made by Jay, on the tattered business card sticking out of his host's shirt pocket.

Realizing what Gabe was looking at; Walter looked back at the letter and joked, "Well I sure do appreciate receiving the lion's share of the credit."

Gabe quickly quipped in reply, "Yes, you earned it - you deserve your fair share."

Walter sat back with his fingers tips tapping away at the same on the opposite hand, maintaining a conciliatory tone, "Thankfully for us, your little press release can remain sealed, assuming none of your people get sloppy. So what is it that you propose?"

"First, let me assure you that my people are good," said Gabe. "They act only if I don't return safely, or if something happens to my loved ones. So, regarding the business of The District, I need your help in completing the shutdown. You had to know that this was coming."

"Oh, I knew this was coming long before you showed up. Even prior to Walker's arrival on the scene, I knew our days were numbered," opined Walter. "Once the founders became leaders, and limits on this new freedom were established, the end became inevitable. I envisioned a greater level of anarchy, something approaching utopia, but events…really certain people, got in the way…"

Gabe interrupted, as Walter's thoughts and voice tailed off, "So you are saying that you all underestimated the human element, probably because you wanted it so badly…You wanted it to work. I get that, but it's done, over, and I demand that you arrange to have the entrance to your 'Grotto' sealed up with concrete."

Walter, "OK, I can do that. Please just give me some time to clear out the dregs, every one of them - I may need to properly place some holdouts. You know some good folks exist in every circle…"

"That's fine," said Gabe as he cut off his elder. "A week should suffice. Please have it done by this time next week. We'll check your work." He stood and reached out his hand and Walter reciprocated with a firm handshake.

"Fair enough, check my work," was the answer. Walter had a final statement for Gabe, "I have a very strong feeling that our paths will cross again someday, likely under more pleasant circumstances."

Gabe nodded with an uncertain smile upon this remark and made his exit.

***

In accordance with the agreed upon terms, Walter assumed his alter-ego one final time as 'Allen' visited The Grotto. He warned that the end of The District was imminent, both the dwelling and the way of life.

Assistance was offered to anyone interested, but everyone genuinely interested in being helped had already heeded Gabe's earlier warning. The rest were content to roam the familiar area and freely forage.

One final Subject remained. Despite Allen's offers and pleading, Smith had no desire to return to a life as 'Connor Ericsson'. All offers to reintroduce him to the mainstream of society were promptly rejected. The only assistance he would accept from his old friend and fellow founder was a generous supply of food and personal item rations, twelve years worth as they figured. One final gift, a hydroponic garden, complete with a fluorescent light and spare bulbs, might buy him more time, if the power supply somehow remained intact.

The big day came, and Smith stowed away under the elevated shower platform, as he saw the lights of approaching workers attempting to clear the tunnel and living areas. He went undetected, emerging from his hiding place just as cement began to fill the tunnel. Smith propped up a sheet of plywood against the undersized opening. He dragged every bit of the heaviest furniture snuggly up against it to brace the support. Allen's calculations proved accurate and, with the void seemingly filled, the crews shut down the pump. The makeshift form held as the stalwart Subject leaned against it with every bit of strength he could muster. This very spot where his world formerly transitioned to the overworld had become so very familiar. Smith contemplated loneliness, the air supply and his ultimate fate.

Soon the supplemental lighting powered down, and the concrete trucks rambled away. The Theater District once again grew dark and quiet, yet with an undertone of freshly found freedom. As Walter Timmons commenced a slow stroll back to his luxury abode, Gabe and Laney took it all in from a safe distance, sufficiently satisfied with the outcome and pondering holidays to come.

THE END

R.I.P. Houston Club Building (1954 – 2014)